Valor

Valor

Stories

Murathan Mungan

Translated from the Turkish by Aron Aji
and David Gramling

NORTHWESTERN UNIVERSITY PRESS
EVANSTON, ILLINOIS

Northwestern University Press
www.nupress.northwestern.edu

Support for this publication came in part through the Global Humanities Initiative,
which is jointly supported by Northwestern University's Buffett Institute for Global
Studies and Kaplan Institute for the Humanities.

Printed in the United States of America

10   9   8   7   6   5   4   3   2   1

Library of Congress Cataloging-in-Publication Data

Names: Mungan, Murathan, 1955– author. | Aji, Aron, 1960– translator. | Gramling,
    David, 1976– translator.
Title: Valor : stories / Murathan Mungan ; translated from the Turkish by Aron Aji
    and David Gramling.
Other titles: Cenk hikâyeleri. English
Description: Evanston : Northwestern University Press, 2022. | "Originally
    published in Turkish under the title Cenk Hikâyeleri."
Identifiers: LCCN 2022020569 | ISBN 9780810145245 (paperback) | ISBN
    9780810145252 (ebook)
Subjects: BISAC: FICTION / World Literature / Turkey | FICTION / LGBTQ /
    General | LCGFT: Short stories.
Classification: LCC PL248.M86 C4613 2022 | DDC 894/.3533—dc23/eng/20220609
LC record available at https://lccn.loc.gov/2022020569

CONTENTS

TRANSLATORS' PREFACE

Her dakikam bir ayrı cenk ile geçiyor.
(My every minute—a new battle taking place.)

—Yakup Kadri Karaosmanoğlu

This book is an experiment in the reanimation of legend—and in the use-fulness of legend for contemporary life. When the "real world" seems poised to sabotage whatever is alive and beautiful around us, legends can reenchant that world with a new dimension, putting liveliness and secret joys again within reach. Adults do not tend to believe that legends, heroes, and icons are theirs for the taking when needed; the social order has convinced them that heroism, grandeur, epic experience, and indeed valor itself are for others. Neither cynics nor doubters, they simply may not entertain the notion that the legendary figures of ancestors—Shahmaran, Jengaver, Binali, and all the jinn of the netherworld—are still speaking to them too. They may think themselves too modest, too ordinary, too modern, or too queer to partake seriously, or playfully, of legend and myth. Not so, says *Valor*. The stories in this collection are a guide for wresting legend back for personal, erotic, spiritual, and politi-cal purposes, and each one chronicles the intense surprises generated by this undertaking.

Murathan Mungan's short-story cycle *Valor* (*Cenk Hikâyeleri*, 1986) has long been regarded by Turkish critics as a classic and a milestone of twentieth-century Turkish literature. The collection vividly reflects the author's multiethnic Turkish, Kurdish, and Arab cultural background and represents his lush poetics, literary breadth, and enduringly libera-tory sociopolitical commitments.

Publication of *Valor* is woefully overdue, now thirty-five years since its initial publication. Among the contemporary Turkish literature avail-able in English, the oeuvre of Murathan Mungan (born 1955) is a glaring gap. Over sixty books have studded his forty-year writing career, includ-ing over twenty volumes of poetry, ten short-fiction collections, eight novels, six plays, and several volumes of essays, screenplays, and edited anthologies. To date, only a handful of his poems and short fiction has appeared in English, and no book-length work has been translated prior to *Valor*. Mungan's dazzling output in multiple genres seems the most likely reason why it has been difficult to select a single work that can effectively introduce his literary gifts in English translation.

Valor begins with "Shahmaran's Legs," which introduces the eponymous and profoundly genderqueer figure of Shahmaran—a mythical half-human, half-snake creature whose talismanic image is depicted on icons, engravings, pendants, and bracelets throughout Turkey's southeastern provinces. The story opens in the workshop of an ageing master artisan, who teaches the young İlyas what it means to make Shahmarans. On one level, İlyas is a boy growing up in a contemporary Turkish city, forced to negotiate society's demands as they relate to commerce, education, gender, sexuality, labor, and vocation—whether as a carpet weaver, a coppersmith, a shoemaker, or a baker. But this quiet coming-of-age narrative soon turns into a battle with something larger than modern life, widening into a world of adventure, betrayal, and desire.

Fate pairs İlyas with a master artisan whose workshop produces Shahmaran panels on wood, metal, and mirrors. This elusive Shahmaran is a mythical pre-Islamic nonbinary figure, rumored to live underground in the ancient city of Tarsus (now Mersin). As Turkish has no gendered third-person pronouns "he" or "she," it was important for our translation not to ascribe to Shahmaran a pronominal gender that was absent in the original text. Today's Kurdish, queer, and feminist activists often invoke Shahmaran as a symbol of their resilience, struggle, and survival against oppression and betrayal at all levels. In this first story, İlyas labors to render an authentic Shahmaran, and in so doing he dramatizes what it means to appropriate this symbolic figure and its lessons into one's own life—lessons such as, "Beauty is what terrifies you the most."

"Shahmaran's Legs," the opening section of the five-part story, frames the narratives that follow. The second story in this cycle, "Ökkeş and Jengaver," chronicles a heart-wrenching rivalry between two teenage boys who love one another passionately and purely but who must set aside their affection for the needs of the village and their families' standing. As in many of these stories, custom (*töre*) seems to be somehow the main character, both protagonist and antagonist at once, yet unyielding in its dictate that manhood is proven through stern enmity, not tender love. The next story, "Kasım and Nasır," pits another pair of men (this time, brothers) one against the other in battle. Like the mythic framework in "Shahmaran's Legs," Mungan introduces Kasım and Nasır's bitter tale of valor by alluding to the martyrdom of the prophet Ali's sons, a seismic episode in the history of Islam, depicted in age-old images on faded plaques that adorn coffeehouses throughout southeastern Turkey. "Binali and Temir" brings the cycle into contemporary times and politics through the enmity between captor and captive in the impenetrable mountains of the 1970s brutal ethnic conflict between the Kurds and Turks. In the final tale in the cycle, Ensar and Jivan are loving friends separated by a river that surges in the winter and recedes in the summer. This continuing theme explores the deeply felt bonds between young men as they are tested by time, war, violence, tradition, mortality, absence, and family. These are relationships in which the greater desire proves to be the virtuous one—longing, desiring, holding out, keeping watch—the stuff of full-hearted valor rather than of sternness, stoicism, or austerity.

The six stories in *Valor* speak to the central concerns Mungan returns to time and again: tradition versus individuality, religious and social dogma, ethnicity and tribalism, the cultural politics of (trans)gender and (homo)sexuality, and the negotiation of fractured, fraught identities. The stories interweave several southeastern Turkish folktales within the expansive spatiotemporal cultural space that Mungan calls "Great Mesopotamia"—the historical home of Kurds, Armenians, Yezidis, Assyrians, Arabs, Turks, and Jews and in various combinations straddling these identities. This collection is a loving tribute to this wide, narratively rich, myth-saturated region—and its multiethnic, multilingual echoes from time immemorial. Sometimes ethnicities are marked in the stories explicitly, but often—particularly with multiethnic cast of characters—they are signaled through names themselves. The modern nation of Turkey plays a rather muted role in the collection, coming up only in the occasional mention of the regional gendarmes hunting the mountains for "outlaws" or, in the final story, "The Serpent and the Deer," through mention of Ankara's ministerial architecture.

The twentieth-century frame setting established in "Shahmaran's Legs" follows the protagonist through his self-actualization in the art of Shahmaran-making and his sexual awakening. Each story is a search for an answer, a reclaiming of myth, and a valiant struggle with the duty of being indelibly alive. The word *cenk* in Mungan's title *Cenk Hikâyeleri* (lit., *Battle Stories*; pronounced "jenk") comes to us as an everyday, unspectacular Turkish word for *battle* or *war*. From the Persian كنج (*jenk*), variants of this word are also found in Crimean Tatar, Northern Kurdish dialects, Punjabi, Tajik, Urdu, and Gujarati. *Jenk* is related historically to the common German word *Gang* which means "walking" or "marching." One is always *going* in this way in *Valor*—embarking on a long, harrowing, and promising journey.

With *cenk*, Mungan has chosen a common Persian-Turkish word for warring activity over other terms such as *harb* or *razm*, which, loftier and more heroic in connotation than *cenk*, appeared already in the tenth-century epic Persian poem *Shahnameh*. *Cenk* is no sublime abstraction. It is an embodied, psychical, emotional experience of profound, prolonged displacement, danger, and doubt. It is something that one goes through, rather than something one looks upon or analyzes.

Mungan is deeply attached to vernacular, plain language like *cenk* and to a natural musicality that accommodates the sonorous lyricism resulting from the vowel harmonies and inflections of Turkish. His stories exploit the line between the figurative and the literal, yielding vividly expressive descriptions that animate the best of poetic imagery. In his short fiction we experience the synthesis of his poetic lyricism and narrative ingenuity, packed for optimal effect inside a lean form and crystal-clear language.

Mungan's attention to the rich particularity of human stories makes his lyricism all the more magnetic. A reserve of private and often illicit memories, ultimately enigmatic and inaccessible for readers, creates an irresistibly subjective core within his writing. At the same time—true to the Turkish lyric tradition—the personal is inseparable from the public and the political. *Valor* draws as much from the author's own autobiography (a young artist discovering and ultimately embracing his identity) as it does from the cultural memory, the stories and myths, of the scarred landscape and the people of southeastern Turkey.

In these stories from the late 1970s and early 1980s, Mungan's sexual politics operate in a tantalizing space where the radical is also allegorized. Their aesthetic value notwithstanding, such narratives are vulnerable to collapse when either side of the allegory/metaphor overwhelms the other. Queer sexuality is an incisive metaphor for the countless disguises Turkish society has traditionally expected most of its citizens to wear. To be part of the glorious republic, or the contemporary pietistic society, or even (the strictly hierarchical myth of) the great Turkish "mosaic," one's difference must be concealed by masks that ultimately disfigure us emotionally, sexually, and linguistically. The mask dictates—but even more frighteningly, becomes—those selves. The "battle stories" in *Valor* are ultimately stories of difficult striving for self-actualization in the face of social violence and rebuke.

The final story in the collection, the self-standing "The Serpent and the Deer," is Mungan's most explicitly gay story in this collection—a remarkable feat for 1983, just as the AIDS pandemic was beginning to engulf the world in fear and recrimination. It is a story of a man cruising in a dark park, looking for a way out of heteronormative constraint, seeking new ways of feeling and being in a world that would rather he disappear. Though the story holds to some of the tools of allegory, it is a strikingly realistic depiction of queer life on the edge of the "closet"—expressing both the profound hope and the boldness to think that another life and another world is possible, whether underground or above.

We chose Nazlı Büberoğlu's mixed media artwork *Melting Memories* (2020) for the cover of this book because its contemporary materials and gestures embody the kind of vivid tensions that sprawl through-out these stories. They are tensions within manhood, within sexuality, within memory, within families, within marriages, and within one's rela-tions with ancestors. There is a strong queer sensibility in *Valor* around adventure—around what is *a-venir*, what is yet to come in LGBTQ his-tory. These stories each take a frozen, closed image and open it over and over and over, insisting on knowing what is yet to be found there. This struggle to open, to reanimate, to give life is the momentum behind each of these tales.

Valor

Shahmaran's Legs

To Bilge and Tomris, for the same and different reasons

1.

My father sent me to apprentice with the Shahmaran maker.

So that I don't waste time on the streets, so that at least I learn a craft. Idle drifters don't end well, he said. Had I known better, I'd have told my father that busy drifters don't end well either.

"You're old enough to go apprentice," he said.

Such was the custom. At a certain age, the neighborhood boys would be sent to apprentice with a craftsman. Whenever one of our playmates disappeared, or didn't show up on the street for a couple days, we knew: he'd gone and become an apprentice. Whether it was at the ironsmiths' market or the coppersmiths' market, we never knew. Then there were the kilim weavers, the carpetmakers, the shoemakers, the bakers, the jewelers, the clockmakers: for each child an occupation that suited his talent, whether at the tailor or the shirtmaker. Every now and again, on special days when we went to the market, holding hands with our mother or father, we'd run into boys we'd not seen for quite some time. For some reason, they'd avoid us, walking away, with a strange look of guilt they didn't understand themselves. Or they'd grin nervously, pretend like nothing was the matter. No doubt, their look of guilt had something to do with being poor, even though we were all children from the same poor neighborhood, and the same destiny awaited us all. I could sense something bothered them about these chance encounters; that's why I began making sure not to take notice of them. They seemed to us like they'd aged, outgrown us while working at their benches and stands, as though they were no longer the same kids we'd been running around with just yesterday, along the same backstreets. They had the faces of men. Did we envy or pity them? I don't know. Besides, we knew sooner or later we'd all end up apprenticing somewhere.

It's my turn then, I thought. I looked at my hands. They seemed, still, like the hands of a kid. I tried guessing my age, imagining my line of work. My hands told me nothing. I thought about my friends who—tomorrow, the day after tomorrow, the day after that, and the day after that—wouldn't see me on the neighborhood playground. Apprenticeship meant separation. Would they wonder about me? Maybe miss me? Who'd be the first to ask about me? Who'd notice first that I was gone? Or would they quickly grow used to my absence? Years later, when I felt depressed, sad, or weighed down with night terrors, I'd often turn to a particular scenario: imagining myself dead. In the scenario, I was more interested in the reactions of my friends, relations, and acquaintances than in my own death. Their immediate reactions, initial sorrows, surprise. I'd be so absorbed in my fancy, in its own reality, that I would soon quit thinking about dying and actually begin feeling a happiness of a certain kind. As if imagining other people's reactions brought me back among the living. Thinking about it now, that day when I was sent to apprentice with the Shahmaran maker, I did want my friends to think that I'd died. But I'd not have named it death. Because I didn't know death—or shall we say, not enough to fancy it.

As for separation: each time, it was for me a kind of death.

Back then, and to this day.

And so, I gathered that I'd be going to apprentice.

In the evening after dinner, I left the table and sat on the sofa, feeling dispirited, weighed down. I saw myself as a person with a job. But somehow the change didn't please me. Rather, I felt a deep, heavy sadness. So this is what having a job feels like, I thought to myself. This was, I assumed, why my father comes home sullen faced, all tuckered out. And just then, our eyes met. Guessing we were both thinking the same thing, I blushed and lowered my eyes.

But the next morning, everything seemed like playacting to me. I saw us, father and son, walking down the street holding hands, two characters in this sad play. Who knows, maybe our whole life was nothing but a sad play. The streets were empty; it would be a few more hours till they'd be filled with my friends' carefree shrieks and laughter. I'd never seen the street as deserted as it was now. Upset, I wanted to cry. I longed to see one of my friends, anyone, as if to bid farewell, exchange a last good-bye. Maybe I was afraid it would take them a long time to notice my absence. Or maybe I wanted a witness, just a witness. What I've always been looking for. All my life. But I saw no one on the street, no one to testify to my abandonment.

"Know your hands' worth," my father said, "the talent in your fingers. You draw a beautiful likeness. If a child your age can draw faces so well, who knows what you can draw when you're grown."

I didn't get what he meant but was happy still.

My master's name was Mahir.

He asked my name.

"İlyas," I said, flustered.

"Are you familiar with Shahmaran?"

I shook my head.

In the evening, I had asked my father, "What's a Shahmaran maker?"

"An artisan. Someone who makes Shahmarans and sells them."

"But what's a Shahmaran?"

It was the name of the strange creature whose likeness hung on my grandmother's wall. Every time we went to kiss her hand, we'd see it. Beautiful and frightening.

The way something could be both beautiful and frightening, I didn't know then.

The first time I saw it, I stared at it for a long time, then averted my eyes. (Grandmother had just forgiven my father and made peace with her daughter-in-law; we hadn't visited her for quite some time.) Grandmother, her house, the objects in it, had always frightened me. She never smiled, and when she looked you in the face, she saw your whole being—at least that's what I thought. As fate would have it, when I brought her the first Shahmaran I made, she was at death's doorstep and died a few days later. She wasn't lucid, but still she stared straight into our faces, as though knowing everything, understanding everything, but unable to speak. I'm not sure if she understood the meaning that one Shahmaran panel held for me—I'll never know. Perhaps she hadn't realized I was the one who made it. She was trapped inside her suffering body. I still feel like I had things I never got a chance to say to her. I'm still sorry she died so soon.

From the way my father described it, I pictured a male being with a female face, a human head on a snake's body, with forty snakes for legs, wearing a gilded, ornate crown. A creature with a long tail curling up and then forward toward its head.

"Is that what I'm going to make?" I asked, alarmed. "Those things are scary."

"Why would someone ever fear something he makes with his own hands?" my father countered. "Why would a thing of beauty that your hands have made frighten you?"

Oh, but it would. My father didn't know back then, and maybe never learned, how beauty, beauty created with your own hands, is in one way or another what frightens you the most.

One of those things you couldn't learn without experiencing it.

As I'd come to know much later.

Something that fear teaches you.

"Shahmaran is the sovereign of the snakes!" I told my master. I paused. I must have said something wrong. "The offspring of the sovereign of the snakes . . ." I tried to correct myself.

My master didn't say a word.

I wasn't sure which of my answers was correct. I still am not.

The father? Or the son?

Not that it matters now.

I added, stammering, "And all its forty legs, made of snakes!"

"Not *made of*," my master said, "They *are*. Besides, you haven't made anything yet, we haven't."

He smiled ever so gently.

"Every one of its legs is a snake," I said. "And its crown is gilded, covered with gems. It's huge!"

My eyes wandered among the countless Shahmaran images hanging on the walls and stacked row upon row across the floor. As I tried to take them all in, one after the next, my master asked, "Which of these is Shahmaran?"

"All of them," I said right away.

He shook his head.

Startled, I didn't know what to say.

"No," he said, "none of these is Shahmaran."

"Then so where is Shahmaran?" I asked, helplessly.

"You'll draw it."

I stared at him, perplexed, unable to grasp what he meant.

"And if you can't draw it, your apprentice will, and if he can't draw it either, then his apprentice will. If you don't think this way, you can't ever draw Shahmaran."

"But all the Shahmarans look like each other," I said.

"So do all human beings."

I fell silent. A long, long silence.

My master was a wise man, and the task before me a difficult one.

"Well done," he said. "You know just when to be silent."

This first bit of praise I received was for my silence, for knowing when to be silent. Then he turned to my father, who, aware as he was that I was being tested, secretly rejoiced that my answers were enough to his own liking as he stared ahead blankly, anxious whether the master shared his view.

"This child is very clever," said the master. "If his fingers are as agile as his mind, it won't be long before he's the most capable Shahmaran maker in the region. He'll draw the best Shahmarans around."

My father laughed a mouthful. He'd been proven right. The happiness he'd suppressed till then spilled out in one big, proud laugh.

I've rarely seen my father laugh that hard.

He was a poor man. We lived in a poor neighborhood. I was one of six siblings. We toughed it out through plenty of hardship. And here he was, laughing his heart out. I couldn't but take some credit for his happiness, and I felt hopeful. This was the first time I saw myself as someone others might take pride in. There in Master Mahir's workshop, with its low ceiling and smells of oil, wax, and soot, I had my first taste of self-confidence. Now, whenever I succeed at doing something, I still see my father's face radiant with that laughter. I tear up but can't quite cry.

Would I be feeling this way if he were still alive? I don't know.

That evening, my father was more generous than usual, buying me sweets and roasted chickpeas. We went back home like two grown men, with big smiles across our faces.

Greeting us at the door, my mother was taken quite by surprise.

I started work the next morning. There were a couple of small workbenches. String, paint, spools, frames, rags, glass panels, moldings. I learned about paint mixing, stretching a canvas, spooling, and other related minor tasks. What I wanted to learn the most was how to draw. My master noticed my impatience and smiled slyly at my eagerness.

On the third day, he had me sit down next to him.

"It's hard to draw something when you don't know its story. When you don't understand it and grasp its essence, İlyas. One shouldn't dare touch what one doesn't know. If he dares, then he should dare knowing it, too. And to dare knowing it is difficult, İlyas. Knowledge can be frightful. Knowing is a bit like being cursed. So I'll tell you the story of Shahmaran while you go ahead and start drawing!"

"Maybe I should listen first and then draw," I said.

"No," he said. "Then you might not be able to draw it. Worse yet, if you understand it all, then you might never be able to draw it, ever. To start drawing, you don't need to know much. Later on, that's when you need knowledge. When you come to feel its absence. You gain nothing by knowing something unless you've felt its absence. When you reach the point when you cannot give up drawing, that's when you dare knowing everything, risking everything."

Of course, I didn't understand all of what my master was telling me. But I could sense things. And draw tentative conclusions of my own. I tried to follow his every instruction without fail.

"At first, you'll look at the white emptiness before you, as if staring at cloudy water. Or you know how, when you look at the sky, the clouds begin to take on shapes before your eyes: a mountain here, a bird or a human form there. This is how the white emptiness before you is like a bundle of clouds. Imagine a Shahmaran figure, try to pencil its outline. It'll look like the ones you've seen before, the ones drawn by others, but don't be afraid. This is the inevitable path you must travel. A way station you can't pass without staying there for some time. What you draw may seem clumsy, childish. It may look like ones drawn before yours, but it still is yours, it has to be yours. Among the lines you borrow from others, your own line, shaky or timid, has to show itself. 'Look at me, here I am!' it has to say. So that it will keep on going."

"Where shall I begin, Master?" I asked.

He smiled. The lines that were just beginning to deepen across his face made creases in the white glow of his skin.

"How true," he said, "I forgot. This is always the first question, 'Where shall I begin.'" As though he was remembering all his apprentices, and himself. "Start wherever you think you ought, as long as you can draw the rest," he said, adding, "Or start whichever way will keep you going."

On the first day, I used charcoal pencil and drew a few Shahmarans on paper. Looking at them, my master smiled.

"None of these look alike," he said.

Then I drew a few more and showed them to him.

"But now all of them look alike," he said.

I couldn't fathom what he was looking for. How was I to please him, I kept wondering. I must have frowned.

"Don't frown," he said. "You're on the right path. A person always draws the same thing, but not one of them looks the same as the next. It shouldn't look the same. And to get where you need to be, you have a long way to go. You're too young, you need to proceed patiently, without getting discouraged, without giving up or getting tired. Braving every difficulty, betraying neither yourself nor your work. A Shahmaran maker must learn this, above all else: to not betray . . . This is what we need most."

I drew a huge Shahmaran.

Was I thinking it would contain all the others?

As if he understood what I was thinking, my master looked at me with a smile, stroked my hair. I felt his fingers sliding softly through it. As if I was being caressed for the first time.

There was no shame, I thought, in being a Shahmaran maker's apprentice. One day I would run into a friend who would be walking arm in arm with his parents in the marketplace, and I would be able to look him in the eye and smile.

I decided I enjoyed this work.

As I write all this down now, I don't feel in the least that I betrayed my master.

I believe I'm still in this business of making Shahmarans.

2.

I pulled up a small chair and sat next to his knees.

"Let's think now," my master said. "What is a Shahmaran? Who is this being?

"What has it been saying for centuries, this beautiful nomad's face, traveling across the mudbrick walls of village teashops, all the coffeehouses of the provincial cities? What does Shahmaran, embroidered everywhere from throw-cushion covers to bed skirts, say to all these people?

"Just think, there are so many Shahmaran makers alive in this country. Every year, they draw hundreds of Shahmaran figures, frame and sell them. All the people who purchase them and hang them on their walls, what do they see in them? Those walls, what memories do they harbor?

"What is the venom hidden in the heart of the Shahmaran story? This venom, tasting of fairy tales, has passed from mouth to mouth for a thousand years. This companionship between the serpent and the human being (which you could also call enmity) goes back very far, all the way back to the days of the first apple."

"What did Shahmaran say to Jamsap?"

"'Haven't I told you, Jamsap, the son of man is traitorous?'"

"Let's start from the beginning."

"Let's return again and again to the truth Shahmaran has been dragging around on those forty legs:

Once upon a time—a time we either don't know or don't want to name—there lived a wise man named Danyal. He was the sort of man never satisfied with what he'd been given, seeking to know more and more, digging beneath all things visible. He refused to limit himself to what he knew or what was his business, as though none of the things visible—or seemingly visible—in life would suffice. He wanted more, trying to reach truths buried deep beneath reality: hidden truths, as he believed them to be. To know, to learn—these were his passions. He had devoted his life (and death) to being a sage. Which is why people had difficulty understanding him. But Danyal had long accepted his solitude. He who dared to know—didn't he also have to brave solitude, brave being cursed?

For many long years, he had given himself over to the study of all kinds of subjects, ranging from medicine to philosophy, arriving at noteworthy conclusions while also developing curious notions of his own. His studies set him ahead of his contemporaries; at the same time, he investigated topics favored by all the wise men across all the ages. For instance, he'd been tracking the secret of immortality, searching for the key to eternal youth, to eternal life. Everything was hidden in the heart of nature. (After all, how much did we know about nature's abundance? All the things we saw, all the things we touched: did we truly know them? Did we know what they hid in their essence?) He made medicinal potions from salubrious plants, which could quickly heal the deepest wounds and cure the sharpest pains. Seeing these small miracles, Danyal was convinced that one day he would also attain immortality.

Except that he wouldn't live long enough. Long enough to attain immortality.

Knowledge, learning, investigation, these are without end, true. But human life ends. What nature offers us is a finite life. Very soon before his death, he called his wife to his side. He had a black notebook by his bed; he'd spent his life filling the pages of this notebook, recording everything he'd learned. When his wife came in, he reached for the notebook. He was holding his entire life in his hand.

He said, I am out of time; let my son take up where I left off.

He said, Human life is short; nothing we know, nothing we learn and achieve has value unless it bears fruit in someone else's lifetime. Otherwise, everything gets buried along with us, underground. I entrust this notebook to my son, as I entrust him to this notebook.

He gave the notebook to his wife, delivering his life into her hands. And he closed his eyes for the last time.

His son was just a child.

Danyal died.

Left his son behind.

This son of his was rowdy, clever, curious about the world. He grew up quickly. When the time came, Jamsap's mother sent him to school. But

Jamsap had a liking for mischief and games, not for books. His mother could think of nothing but the black notebook lying at the bottom of the chest. Once Jamsap had figured out his alif-bas and learned to read, his mother would hand him that black notebook so he might fulfill his father's wish by taking up where his father had left off. But when her son kept on skipping school, escaping home and everyday life to spend his time under the trees, or along the riverbank, or in the woods, his mother came to realize it had all been wishful thinking. And little by little, she forgot about the sad little black book sitting alone at the bottom of the wooden chest. She had to forget about it. Giving up on his schooling, she put him to work. Saddled him up a donkey and sent him off to the forest. The boy and his friends began chopping and selling wood. An axe on his shoulder, a whistle between his lips, the donkey underneath him, Jamsap went to the woods every day, chopping wood and beginning to earn his daily bread. In time, his mother grew used to him. Jamsap wasn't the son Danyal had imagined or dreamed about. Had Danyal lived, maybe Jamsap would have lived up to his father's hopes—or maybe he still wouldn't have, but there was no point in thinking about all this any further. Besides, a son is not a disciple bound to carry on his father's unfinished pursuits. Fathers should stop viewing their sons as hounds. A son is not a hound. A son is a son.

Jamsap was Jamsap. Nothing to be done but to accept him as he was. An honest-to-goodness human being. Complete with his own destiny.

Jamsap and his friends went merrily about their days. They turned work into play. Chopping wood for them was nothing more than a happy excursion. At their age, everything was play. Having faced none of life's commonplace troubles, unaware of all the choices, questions, crippling anxieties, they merely lived, assuming life would unfold of its own accord. They were blinded by innocence, its pure joy. They knew nothing about the world, about themselves, or about others. Their strengths remained untested; neither their own limits nor those of others had been tested. Treating life as a carefree adventure, they were full of health, energy, and joy. They'd not yet tasted betrayal.

On one of those happy-go-lucky days, they'd climbed up the hilly forest, to the edge of the steep rocks, ready to hack at the unyielding trunks of the oldest trees that had been baking there in the sun. They were drunk with ambition. Determined to cut down all these mighty trees, leaving none for any other woodsmen. It seems they thought they could subdue this mighty forest all by themselves. Passion knows no acreage; this is something humans must teach their passions, for it is the only way they can cope with it.

Soon after they reached the base of the rocks, rain clouds surrounded them from all sides. A relentless downpour followed. Amid the dense bushes Jamsap noticed a small cave, its mouth covered by wild overgrowth. Braving the thorny branches, he entered the cave, his friends running in behind him. Sometime in the long hours they ended up spending in the cave (the rainstorm wouldn't let up), Jamsap began to scratch at the ground with a stick, digging up the soil until he'd reached a slab; scouring further, wiping away the dirt, he uncovered a marble lid. All of them huddled around the lid as they lifted it and found themselves staring at a huge well of honey.

From that day on, they quit chopping wood and instead became honey traders. They'd ride their donkeys, climb through the forest to the hilltop, enter the cave, lift the marble lid, and fill their tin containers with honey to sell at the market.

The honey well was their secret. The boys had promised each other to tell no one. They would keep the secret till death.

Days turned into weeks, weeks into months, and finally one day the boys noticed they could see the bottom—of what they'd thought was a bottomless well.

And from the mouth of the empty well rose the mists of a fairy tale.

On their last trip in, Jamsap was once again lowered into the well with the aid of a rope tied around his waist to scrape out the remaining honey—just enough for a few containers. But once he'd filled those tin containers and sent them up, his friends reeled the rope back up and closed the marble lid, leaving Jamsap inside, to the mercy of his fate.

Now let's pause here and catch our breath a little. Why did Jamsap's friends leave him trapped in the well? One legend holds that it was to claim his share of the profit for themselves. But this is not very convincing, since those few last tin cans wouldn't make anyone rich. Especially when you consider the number of his friends: true, none of the accounts tell us exactly how many there were, but the reference to "friends" is intended to make us think there were at least a few of them. So it sounds even less convincing that Jamsap's share, now divided into even smaller fractions, would be worth anyone's greed.

So why did they do it?

Let's think.

First, we might say, to nudge the plot forward.

Then, we might say, since the days of Joseph—and even before him—people have been betraying those they lower into wells.

We might also add that these boys had reached the age of betrayal. It's hard to hold on to a shared secret—to tend and protect it, if you will.

They wanted once and for all to bury everything in the well (*their* well, that is)—both their shared secret and the person responsible for the secret. (Consciously or unconsciously, everyone viewed Jamsap as the "owner of the well" since he was the one who'd found it.)

We might say they chose betrayal as a means to forget, once and forever. Betrayal is a natural impulse among humans, after all.

Jamsap spent many hopeless hours after realizing he'd been left to his own fate inside this blind well. Every hour spent waiting is a hopeless hour, isn't it? Then he understood: he had no choice but to bear the burden of his fate. The well he'd uncovered could ultimately become his grave, but it would take him some time to recognize this. Only a miracle could save him. He had to do something besides just standing there as if his hands were tied. He began feeling the walls, looking for a way out. For whatever reason, he kept remembering the joy he'd felt the day he first uncovered the well. His entrapment, he thought, was this erstwhile joy taking revenge on him. Sooner or later, every joy exacts its revenge on human beings. He scraped the walls with his fingers, tried to scratch at the soil with his feet. He had to escape this grave, escape it at all costs, find himself in another grave, if necessary, just to escape this one.

How long this exhausting struggle lasted, even he could not remember. After a while, he lost all sense of time and space. Only much later did he notice on the wall a glow the size of a pinhead. An illusion perhaps, he thought at first, his eyes playing tricks on him. He looked again— this time, from another angle. No, he wasn't mistaken. There was light. He began digging around it. The wider the hole became, the stronger Jamsap's hope for escape. In time, he managed to dig an opening large enough for his body to squeeze through.

This was his first victory.

An immense garden stretched before him.

It was a fairy-tale land.

Or a fairy tale about a land.

He sensed it right away; the magic of the garden seemed as if spirited from a fairy tale. He'd managed to pass through the hole he'd dug, and now his feet were standing on the soil of another land.

In the realm of another era, in the clime of another region.

He was standing on Shahmaran's land.

But he wouldn't recognize this until later.

For now, he was experiencing the spell of his discovery, the miracle of a spirited hope. The garden stretched and stretched and stretched out before his eyes, like a magic incantation.

My master paused here.

"Enough for today," he said, "We'll continue tomorrow."

I said not a word.

At night, I must have fallen asleep, dreaming of Shahmaran's land.

I'm watching my master's hands.

The way he holds the pencil, how he draws a line, the quickness of his fingers . . . His hands flow like water across the canvas, fluttering like the beating of dove wings. The lines and the colors seem to glide under his pencil. My hand trembles as I watch. My poor, tiny hand. Clumsy, insignificant. I admired my master but resented the way his hands could move like wings. I felt at once angry, resentful, jealous.

My master had told me, "Everything, everything should be discussed between a master and his apprentice. Nothing should remain unspoken. This is our custom."

Yet I hesitated to express all my feelings. I was ashamed that I could feel them about my master. At the same time, I was unable to control them. After much thinking, I decided I would not tell him what I felt. More accurately: I would postpone telling him. I thought, in time, I would gain experience so that my hands would flutter across the canvas like his. Then I would not fear anger or envy.

We would be equals and, once equals, I would love him freely, without anger or envy.

That's what I thought then.

But with experience . . .

"Where were we?" he said.

"The land of Shahmaran," I said.

This was a fairy-tale garden, but a garden fairy tale too. Now it broadened into a view of a narrow-veined marble courtyard that stretched as far as the eye could see, defying the human sense of horizon. Behind the tall columns circling the courtyard was a sky, maybe of a different color; a second sun was heavy on its way down. At the center of the blue-and-green-tile-framed pool was a colorful bubbling fountain, lending the whole place a hushed coolness. It gave Jamsap hope. He hoped in this coolness for a miracle, one that would bring him back to earth again. All at once he grasped why heaven is always depicted as a garden, vast and wondrous. He understood his long-held hope for heaven. How very many things one could come to grasp just from being alone, and inconsolable.

Such was the power of silence.

(Thinking about the garden and heaven, his eyes scanned the garden as well.) He could not see a single apple tree in this huge garden. An omission, he thought. A big one.

Slowly, gravely, Jamsap made his way toward the middle of the garden. There, looking toward the courtyard, he saw, elevated on a marble pedestal, a throne whose grandeur and beauty dazzled the eye. The throne was crowned with ornate jewels of innumerable color and embellished with inlaid mother-of-pearl and wrought engravings. It bespoke an infinite and unbridled power, a steadfast sovereignty. When he reached the steps at the throne's base, he saw a formidable number of daemons, serpents, and dragons meandering around the garden in a fashion that quite befit this garden dream.

Silence splits open at its most fearsome seam.

He'd happened upon this garden earlier, and now—as the coolness and hush began to set in—he was overtaken by a feeling of having escaped, and he surmised he would be back home by the time evening fell. But now it was fear he was feeling, a bewilderment that erased everything, and it left a thick, deep disconsolation in its stead. Perhaps heaven wasn't such a reassuring place, he thought. The notion was forming in his mind that no thing and no place would alleviate a human's endless unease—except death, that ultimate silence. After death, living was neither here nor there.

Varicolored vapors rose suddenly into the air, each forming a wafer-thin rainbow against the sky, then dissolved inside a pure-white haze. A moment later, it all vanished from sight (from Jamsap's sight at least, along with the serpents, daemons, and dragons), everything subsumed within the haze. Tufts of white circled the entire garden. A while later the vapor settled and, as everything began to assume its original shape, a giant daemon loomed within the haze. With grand solemnity, it carried a silver tray, set it before the throne, then retreated deferentially.

Upon the tray was the sovereign. With the head of a woman and body of a snake.

Leaving the tray, the noble creature glided onto the throne.

Jamsap fell under a spell. He collapsed to his knees.

This, he knew, was Shahmaran.

How often had he seen its likeness engraved! None of them captured Shahmaran's likeness, but all of them bore some aspect that evoked it. Alas, Jamsap did not know Shahmaran's story. He'd never heard it, never listened, hadn't even ever been curious enough to ask. If he'd known this story, if he'd known about this place in the story, would everything have turned out differently? This is something we cannot know now. Not anymore.

"Welcome to my country," Shahmaran said. "Don't be afraid; all the snakes, dragons, and daemons you see around are my friends, my helpers. You will come to harm from no one here."

Which meant, thought Jamsap, that each of them was "no one" for Shahmaran.

In everyone's lives, there were always "no ones."

"My name is Yemliha. I am the padishah, sovereign of all the snakes on the face of the earth. The son of man and his subjects know me as Shahmaran. You enjoy asylum here with me; no terror shall threaten you. You must, however, report to me how you came here and what it is that you seek."

Jamsap spoke, conveying to Shahmaran in succession all he'd experienced before arriving here.

Shahmaran listened to Jamsap carefully, pensively, and said, "So this means the son of man has yet again discovered this place of ours. Which means he will no longer look upon us kindly."

Jamsap burst out, "If you're talking about my friends who abandoned me to fate and left me in that well, there's no reason for you to be wary of them. What they wanted the most at the well was just to leave me to die. They're just traitors."

"I'm speaking neither of them nor of you, Jamsap, no," Shahmaran said. "I'm speaking of the son of man."

"Aren't you being unjust, treating all as one?" asked Jamsap.

"No," Shahmaran said. "The son of man is traitorous. It is for this reason that not even one human can know about this place of ours; our secret must not be made plain. For we are creatures bound to our secret life. Think of it, how fearful you must have been of us when you arrived here. I, too, was afraid when I saw you. Note that I didn't say I was afraid of you. I've had a change of mind when it comes to the son of man. Many years ago, I once placed my faith in him. Just once, I gave him a chance. I paid a great price afterward for my faith. That's why, dear Jamsap, I do not intend to entertain betrayal again. Having tasted betrayal once, a part of the heart is destroyed and can't be recovered; something that has broken deep within vanishes. When your love, faith, and belief are met with betrayal, it is an ache you cannot bear, cannot abide, cannot sustain. The heart decays fast. When the son of man is near, I must think not only of myself but of safeguarding and tending to my charges. I can't allow my weakness to jeopardize their safety. You understand, don't you? Maybe this is an injustice, or perhaps it is selfishness, wickedness."

"I want you to have faith in me," said Jamsap.

"I want that also," replied Shahmaran.

There was a long and seamless silence. With the setting sun, the garden was dimming, and all the daemons and snakes in all corners of the garden listened quietly.

The silence lasted for a while longer.

It was the kind of silence that bled from within.

Gathering all his strength and hope, Jamsap broached the one vexing question they had not yet spoken of but that lingered between them everywhere they turned. "So, venerable Shahmaran, are you going to send me back to earth?"

Shahmaran remained silent. Feeling a need to speak again, Jamsap continued, "I swear I shall not tell anyone about this place of yours..."

Jamsap, so recently seduced by the sense that he'd been saved from that dark well, and that he was now simply making his way home as evening fell, suddenly felt as if caught in a trap with no escape. The things we think we've been holding in the palms of our hands, how they slide away; the things we've carried, we've caught, we've touched—how fast we lose them, he thought, how quickly we find we've lost them.

"Believe me, what else can I say?" he implored. "I want you to believe me—more than I want you to release me. Believe me, I'd die before breathing a word about your whereabouts. I won't tell anyone. It's enough that you send me back to earth, to my home, to my hearth."

"But think about how the road that led you here was one of betrayal, dear Jamsap," said Shahmaran. "This is not a good beginning. You came here as the consequence of a betrayal; your path now is marked with wickedness. Once you've known betrayal, it continues throughout your entire life, changing only its guises."

"How can I make you believe, I don't know!" Jamsap said from deep within.

"What would you have me believe?" said Shahmaran. "Whatever oath you make, as the Jamsap of this moment, you may even get me to believe it. But the one who will one day commit betrayal will no longer be the Jamsap of this moment. How can you make a commitment in the name of a future Jamsap? Even you don't know him..."

Inconsolable, Jamsap began to weep.

"Listen, though," said Shahmaran. "I'm going to tell you the story of Belkıya."

"Belkıya?"

"Yes, Belkıya, the first son of man who betrayed me. Are you ready?" said Shahmaran.

"Ready," said Jamsap.

"Are you ready?" asked the master.

"Ready," I said.

"Then we'll pick this up again tomorrow," he said.

The nature of Jamsap's captivity was still not quite clear to me. This business had a flavor of adventure to it. Up until he fell into that well, everything Jamsap did was adventure—his life had begun! Whereas for me (or, let's say, for us, for those who listen, for those who write, for those who read) it was all about the time after he went down into the well . . . All of us, we're all spectators to someone else's fate.

Who knows? Maybe writing, reading, listening was the antidote holding the inevitable at bay.

Or sometimes holding it close, too.

As we draw or write, the spell rubs up onto our hands. The spell of what we've created rubs up onto our hands, turning distances into proximities, making proximities distant.

That night in my bed, I imagined the start of Jamsap's adventure, and it filled me with excitement. What would happen next concerned me as much as it did Jamsap.

I was thinking of Jamsap while drawing Shahmaran.

But I wasn't fully aware.

The possibility did occur to me while drawing Shahmaran's face that, in the story, I was more interested in Jamsap than in Shahmaran. What was I to do with this face? A lot of the Shahmarans I drew looked much more like Jamsap than like Shahmaran. Like my Jamsap. Eyes widened with worry, a face that had surrendered its fate to another. A captive expectancy . . .

Later, much later, I thought about how the Shahmaran I'd drawn, unknowingly, was in fact correct. Because wasn't Shahmaran a captive too?

A sovereign held captive inside an eccentric identity. That magnificent, holy, beautiful being did not fully belong either in the world of humans or in the world of snakes. Stuck somewhere in between, waiting silently and alone, in its own hell. Even the subjects' rebirth was bound to the sovereign's death.

All of the figures I drew while thinking of Jamsap had something in them redressing a wrong. Sometimes, when humans get back on track after a transgression, they take steps to make amends.

My entire life had become a Shahmaran story. During the days in the workshop, where colorful yarns, spools, and frames gave it an authentic feel, and then in the evening at home preparing for sleep in a void thick with darkness, I devoted myself, enmeshed myself in various Shahmaran stories. I was unable to deduce anything from the story of my own life. All of that was far removed from me. Or seemed so.

Years later, after I'd paid a much higher price and faced even greater suffering, I grasped how my entire life had been a Shahmaran story.

As I became more acquainted with its beauty and its death.

As I had not yet been lowered down into the well. Had yet to discover my well.

But it was there.

3.

What Shahmaran Told of Belkıya's Betrayal of Shahmaran

Once there was a ruler named Yusha. Having devoted most of his time to the study of the Old Testament, Yusha had read in it somewhere that Moses was not the last of the prophets. That there was a more recent messenger of God, with superior qualities, good humor, and holy justice.

At this point, Yusha was absorbed by a single thought. It occurred to him that it had been quite some time since the last prophet. He feared this new message, should it become known, might threaten his own mandate to rule. His tribe considered their knowledge to be the world's only and absolute knowledge, the world's only and absolute truth. They were poised to believe and profess it until the end of time. Acknowledging another truth was going to unleash confusion. History's vicissitudes would come between the people and their beliefs. The son of man does not care to believe that the generations that come after him, and their ways of living, may change. He begrudges them. Were immortality an option, he wouldn't begrudge them. If this truth, hidden in the pages of the Old Testament, were to see the light of day, the people of his tribe would learn about change, about transformation.

But

once one sees the collapse of absolute truth

no ruler will ever again be obeyed.

And so, Yusha conducted himself like any sovereign trying to outrun history. He ripped from the viscera of the Old Testament the pages that spoke of this topic. To diminish the Testament was to save it, he thought. He put the ripped-out pages in a silver case and set his seal upon it. After which he put it in a tiny room, which he locked and bolted shut. But this didn't suffice; it could never suffice to just lock up such a profound secret. He had the room walled off to hide it.

This way, he thought, the truth would remain secret.

But knowledge—like air, like water, like the sun—belonged to humanity. No one person's might could withhold it from people. Prohibitions don't extinguish truths, they just defer them. Besides, truths will one day take their certain revenge against those who have betrayed them.

A few years later, Yusha died.

Died without telling anyone a thing.

The throne passed to his son Belkıya.

How could Yusha have known that the truth he'd labored to hide from everyone would eat away at his son even more?

One day, pacing around his treasury chamber, Belkıya found the room behind the sealed-off walls. With great excitement, he read the pages that had been missing from the Testament. *"The scripture had waited in darkness and secrecy through the years; it attained an entirely new beauty."* He sensed these pages would compensate for all the absences in his life.

The truth dazzled Belkıya's eyes.

It made him forget everything.

Now he knew something no one else knew.

He was caught in the spell of knowing something no one else knew.

He handed over his crown and his throne to his brother and became a wandering hermit, devout only to the truth he sought.

One day, trying to reach the edges of his wilderness, Belkıya came upon a seacoast. The sea conjures adventure in all its forms. He saw the sailboats, blown by the winds of fate, the great ships. He saw the seamen, with sun-kissed skin and moss-colored eyes. Belkıya boarded a ship and set out on the open seas. The ship was going in the direction of Damascus. Once on the soil, he would look for the herald of the end days.

Perhaps the herald of the end days didn't himself know that he was the last prophet. Belkıya would explain this to him.

The ship was headed straight toward Damascus.

Belkıya was headed straight into his dreams.

A few days on, the ship came upon a deserted island. It was a silent island, full of fruits and herbs and dense, green bushy plants and streaked by moist sea breezes. It stretched out over the sea like a good-natured cat.

It was known among the seamen as the Island of Sleep. The narcotic scents of its tropical flowers, the fleshy wide leaves of trees no one knew the names of, the island's deep and absolute silence lulled people into sleep.

The seafaring men scattered to all corners of the island and replenished their provisions, gathering edibles they didn't know the name or taste of. For a while, Belkıya went along with them gathering food and then later, as suited his habitual fondness for solitude, he took his leave of them, seeking some repose under a tree for his tired body. Still dizzy from the sea journey, he lay his head against a trunk and closed his eyes. Soon Belkıya was swept into sleep by the overpowering scents of the pastel-colored flowers and the sweet lullaby of the sea breezes.

Hours later, he opened his eyes and saw that everyone had gone, and he understood that the ship had taken to sea and left him, forgotten, on the island. With a last shred of hope, he went down to the shore, but it was deserted. The Island of Sleep had abducted someone yet again. One more traveler had been plucked from the ships that visited its shores. *"The footsteps of solitude always lead the son of man to the same place. Wander as he might, Belkıya kept choosing to return to the shadow of that great tree."* This was the circle of his fate.

After a few hours spent in desperation, he found an old boat among the reeds, and with it he again took up an adventure with an uncertain end. From here on, he'd leave his life up to the currents of the sea. Swashing to-and-fro with the current for a few days, the boat suddenly struck land—on the island where I live.

This was my island. When Belkıya made landfall and began wandering around, he came upon one of my daemons, and then another, and another. However fearfully he tried to escape, the landscape swarmed with daemons and snakes.

I called out to him, "O son of man! Fear not the daemons and snakes you see. Come close, by my side. Don't hesitate, come closer."

As he approached, I asked, "What is your business on this island, which no human foot has yet touched? Where are you from; where are you going? What do you seek in the middle of this open sea?"

Belkıya explained his story at great length.

His dignified and grave look made an impression on me. He was clearly a noble person, full of heart.

As soon as I saw him, I loved Belkıya. And in fact, it's only at first sight that I love at all.

"My name is Shahmaran," I said. "This island is my capital. No human has ever set foot upon it."

And thus was my spell undone.

And now Belkıya wanted to escape, from me . . .

"No way," I said. "Not ever! Whichever son of man sets foot on my island must spend the rest of his life here. If I release you now, people will find my place; this will be the end of my race."

"I shall never reveal your place to anyone, not a soul!" said Belkıya.

I smiled. "You can't be so certain, Belkıya," I said. "The son of man betrays; we have been taught a lesson in this matter."

"And have you tested this? What you've learned?" he asked.

"No," I said. "What good would it do anyone for me to test it?"

Belkıya wasn't listening to me, just imploring me at length. Even his imploring was noble, uncompromising, and grave. It was as if, more than just imploring, he was seeking justice.

Belkıya said, "This is not my home."

I said, "But you can't go home."

He responded, "Who knows, maybe a home is what I'm looking for. And think of my luck—casting off my crown and throne, and now, how am I to find a place for myself on this island?"

I thought about it—Belkıya wasn't quite your ordinary human being. He was chasing some truth. A thought, a belief, a person. Someone like this would stare down death just to protect his secret. Someone like him knows how to hide a secret, to defend it. He's careful with his words, as he's careful with his soul. He grasps the sanctity, the importance of a secret or of a cause. (That's what I thought back then.) But when later he betrays me, I have to recall that very moment: inconstancy is in the nature of the son of man . . . In short, I couldn't anticipate Belkıya's betrayal. Was it right to be so trusting of someone who was so unlike normal, everyday humans? I didn't know. I was unsure. What was worse, Belkıya could sense my indecision. He kept coming for me, kept insisting.

It wasn't Belkıya's betrayal itself that frightened me so much as the thought of his capacity for betrayal. More than testing the son of man, I'd sensed back then that Belkıya was himself being tested, and I feared the "feeling" at the heart of my decision.

Because ultimately when all the differences among humans dissolve, I will face their very nature: their untrustworthiness.

And so, those who say "May the snake that doesn't bite me live a thousand years" are missing a certain truth: one day—the day of our awakening, that is—all snakes will bite.

"What day is that day?" asked Belkıya.

"The day I am killed," I said. "Or the day when all the snakes in the world learn of my death . . ."

Belkıya's visit lasted a few days more. As I told you, there was nothing more I had to explain to him.

It was a few days later when I put Belkıya in a boat and released him. I showed him the direction to go in and wished him Godspeed, and he left. It was the last time I saw him. But I never forgot.

When we were taking our leave, I said, "This has been our first and last meeting."

First and last . . . Everything, that's it.

And yet, I so wanted to see him just once more, once more, once more, always once more. No, I couldn't want this, because it could only happen by virtue of a betrayal.

As a matter of fact, I would see him much later—in the moment he would betray me. But this was not the Belkıya I'd met, whom I'd released, whom I'd bid Godspeed to, whom I'd loved. His treachery had comingled with his faith. What is most important for a believer to learn is patience. The truth, the fantasy that Belkıya sought—he was trying to wedge it into his own lifetime. And yet, most of "our truths" and "our dreams" exceed "our lifetimes." This is what Belkıya did not realize. That thing he devoted his hope and his life to, he wanted to achieve it within his own lifetime. He could not bear the weight of a belief whose time had not come. Besides, who knows, maybe the herald of the end days had not yet been born when Belkıya had sought him out, or maybe there were many such prophets. Knowledge of his own mortality, that selfish knowledge, opened the door to Belkıya's impulsiveness, which compelled him inexorably toward the truth he was following. These were all things Belkıya didn't know. His betrayal, his patience, and his ignorance had a price.

And he succumbed to Ukap's ambition.

Who is this Ukap, you might ask.

A Jewish scientist from Beirut went by the name of Ukap. A scientist who was not wise. He'd fallen for the dream of the Seal of Solomon. He read the old scriptures, the black books, the scrolls, the written wisdom, and he came to possess all sorts of knowledge filled with secrets.

From these sources he learned that the prophet Solomon wore a seal on a ring on his left hand. By virtue of this seal, the prophet Solomon maintained power over all the animals, spirits, fairies, and humans. With this seal, he could influence them all and keep them all under his spell. He who possesses this seal rules the whole world. Now, Ukap's thoughts swirled around this seal's orbit. Laying hands on this seal, ruling the whole world, making all his dreams come true—he wanted it all. Gathering together all the knowledge he'd acquired from the old books, he looked for a way to acquire the seal.

The seal, in its form as a ring, rested on the middle finger of the prophet Solomon's left hand.

All these years, Solomon's pristine corpse was preserved on a lofty throne.

This throne was located in a great cave.

This cave, furnished like a palace, was located on an island far on the opposite end of all the seas.

Therefore, to get to this island, one had to cross the seven seas.

And to cross the seven seas, one needed a particular herb. An herb we've known, one we've seen but didn't pay much attention to, one whose secret no one knew at the time. The herb that, when boiled and rubbed on the soles of the feet, allows one to walk on water as one walks on land.

And to find that herb, one needed to find Shahmaran.

The island where Shahmaran lived. On that island, all the herbs could speak. They revealed their secrets, disclosing what they were good for.

Which means that the way to the Seal of Solomon had to go through this island.

And so, what Ukap was hunting for, the trail he was following—or at least the first stop of the hunt—was Shahmaran's hideaway.

My hideaway.

In the course of his journeys, Belkıya's fame had spread throughout Jerusalem. It was said that he had traveled far, seen much, that he was a person of wisdom, a man of faith, praise that spread from one mouth to another. Someone who has traveled far and seen much—at least in those days and especially for those who had never seen another land, who lived and died in the same place—how strange he must have been. He was surrounded by probing minds. Everyone wanted to listen to his stories. Distance is a thing of wonder for the sons of man. Distant lands, distant countries have been the son of man's most magical dream. In distances, the son of man finds his symbols for death and time.

Ukap was among the people crowding in around Belkıya. He listened with great care to what he revealed, angling to find the gaps in his stories. He was able to surmise that Belkıya may have seen Shahmaran and that he may know the way there. Ukap teased open Belkıya's thoughts ever so gently, without giving himself away, and could see what they meant: someone knew the location of the Seal of Solomon, someone else knew the location of Shahmaran. Putting these two pieces of knowledge together amounted to having the entire world in one's hands.

Ukap had a greed he did not know how to satisfy. His heart was like a great whirlwind; it wanted to swallow the world whole. He thirsted for power. He was hopeless and miserable, like all those who thirst for power; he led a broken life, and he was not liked by other people. Always suspecting that his rights had been impugned, that his capabilities and value were going unrecognized, he behaved as if every human, and humanity itself, owed him a great debt. He felt a boundless disgust and hatred for life. He knew much, he'd read much, but all of this he'd acquired for the sake of himself and his greed. Knowing was, for him, something like collecting money. There was no love for what was known, no righteousness for it. What he knew was for himself alone, and so whatever he knew flowed into nothingness, reached nowhere, and became nothing; it gathered within itself and suffocated.

His whole world was made up of himself and his whirlwind.

But Belkıya was unable to see Ukap's true face: "*Love made his eyes blind, he could have used me for his purpose even. What is the use of love otherwise?*" He was drawn into the charisma of Ukap's thoughts, into the force of his thoughts, which made everything quicken and grow virile, and Belkıya's own impatience was a perfect match for him. "*Belkıya was fooled; he thought he was on the verge of finding what he sought.*"

Belkıya gave me away.

Had he forgotten the promise he made? No, not that.

He thought any path whatsoever was acceptable if it led him to his goal. And yet there was no possible goal left, none that would have made any and every path acceptable. As with many things, Belkıya had no way of knowing this, and so he availed himself of every last thing. But what was to remain after? He didn't give that any thought at all.

They made their way to the island in secret. Putting out an iron trunk with a crystal bowl of milk and a crystal bowl of wine, they concealed themselves and lay in wait. Snakes being snakes, Shahmaran can handle neither milk nor wine. I drank the milk, then the wine, and I was soaked drunk for sure. When I came out of it, I was in the iron trunk in the middle of the ocean. I gathered I'd become the bait, the prisoner.

But I hadn't yet seen my captors, and I wouldn't see them still for a while yet.

From the trunk, I called out, "Hey, my captors! What is your aim? For what purpose have you kidnapped me? What do you want from me?"

Ukap answered me (from then on, it was always he who answered). "O Shahmaran!" he said. "Stay calm, do not fear! We shall do no harm, neither to you nor to your charges. You are not our aim, you are the vehicle for it. We are looking for something. An herb. You'll simply help us find it. After finding it, we will leave you where we found you, have no doubt. You are not our prisoner; you are our guest."

"What herb do you seek?" I asked.

"An herb that allows you to walk on water as if on land," replied Ukap.

"What will you do with this herb?"

"We shall cross the seven seas and reach the Seal of Solomon. In this way, the whole world will be in the palm of our hands. We shall conquer the world, the entire world . . ."

I could already understand that Ukap would become the victim of his own passion. People who wish to conquer the world meet their end in a fire that engulfs them too. They die in the worst of their regrets. We've seen many such specimens, and we will continue seeing them . . . Even in that moment when they think they have conquered the world, they're experiencing the climax of their delusions. They succumb to the wild enthusiasm of the people, to their fanatical genuflections and unconditional surrender. The power of their authority blinds the rulers, and soon they can see nothing at all. This, too, is their fate. I tried to summon Ukap's likeness before my eyes: his sharp chin and pointed beard, his huge, fearsome eyes, which looked upon the world in bewilderment and suspicion; every line on his face signaled another unfulfilled ambition. His hands quavered, and no amount of will, intelligence, mastery, and renown would ever be enough for him. Such a person who cannot conquer himself—what, pray tell, is he to do with any world he might conquer? We've seen many such specimens, and we will keep on seeing them . . . and this is why I didn't fret over him.

"You are not our prisoner; you are our guest," he had said.

This mandatory hospitality lasted exactly forty days. We wandered and made stops throughout the mountains, among the cliffs, the vineyards, gardens, plains, and meadows. In the end, we found the herb.

They boiled it immediately and put it on the soles of their feet. And, lo, we walked back to my island.

They hadn't taken me out of that trunk until just then, and when they did, I saw Belkıya. And I understood everything.

When our eyes met, he hung his head.

I took stock of myself inwardly: there was nothing within me that felt like a longing.

This was not the Belkıya I'd loved.

"I told you, Belkıya," I said. "The sons of man betray."

He made no sound.

He clearly had no remorse but suffered still.

4.

Even in the midst of this betrayal, the difference between Belkıya and Ukap had made itself plain. The betrayer understood my suffering.

Belkıya's shame would pass, that I knew. After leaving this place, and as soon as he was whisked away from the fact of my existence, he would forget every last bit of it. (He'd forgotten it all before, too, of course.) Love had made his eyes blind. He thought I didn't understand him, or perhaps he didn't even consider this a betrayal at all. And yet, once you've begun to behold betrayal, it mars everyone and everything, no matter where you may be.

"Leave the Seal of Solomon alone," I said. "Its time has not come. It shall not become yours. Because it belongs to everyone. Because you do not know how to wear it. It is such a boundless power, and the responsibility for such a boundless power requires wisdom and virtue. And even so, whatever it may mean to the son of man, no matter who he is, it will seduce him, and he will succumb to his own frailties. This is why it must belong to everyone. It's not, as you always thought, somewhere across the seven seas, but here, right before your eyes. Indeed, the things whose value the son of man is the least able to acknowledge are right before their eyes. For instance, when you were all walking with me along the mountain ridge, you didn't even notice the chances you were missing; your eyes were tied and bound in such a way, closed to everything else beyond that one thought you'd sunk yourself into, and you didn't even grasp the greater and more important chances you'd missed, because your eyes could see nothing but the one herb you were searching for."

"Which chances did I miss?" shot off Ukap. His sanguine eyes bulged open.

"For starters, capturing me is not an easy feat. Since you succeeded, you ought to have been better able to seize this once-in-a-lifetime chance. In all the places we passed through, we came upon hundreds and thousands of herbs. All of them spoke, revealing their secrets.

One said, I am the herb of youth; anyone who boils my essence and drinks it shall never age. You didn't even listen.

One said, Any material you rub me against turns to gold; you will never want again. You didn't even listen.

One said, I am the herb of immortality. I grant immortality to the son of man. I am his oldest dream. Anyone who drinks my essence cannot die. You didn't even listen.

You didn't listen because you were locked on that single thing you sought; your ears heard only what they wanted to hear.

You want the Seal of Solomon so much that, even if you obtain it, you won't know what to do with it, how to use it. For those guided only by ambition, there is no such thing as an aim. Ambition is the only absolute, ambition, no matter what. In other words, contrary to what everyone thinks, ambition is an aimless thing. I'll tell you this for the last time: give up the Seal of Solomon. If you insist, your fate will be death.

Ukap almost begged that we go back, that we look for those herbs. I could see a plaintive remorse in his eyes.

But I could only laugh at his pleading.

"The bait is set once only," I said. And then I added, "Chances are like bait."

Knowing what set Belkıya apart from Ukap, I sidled up to Belkıya.

"Are you sure you want to go?" I asked.

He hung his head, and his eyes averted my gaze. I understood he'd go on to the bitter end. He would risk it all.

I said, "Belkıya! You don't know; Ukap and you are not after the same thing. You love and seek, whereas Ukap loves nothing and no one. I wish, for this reason, to do you one more kindness. I've got just one more piece of advice, which is just for you. If you succeed in making your way there, do not take hold of the Seal of Solomon, let Ukap attempt it. Only in that moment will you understand the reason for this. This is the last and only thing I can do for you. Make sure you do not forget these words of mine."

And they started off into the distance across the sea, like two blue Bedouin. They disappeared into the horizon.

I gazed after them for a long while.

Which Belkıya was this?

Leaving them to begin the ordeal of their adventure, I returned to the company of my daemons. I explained what had happened to me. Since our location had been found out by the son of man, it behooved us to find a new place, a new secret . . . My daemons and snakes and I put our heads together and thought . . . and we came to this place you see here. We've spent many long, quiet years here. But now humans have yet again set foot on our soil, which means perilous, fearsome days are coming. They will no longer leave us in peace. Humans subjugate every other creature on the face of the earth to their will. The only ones they haven't been able to master is themselves; they can't do it. Their power conceals this powerlessness. This is why we do not relish coming face-to-face with them. Until the day of our awakening, we shall hide.

I was now in the latter stage of my apprenticeship.

I was not sure whether to tell my master about my feelings, and this fact weighed heavy on my heart. I'm not sure when I started to feel that my master was a rival or a threat to my existence. One day, another one of those days when he'd been telling Shahmaran stories (we were probably past Belkıya's betrayal and the Seal of Solomon by then), he was standing heavily at the head of his workbench—his back turned toward me—and he picked up the story again. Suddenly I thought about how close to dying he was; his shoulders sunken, his back hunched; the more wildly his hands flew about, the heavier his body seemed. His crooked back, the hunch slowly overtaking his shrinking body, these made me secretly happy. My master was going to die. Before my eyes were those immortal Shahmarans he drew. From here on, I would draw them, each one more beautiful than the last.

Unfortunately, these disgraceful feelings were true. I loved my master.

For the first time, I learned of the desire to kill the one who conceived, gave birth to, taught, and raised me, of the brutal wish to kill him in order to be him. "Learned" is not quite right, I should say, "I sensed." Later on, as our master-apprentice bond developed, I understood that my master posed the greatest barrier to my own growth. I was standing in the shadow of a great sycamore, and I would always stay in that position. On the other hand, the person whom I most wished would see my mastery flourish was my master. I wanted him to see this, to recognize it. Which meant, I wanted something impossible because he was aging.

Which meant, a death of a different kind.

In any case . . . There was still time till I would understand that patience is the most crucial part of becoming a master.

What Jamsap Asked

Jamsap, who had listened to Shahmaran with great care, balked at this point in the story: betrayal at the hands of the sons of man.

"O Shahmaran!" he said. "Fine, you're right: I, too, am a son of man. You doubt me too. But your doubt hasn't been put to the test. You do not know me, you only know Belkıya, and you lump Belkıya and all of humanity together."

"Yet the price of testing you is very high, Jamsap. Your fate alone is not all we're talking about here, you see. And if it were only my own fate I would be putting into your hands, that would be no trouble at all. But do not forget that all of my charges' fates are tied to this; the time of my death is the herald and symbol of our rebirth. If I die too soon, it will serve no purpose at all. So long as the Seal of Solomon has not passed into human hands, my death must not occur. I am required to guard against my own death, do you understand me?"

"But so long as I am in this place, you will not get to know me. An untried, untested friendship is a false fate. I am in your domain and subject to your judgment. Surely my existence or my friendship will merit your trust. But in true love there is always fear of loss. It is a feeling that makes the beloved something other than a possession. Send me away, Shahmaran, test me, give me the chance to prove to you that not every human is Belkıya. This is something you will never learn so long as you keep me here."

"You are far too callow, Jamsap! You trust yourself so! You haven't tested and tried yourself either! How is it that you know yourself? True, it is my domain here, and you're here under my jurisdiction. But the demands of your world, would they not change you? Drag you into betrayal? How long can you stay shielded from the things that emanate from your world's lands and waters? Is it possible even? You are going to want to speak of me, of here, of what you have experienced; your heart will find keeping this secret too constraining; you will want to share what you've lived through, what you've seen, with others. This kind of a fable does not stay a secret, Jamsap. One word, one hint will leave your lips, and that will spoil everything. You see, I just don't want to live with this doubt, Jamsap. No one ought to cede his fate to another to such a degree . . ."

Jamsap understood that Shahmaran would keep detaining him and not desist easily.

"Let not your heart be troubled, Jamsap," said Shahmaran. "When summer comes, we'll retreat behind Kaf Mountain . . . Now that you have begun this fable, live it to its end. See what's behind Kaf Mountain; it's even more beautiful there than it is here; it's more pleasurable, and you will pass the time there in lovely ways. In the meantime, I will tell you a portion of Belkıya's story each evening."

"How long will this last?" Jamsap asked.

"One thousand nights," said Shahmaran.

The Seal of Solomon

The time of a fable is long
Belkıya and Ukap started on their journey upon the
desolate ocean desert like two Bedouin crossing the
seven seas.

Then they reached Solomon's island, reached Solomon's cave, reached Solomon's throne.

Belkıya recalled Shahmaran's words; he did not draw
any closer.

Ukap, who'd for years been ablaze with longing for
this moment, threw himself forth without a thought . . .

Approaching Solomon's island, Belkıya was thinking about the Island of Sleep.

He thought about Solomon's sleep.

About those who wait in sleep, about those who wait for sleep.

How could he sleep in this intense light? Doesn't sleep desire darkness? How many more leagues of the journey were there left, and yet the light from the island overwhelmed all of the sea, all of the distances, all of the dreams.

As they drew closer to the island, they adjusted to the light, although they also felt its glare all the more violently.

Surrounding the cave were thick bushy plants, wondrous woods, and salty, socking winds carrying the scents of a thousand and one spices.

Everywhere, every part of the island, was dazzlingly bright.

A brightness nearly as blinding as darkness.

Their eyes had to adjust to it like adjusting to darkness. This was when Belkıya understood how Solomon could sleep. The two trundled up difficult paths. A large, broad, and frightening spiderweb covered up the mouth of the cave. (In the holy books, this spiderweb appeared in the stories about the later prophets, especially the last messenger whose cave it kept hidden.) Quietly tearing through the web, they entered. A coolness that had waited years struck their faces. On the other end sat the prophet Solomon upon a grand, solid-gold throne. He sat as if he were sleeping, not dead. The beauty of the dead man illuminated his young, perfectly preserved body. The cave was furnished like a palace, filled with silks, velvet, trimmings, cords, pearls, engravings, embossments, gold coins, silver, marble, and porcelain, and surrounding the chamber were heavy drapes that fell all the way to the floor. Now and again, everything undulated in the soft cool breeze, making the grandeur ever grander. Amid so many precious things, the dead body seemed all the more like a person asleep. His copper skin appeared translucent in the dense sunlight, and there was a silk garment upon him, open from collar to chest. He waited with his hands folded over his sternum. The curls of his lips hid a vague smile. The fate of the seal was tied to the fate of the dead man.

Which meant the world was in an endless sleep.

Which meant everyone awaited an awakening.

From its place on his clasped, folded hands, the seal—in the form of a stone ring—blazed dazzlingly in all the four earthly directions, first within the cave, then upon the island, then upon the seven seas, and then it illuminated the entire world anew. It was a light waiting for history, waiting for its appointed time. The two men went straight for the long thin finger that wore this seal—and then Belkıya recalled Shahmaran's advice. A sharp pain went through his heart, and his feet called him to step back. Ukap had however forgotten the entire world and was shaking from head to toe. He was directly in front of the Seal of Solomon, his years-long dream only paces away. Just steps in front of him were all the distances, all the dreams. He reached for the ring, and when he touched it, a monstrous winged serpent appeared with a mighty, earth-shaking sound. Its breath carried a hellish flame. Its repulsive eyes flickered and burned as if in its mouth a door opened onto hell.

On the one hand, the dazzling invitation from the light of the seal.

On the other hand, the repulsive glare of death burning in the eyes of the giant serpent.

For Ukap, this was a dilemma merely of the visible realm; his passion prevented him from seeing it in any other way. And so, he advanced directly toward the ring. Belkıya could sense what was about to happen, but there was nothing to be done now. Nothing could hold Ukap back. It was not the ring he was approaching, but death. Ukap took his last step, and the serpent's growing, intensifying fire breath furled around his entire body. The last thing Belkıya saw of Ukap's giant body, wrapped and whipped with flame, was a thin transparency hovering towards nothingness.

And that was it.

That was everything.

Had Ukap really lived his life for the sake of this absence, this nothingness, which lasted just a few seconds? The body that had given his life meaning evaporated, within a few seconds, into a thin transparent flame.

All at once, Belkıya heard a thick, full, mysterious voice. From behind the columns a giant man, or rather a shadow that resembled Ukap but wasn't Ukap, called out:

"Son of man, why do you cast your souls into peril for things whose time has not yet come? The Seal of Solomon must wait. The son of man, with his foul and bloody history in recent times, has shown that he cannot wear the seal. It will take many years yet to grasp the source of this light. Do you think you are mature enough to take this power into your hands? You could use this power for wickedness. This would be the end of humanity. With your premature zeal, you court disaster for your own kind. You will make humanity miserable. Let this be a lesson to you. Now go and leave this place!"

Belkıya now understood what Shahmaran had said.

Finally he understood.

So he left the cave and went down to the shore. He had never felt so alone. A narrow beach, an endless sea. . . . (How difficult it was to return. How returning was always so hard and long.) Alone, terribly alone. And history's emptiness, stretched out before him, was beyond time and space and beyond any kind of thought.

There was nowhere he'd be arriving.
There was nowhere he'd be returning from.
Only a long, utterly long journey stretched out before him.
But he felt so tired, so worn out.
He'd used up all his journeys.

What Jamsap Asked

"But you had dropped Belkıya and Ukap on the shores of your own island and then left, so how is it that you know what became of them afterward? Why do you know this?"

Shahmaran smiled. "You are right to ask. But don't forget that Belkıya had come into my life once already. I was curious what he'd been going through, what he'd been up to. When you experience a parting of ways, you wonder how the other's way has turned out. His fate was of interest to me as well. Years had passed. I sent one of my jinn to his palace. Before a large gathering in the great hall, the grand vizier was reading from the book Belkıya had written about his life. It seems Belkıya had nothing else left to do but convey to others what he'd experienced. My jinn, wrapped in the form of a white Arabian steed, carried the vizier on its back straight to us here. I took the book from under the vizier's arm and sent him back. Belkıya had shut himself up in a hermitage and entered a period of contrition. He gave himself over to writing, and he wrote for years without pause. So that's how I came to know what became of him."

Jamsap fired off, "So why did you release the vizier?"

"I only needed the book that was in his hands. He'd brought Belkıya's life back to me."

"But didn't you fear the vizier would betray you and reveal where you were?"

Shahmaran laughed. "There was no spell of affection between us for him to betray. There is betrayal only when affection is at stake. That's why I will not release you as easily as the vizier."

One of the daemons knelt down and requested Shahmaran's permission to speak. It pled for Jamsap to be forgiven and returned to his world and his home.

"It cannot be," said Shahmaran. "At the least your kind must not learn how to forgive."

Belkıya journeyed all alone for days, for weeks, for months across the seas. This is how he came to know great despair. The pain in his heart was as deep as an abyss. At the end of his wandering, he reached another coast, another shore. A barren, honey-colored plain and endless dunes reached up to hills glittering under the sun's golden light.

His was a life unmoored and aimless, a life without peripheries.

In other words, he was standing at the onset of a new emptiness.

After journeying across this barrenness for a while, he came upon two armies of jinn. Since his childhood, he'd been in thrall to such visions. This now proved that the honey-colored beaches, the sun that burned differently, the unreal figures of the warring parties, the ease of killing and dying—this mythic aura still endured. (Which meant that he was not yet among the humans.) He watched their battles for a while. It seemed that war was for them still an instrument of negotiation: the lifeless bodies strewn across the sands, the streams of blood that were still absorbed completely by the sands, the instruments of war that resembled spears, axes, and arrows, and the deadly, immense endlessness of the battlefield . . . As if he stood outside of everything, he had lost all sense of touch. Belkıya remained gripped by the spectacle for a while, and then everything went silent. All the sounds and apparitions faded away. Either the war found its ending in a defeat for one side, or there was a truce. Death seemed so remote, Belkıya felt so far beyond its reach. After living through a solitary adventure like this, death remains outside everything. A person falls away from everything.

And then the jinn saw Belkıya. (He had a seashell propped up against his ear, hoping for a sound to rescue him from his silence.) They brought him to the chieftains, and he explained to them all that had occurred. How estranged we become from our experience when explaining our life to others! When he'd finished telling them his story, he wanted them to let him go, to permit him to continue on his path. The chieftain of the jinn army eyed Belkıya for a good long while, then made him his guest for seven days and seven nights, watching him, getting to know him, regaling him, believing in him. Come the end of the seventh day, he had a pale-blue steed saddled up for him.

The chieftain said, "This is my horse, which rides a half-year's journey in an hour. This horse shall bring you to the land of my vizier Amr. He will drop you at the start of the road to the border with the humans."

Belkıya thanked him, climbed onto the back of the steed, flew up through the tulle filaments of cloud, among the harsh winds, and over the high mountain zeniths until he reached Amr's land an hour later. Amr recognized the chief's steed and inquired as to Belkıya's wishes. Belkıya explained to him all that had happened. While explaining, he grew distant from those experiences. He had yet again become someone else.

He realized that explaining was a kind of magic spell. Perhaps what propelled Belkıya to write down his life was the delight he took, the fact of having been estranged from himself while explaining to others all he had experienced. The vizier Amr then also hosted Belkıya for seven days and seven nights . . . After that he placed Belkıya on yet another steed's back and guided him to the border with the humans. Then Amr turned back.

During the whole ride there, they spoke of nothing.

Belkıya was yet again on a threshold.

What Jamsap Asked

Jamsap said, "People can only be happy while they're among their own kind. This is the case for everything alive in nature. I am utterly alone in this place. No matter how warmly I am hosted, from start to finish I am a stranger among you, someone else, an other. You know so very little about life when you live as a constant stranger; it turns out that living as a constant stranger is a corrosive feeling . . . It's living at a distance that no 'closeness' can remedy."

Shahmaran smiled, and said, "Well then, do you know what it means to live in secret, my dear Jamsap? Believe me, the ordeal of living underground is no less wearying. The acreage of this garden is as far as my sovereignty reaches. Beyond this place, everything is immediately full of danger for us. I didn't know that being here, that being with me, had made you so unhappy."

"Please don't misunderstand me! I'm not unhappy because of being with you. On the contrary, this makes me very happy. My unhappiness is about being here."

"But the thing is, you can't be with me anywhere else but here . . ."

"Some loves only exist, dear Shahmaran, in their impossibility," said Jamsap.

"Who knows, maybe love is an altogether impossible thing, dear Jamsap," said Shahmaran.

Some days I liked my master a lot.

And some days I hated him.

I'm not quite sure why; a range of feelings groped at my heart. But it wasn't just because we did the same work. I understood this early on. To the contrary, our relationship was a quite intricate thing. In a very short time, a bond between us had formed, and then grew and strengthened. Like all bonds, it wore on us. Both my love and my hatred for him frightened me. For both were very powerful, and as they flowed into one another, they caused me great pain. Their power, so tenacious, seized me and began to transform me from head to foot. This too made me furious. I couldn't recognize myself anymore. It was as if I'd let myself slip out of my own hands, as if my own self escaped my grasp, I was someone else, and I couldn't turn back. I was resisting something, that's for sure. Was I afraid of growing up? Of loving? Of changing? I owed my master many things. Debt was culpability. The weight of this burden had begun to crush me. This master, who'd instructed me about my own self so very early on in life, was soon faced with this self recoiling from him.

Ours was a father-son relationship. With him, I experienced something I could not experience with my father. He filled up the absence of my father. I couldn't grasp that he'd taken my father's place, and this led to an angry resentment, a devastating indebtedness.

My master and the story he told began to envelop my life, all of it. My life was out of my hands. In the Shahmarans I drew, the reds deepened, the lines toughened, and there was the strained feeling, as if readying for battle.

I was looking for a way out.

Belkıya was looking for a way back.

Belkıya at the Great Wall of China

Belkıya continued on his path, alone. He climbed hills, crossed rivers. He asked for directions from the giants, fairies, and jinn who came upon him along the way. It wasn't quite clear why they were giants, jinn, or fairies. They appeared tired, heartsick, defeated. It was as if they'd given up on all the worlds.

Belkıya finally reached the Great Wall of China.

Its height stretched to the sky, its length yawning to the horizon, and not a single gate in sight all along it. It seemed to cordon off all the worlds and all the human beings from one another. And yet, Belkıya was craving touch. He had touched no one and nothing for such a long time. (He hadn't even touched the Seal of Solomon.) An immense wall had been erected long ago between humans and all the worlds. Now, the wall he was looking at made him recognize the invisible wall that had stood before him throughout his life. All grand dreams ushered in cursed adventures.

The path along the wall went on for days. Not even the smallest gate, not even a door or any other kind of hope, opened before him. (He'd spent his whole life in front of a wall like this . . . He understood this when the Great Wall of China materialized before him. The wall summarized his entire life . . .) Walk and walk, and it never ended, never exhausted itself, this wall; it extended perfectly straight, it neither curved nor bent. It stretched straight toward the horizon. It offered not the slightest glimpse about what or how much land or territory or volume it encompassed. It betrayed not a hint. As if it were reaching up to infinity, as if sweeping Belkıya toward all the forms of hopelessness in the world.

There were no magical journeys here like there were in the world of the giants. Humans countenanced hopelessness with such ease. He had reached the nadir of everyday existence. In short, this was a confining, depthless, tedious wall.

Life began behind it . . . or ended behind it . . . he didn't know.

Days later he met an ancient sage.

This was the first human he had seen in, how long had it been? A sage with white hair, white beard, and a white collarless shirt, squatting at the threshold of a door, as if he'd been there for a thousand years, mumbling little prayers now and then, gazing at the sun, swaying backward and forward, then falling silent for a long while. Belkıya rejoiced at the sight of a man and a doorway. He quickened his steps, reached the man, and sat next to him. The elderly man recounted everything step-by-step, building up as he went.

"This is the only door in the Great Wall of China. It is closed three hundred sixty-four days a year. Each year it opens on the first day of spring, when Dhu al-Qarnayn comes and opens the door. Then it is closed again till next spring . . ."

"Spring is approaching," said Belkıya.

"Approaching indeed," said the old man.

Belkıya grew warm inside. He'd seen a human being, and he would come to see many human beings on the first day of spring.

He put his hands on the man. Touched him for a long time.

His fingers felt a chill.

"Talk to me, Grandfather," he said. "It's nice to talk when you're lonely; a human being becomes someone different when talking."

They talked, and every day they looked around for the nectar of life, which the sage said was to be found all around the Great Wall of China.

In those days a journey lasted a lifetime. While studying at the Bukhara Seminary he'd come upon a section of a book that talked about the nectar of life. After that, he sought to learn more about it. The books he read described people who, determined to accomplish something in life, chased after the nectar of life. The nectar—which they used to call "the elixir" in the old days—granted eternal life and well-being to anyone who ingested it. To this day, only one person has attained this good fortune, and that was the Prophet Muhammad Aleyhisselam. He became translucent, vaporous, immortal. In all the written texts and in all the rumors that traveled from tongue to tongue, the nectar was said to be found in the vicinity of the Great Wall of China, and it was this nectar, or the dream of it, that led the old man to take this path and that had aged him so.

He had set upon this road in those days when a journey lasted a lifetime, and after so many years, he now sensed within him, here, by this wall, that he had come to the end of his life. On these last days before the beginning of spring, he was still searching ceaselessly, spending his last days in these surroundings. Spring was approaching. When uttering the word "approaching," the old man felt a sorrow so strong it was almost joy, but in his voice, there was more of the sorrow. To obtain immortality, he'd given his life and been defeated. He was at the end of the path, standing at the threshold of the door.

And he stayed there, until Dhu al-Qarnayn appeared on that first day of spring and opened the door.

Belkıya rejoiced to be surrounded again by humans. He always thought everyone he came across would be surprised to see him, no matter where he was in the world, and that they would greet him with equally great interest; but now everyone was just going about their business, not even turning around to look. This side of the Great Wall was as silent as the other. Now the loneliness he felt was deeper, thicker. An abyss ached inside him.

He kept on the road. This time he was headed to his country.

Belkıya was going back.

Whatever going back meant, that's what he was doing.

What Jamsap Asked

"He's going back," said Jamsap. "He's returning to his country, however lonely he may be, let him be lonely among his own kind again."

"Understood, Jamsap," said Shahmaran. "I can't keep you here, it's impossible. In the stories I tell you, you're always interested in those who go back . . . Who knows, maybe all stories are stories of return. And if I am silent on this topic, don't mistake it for cruelty; I too am searching for a remedy, a path, a solution. Both of us are suffering. But if you please, wait for the end of the story, as we have come to the story of Jahan Shah."

"Jahan Shah?" asked Jamsap.

"Yes, Jahan Shah," Shahmaran said. "He of countless love stories told over coffee in the winter cold, he of the deserted roadhouses, he who romances hearts on wintry nights and adorns dreams; you must have heard the story of Jahan Shah and his beloved Gevherengin . . . Their images hang on the sooty walls behind the coffeehouse stoves. Well, now you shall hear this story from me."

Jahan Shah

On the road, a gleaming white marble building appeared before Belkıya. It rose up in the middle of the steppe like an incantation, dazzling the eye like a desert dream. At the door stood a young, beautiful man in shining white silk and with hair and beard that appeared not to have been cut for years.

He stood worlds apart, as if near death.

"Welcome to these climes, stranger," he said. This phrase pleased Belkıya.

"Asian people are identified by clime, not country," he added, smiling. "Just four or five paces across borders, sometimes even none; just four or five paces to cross a trench or a rampart, but between climes stand centuries and worlds. For instance, my waiting at the front of this building, or your journey, these things may not be comprehensible in another clime. But we can recognize one another by the steppe or the silence we carry inside us, or by the tales the travelers will tell about us on long nights while on the road."

Their eyes met.

Already heroes of their own fairy tales, the two greeted by touching each other's fingertip.

Jahan Shah hosted Belkıya in his home. They ate, drank, communed. First, Belkıya told his story. Jahan Shah listened, posing no questions. Nor did he say anything. From the light in his eyes that glimmered while listening, it was obvious that he knew very well what Belkıya was speaking about. They knew each other through their own experiences.

A while later Jahan Shah began his account. (Humans back in those days recounted their lives to one another.)

His name was Jahan Shah. The only son of Tahmur, the Shah of the Rose Gardens.

"For many years, my father Shah Tahmur had no children. For this reason he went around longing and lacking. One fine day, a vizier named

Hajjaj, a master of geomancy, gave my father the good news. He said, 'The padishah of Horasan has a girl. She's an only child too. She was conceived despite a thousand and one difficulties and by way of a thousand and one spells. If you marry her, you will have a child . . .' And lo and behold, I was born. They called me Jahan Shah. The entire palace was mustered to raise me. One day, having grown old, my father turned over his throne to me. And I was of age and maturity to assume the throne. But I had a passion. It was a mad, deep-rooted passion for hunting . . . Why hunting, you'll ask? Because everything, I mean everything, had been handed to me since the moment I was born. There was nothing missing, no lack. To own, to gain, I had to endeavor so little, make so little effort. Even my most modest wishes were fulfilled before they ever had a chance to deepen. And so, the hunt was more important than anything else. It was the only relationship I established with life, one could say. Various things I didn't know awaited me there; I didn't know what would emerge and why, or what I would encounter. I didn't know what would pounce out at me from behind which tree, from which hollow. There was the spell of unknowing in the hunt. Hustling after an animal for hours and setting traps pleased me. When hunting, I was able to achieve something by my own effort, my own power. I came face-to-face with my own effort, tested my own power. I tasted a kind of solitude.

On one of those endless, tireless hunts, in a secluded part of the forest, a stag leapt out in front of me. As far as I'd seen of stags, this was the most beautiful, the most gallant, the proudest one. As if it weren't just one stag but symbolizing all stags. In its slanted, dreamy eyes there was a sense of pride, of love. Up on its long, slender, forked antlers it seemed to carry the whole world. This stag had to be mine. I'd never desired anything this much in my entire life.

We gave chase to the stag on horseback for hours. Once seen, it would disappear again. Keeping up with it, catching it, was impossible. But, in this way, it gained even more of my affection. Most of my footmen had returned to the palace. Because they did not share my passion, they grew more easily tired, muddled. They were constantly waiting for my "Turn back!" command. We came to a shore, and it was difficult for me to even recognize the fact that this was the sea. My eyes could see nothing but the stag, which, bouncing and bustling back and forth at the water's edge, threw itself, undaunted, into the sea, swimming out to an island. It turns out it was the island of stags, and to this day no son of man has ever made it out there. How could I have known this?—but if I had, would it have changed my decision? I don't know . . . where passions are concerned, there is no place for such worries, as you well know. Passion is naked and singular. It exists with and for itself alone. Most of the horses had foundered. Most of my footmen were distraught from exhaustion. We immediately prepared a skiff, and the still agile among my men joined me on our way to the island.

How was I to know that shooting a stag would unleash a curse? As we were rowing back with a dead stag on my lap, the sound of the wind began to change. This was no longer the sea we knew and recognized. A tempest broke out, and for days our boat rocked and lurched in the middle of the sea. The storm resembled a typhoon: we didn't capsize or sink, but we feared and suffered. Some days later the storm abated. The wind brought us to a shore, and I understood that we were now in another clime and I'd now begun a long, cursed adventure.

The ones who had returned earlier had told my father about all that had happened. Hajjaj the geomancer consulted the sand grains and said, "He's alive, your son, but he will only be able return to his country years from now, after enduring many adventures."

Beyond this, there was nothing left for him to do but console my father and wait.

Among the Apes

Advancing for days from the shore, we saw a castle of marble with iron doors. The castle was empty, and we believed it abandoned; we passed through the houses, the alleys, the courtyards. Finally, we entered the palace, which was also empty. What caught my attention were all the buildings made of marble and the echoing sounds of water. Crystal-clear, immaculate sparkling water was flowing everywhere. Passing through steep gutters and narrow canals, it poured into wide pools, and from there spread throughout the city. We entered the great hall of the palace, and there in the center was a magnificent grand throne studded with precious stones. My men immediately set me on the throne and surrounded me, just when we noticed a crowd of apes advancing toward us. We winced, but wincing was unnecessary as they immediately came forward and kissed our robes and knelt before us. But what business did apes have with a civilized city like this, with its advanced and orderly structures? What were they seeking? They couldn't have made this civilization themselves, but perhaps they had overrun it and killed the original dwellers? But they did not have a warring disposition. Soon, seven dogs the size of mules showed up. All of the dogs were harnessed. These apes—who were, I'd learned, to be my subjects—produced strange sounds, maybe trying to explain various things with their hands and arms. In any case, we mounted the dogs and made our way toward a hill. On the hilltop, a monument reached up straight to the sky, sparkling as it caught the first light of day.

It was a tall marble tablet.

The inscription explained everything:

O humankind!

I, like you, ended up here by roaming the path of my fate. I became the padishah of these apes. The whole region came under my command. Unlocking its secret took me many years. Long ago these apes used to be humans like us. They established this city, but they ruined it from one day to the next, they squandered what they valued, forgot their truths, and were eaten up by their meanness, torments, doubts, and defeatism. Trust remained among no one, and everybody began to fatten themselves on the blood and labor of others. Enmity, cruelty, torture, lies, and tyranny became facts of daily life. And they martyred the very prophets who sought to show these people the way again, to restore order. Much was sacrificed in the end. By then, they had summoned the wrath of God. Based on the reasoning that they had no right to humanity, as punishment they were returned to their origins, changed back into apes. Being their padishah is both tough and easy. They're quite dependent on humans, as their pasts reoccur to them in memory, and they most certainly wish to become humans once again. But they will not love you. Animality is not for loving. Governing them comes with some conditions. They cannot govern themselves, as they've grown used to living under the command of another. When left alone, their minds cannot be shielded from confusion. If even just one person leads them it's enough: no matter what they say or do, they will cheer, for they are apes, after all. They do not have their own thoughts, their own feelings, their own wishes, their own values, their own truths. They don't love each other; they just imitate each other. They deem it a virtue to resemble one another, to be precisely like each other. This is why no one among them can become a chieftain.

Do not think of launching a war from this place, for if you go south, you'll find the land of the ogres. As you know, they are creatures who've been unable to find their place on earth. Toward humans they hold an eternal grudge, but they despise the apes even more. Because the apes had their opportunity to be human and squandered it. This is why they perpetrate frequent attacks on the land of the apes.

If you go east, you'll encounter the rage of fire and flame, as this is the land of the volcanoes. Fire and flame have no memory. They live by burning. This is why they have neither history nor future . . . Seeing again all the things that they thought they had burned out of existence drives them to madness, intensifies their rage.

In the north is the land of the ants. These are ants of an advanced kind. They are the size of dogs. Creatures who exist through work alone, who do not love themselves except while working. Their world is crammed, very small. They don't like to be bothered by each other. Even though they move in herds, most have never met one another. Diffident, discontented, dejected. They harbor a broad unhappiness and rage. They don't like humans in the least. As soon as you arrive, they will tear you to pieces and eat you.

In the west, you'll fall beyond the seven seas; this is the path of death. No one who has tread there has been seen alive again.

Your best chance is to remain here.

To die here.

Where the inscription ended, just below the tablet, was his tomb.

I understood there was no way to escape from here. There was no other hope but to get used to my new life. Even if I was the padishah—among breeds not my own—I was not happy. I spent my days getting to know the surroundings and looking for paths away from here that would save me. I waited for spring. In the meantime, we made war against the ogres now and then. These were bloody wars, but each time my appearance startled them and caused them to retreat. The apes now trusted and believed in me. They were happy to the extent that they thought me happy. In the spring, I went north with my men and a few of the apes with the aim of surveying the borders. I thought and wandered a great deal, finally setting out to find those escape routes to the north. I knew this would be a dangerous venture.

The other directions led to death, and death only.

But the north at least provided humans with the opportunity to make war. They may survive at the end or they may die, but there was always in it the imminence of struggle and battle. The north provided the chance for a more humane struggle. Death and a bit of hope . . .

At the border, we held a festival ample with wine. The aim was to get the apes drunk and render them incapacitated. We gathered around a great fire to eat and drink, and lo and behold, the apes all petered out. My men and I began our trek at full gallop toward the land of the ants. The route took days. Nothing yet in sight. Not one building, not one ant came into view. Everywhere was empty, silent, and frightening. The suspense itself was much more draining than everything else, as if, at every turn, we were waiting for the enemy to jump out at us and for the war to begin. The certainty of war was far preferable to the eerie silence.

We'd reached a clearing with a stone basin when ants the size of dogs ambushed us. Their mouths were huge, pincers strong and teeth sharp. Some of my men were dismembered and devoured before my eyes. The rest of us managed to evade them and continued on our way. Now we were on the alert, knowing that they were following our tracks. A few days later, we met our next attack. This time they were more numerous and brutal, full of rage and disgust that they had let us slip out of their grasp. My remaining men and their horses were torn apart. I was the only one among us able to wrest myself from their grasp, and I began running like a madman. I don't know how far I'd run when I came upon a river. On the other side of the river was a charming little city with gleaming white buildings. The river cut off my path and offered no crossing. I searched for a bridge, a crossing, while also keeping an eye on the ants. If they caught up, I would throw myself into the river. Right then, I recalled the stag. He too had stood at the edge of the water like this, with us on horseback coming up behind him. Back then I was the hunter, now the hunted.

And what I was unable to understand then, I understood now.

We both had been standing, inconsolable, at the water's edge. At that moment I realized that all my adventures had led me to this water's edge, had brought me face-to-face with that stag. This was perhaps what fate had foretold to me. All human drama arises from how one's own history intersects with the history of others. It was at that water's edge that I first had this thought.

Just then, an old man appeared on the other side of the river. "Don't fret, stranger," he said. "In the evenings, the river runs high, which is why they call it the Night River. During the day the water recedes and, if you survive till the morning, you can walk across the dry bed to this side. Now, night is approaching, and the pulse of the river is raging more than ever."

There was no other hope for me but to wait for the morning, as instructed. And so it came to be that come morning, the water receded, the sound of it diminished to a hush, and the riverbed dried up. I crossed to the other side and entered the town.

Everything was closed, and everyone was shut up in their homes. There was no one to speak to. It occurred to me at first that this might be a cursed city. After a while, I saw a half-open door and decided to walk in. The owner of the house, his wife, and their child were gathered around the table, eating. They invited me in too. I asked, and they replied.

"The name of this city is Nehrevan. We are of the people of Moses. Among the days of the week, this is Saturday. It is a blessed day. Long ago, God forbade us to fish on Saturdays. We cast our nets on Friday and retrieved them on Sunday. This was a small act of cunning for humans, and perhaps God grew angry about our cheating and punished us. He cut off our water, and this is why the river dries up every day. The water surges only at night."

I spent the night among them.

The next day, my host took me to the market. I had only been looking for the way back to my country, and yet I was now mixing among these people. I trembled with delight; I'd missed my homeland, my people, my customs. Everyone gathered around me and listened to me in the market. I related what had happened to me. What I described piqued everyone's interest, and they took me for a fairy-tale hero.

Just then a barker made his way through the streets, calling out, "Win a thousand gold coins and a beautiful bondmaid! Follow me!"

This invitation caught my interest. The power of gold might make my return easier. Lining up behind the barker, I found myself walking alongside a merchant. By the evening, we were at the head of a great and gorgeous banquet table with wondrous dishes, various sweets and salty bits, and ample drink. Behind it was a young and tender bondmaid, whom they sent to my side. How long since I had been with a woman!

It was a happy, pleasant, and colorful evening, one I would have to pay for the next morning.

That next morning, the merchant and I rode on the back of camels for what seemed like ages, until we arrived close to the peak of a very tall mountain. Right there, the merchant slit open one of the camels and disgorged its stomach. And, handing me a pouch of gold, he said, "Now you will climb into the camel's stomach and wait. It won't be long until the eagles begin to flock around the camel's carcass. They will pick up the carcass and carry it to the summit, up to the craggy cliffs. Once they set you down there, climb out of the camel's stomach. When they see you, they will be startled and scared off. Since the old days, there have been precious stones and jewels there. Gather these in a bag and throw them down to me. Once you're done with the stones, you will climb down too. Climbing up is arduous surely, but coming down is easy, as with any summit."

I hesitated at first, but I had already taken to the road, and turning back was unthinkable. In our clime, all roads expect to be taken once, and none allows return; either death or destiny awaits us. We travel the roads already foretold.

I crawled in the camel's stomach and waited, and the eagles came and carried off the carcass. Once we'd reached the peak of the mountain, I got out and scared off the eagles. Everything was as described. In all directions there were precious stones and jewels. After gathering them up in a sack, I tossed them down. Soon after I saw the merchant get on his horse and head off, ever farther away.

I understood. I'd been cheated!

Just as humans betray you while lowering you down a well, they betray you by bringing you up a mountaintop.

I'd been left all alone.

The descent wasn't easy, as the merchant had said; it was almost impossible. Steep cliffs and sharp crags extended out in all four directions. One wrong step could lead a person off the right path to his death. There was no stone I could anchor myself to, step upon, glide over, not even the slightest indentation or protrusion that gave me hope for going farther. I looked around me, trying not to panic. One of the cliffs was less steep than the others. The best beginning might be from there. Whatever the case, I had to start somewhere on this slippery terrain, for waiting here without moving—and for what?—was nothing other than death. No hope would come from elsewhere. I could bake, scorched from the heat, or die of starvation. Already with my first step, I puzzled over the sun-whetted slopes of the rocks with my hands, arms, teeth, and skin. From head to toe, I was cut up all over and covered in blood, but in the end, I'd somehow made it to a flat surface. I had succeeded!

The sandy color of the clearing, its air, and its barren features hinted at the beginning of another fairy tale. As if I was living an endless chain of dreams tied to one another.

For a while I walked across a flat terrain, and much later a gleaming white marble palace rose up in front of me. In the courtyard stood an elderly saint with a milk-white beard, as if he'd been standing there for a thousand years. He was wearing a white collarless shirt and sash and a shawl that reached down to the floor. His hands were clasped at his abdomen (his index finger in the air, as if indicating something in the sky), and he smiled at me. I ran to him, kissed his hand and his hem. I wanted to ask this person with the saintly face for help so I might discover my way.

We sat by a pool, listening to the sweet sound of the fountain, which gave the surrounding courtyard a sensation of coolness. I explained what had happened to me, and he listened with interest. Shah Mürg, as this was his name, stroked his beard with his index finger, occasionally stopping and smiling. In all of his gestures there was an erudite fullness, a settledness.

This place, he told me, was a sanctuary for birds.

Solomon, the prophet, had offered this place to the birds as a sanctuary. Shah Mürg explained that birds from the world's four directions met here each week. From faraway countries, from their various seasons and various migrations, they spoke about themselves in their own languages.

Shah Mürg took me around the palace, and I was mesmerized. Toward evening he said, "I am going to a conference of the birds." So that I would not grow bored, he put into my hand a bundle of keys, which were the keys to the forty rooms of the palace. "Take in the rooms one by one, enjoy them, look for something to eat and drink," said Shah Mürg. "But pray, do not open the fortieth room, the one with the iron door! Just don't touch that one, or you'll regret your decision!" After he'd gone, I did what he said. I took in each room one at a time, strolling about. Each room was undoubtably its own world, each possessed of its own endless beauties, fineries, and details. Each differed from the next in how it was arranged and ornamented, but I was unable to savor any of them, as my mind was always on that fortieth room. Ever since I held that bundle of keys in the palm of my hand, I couldn't keep my eyes from that fortieth key on the ring. In my eyes, that was the one I cherished, the one that urged me onward. This is why I was never able to taste the sweetness of the places I was visiting, and I felt restless. In solitude, my desire burgeoned. The secret of the fortieth room made me forget everything, the spell of its unknowability blindfolded my eyes, and I could no longer see the other rooms. I made my decision: whatever happens, I was going to open the fortieth door. I'd decided to live this story through to its very end.

And so I opened the iron door.

The fortieth spell of the palace with forty rooms took hold. A garden of extraordinary beauty opened up before me and drew me in. A marble pool, so beautiful that it couldn't be real, a porphyry portico with its back to the setting sun, plush couches, silk shawls, canopies of atlas fabric redolent of the *Thousand and One Nights*, undulating quietly in the evening wind. Tree branches entwined, the flowers swayed about coyly. Soon three white doves appeared gliding against the sky. Their wings touched one another in flight. Descending, they united, swooped down to the garden, and set themselves down on the rim of the pool. They shook themselves off and their wings fell from them like garments, leaving three beautiful girls. The smallest of them—I fell in love with her as soon as I saw her. They disrobed and entered the pool, rinsed off, and swam . . .

My eyes were dazzled by the beauty I saw.

I fainted right there in my hiding place.

When I came to, Shah Mürg was standing above me. He surveyed me with displeasure.

No longer were there three doves around, nor three girls.

I wanted to make peace with Shah Mürg, and I told him what had happened. Shah Mürg's face wore the expression of someone who'd predicted what had transpired.

"I told you already, Jihan Shah," he said.

"If what I've done is a sin, then I've already begun to reap the punishment," I said, asking for mercy, asking for a remedy.

Shah Mürg recounted their story. These were the daughters of the fairy padishah. The name of the youngest one was Gevherengin. Their country was located beyond Kaf Mountain. Once a year they would come, bathe in this pool, and leave. Every year, the same day . . . For years it had kept on like this. I had no other choice. I had to wait exactly one year. Shah Mürg said, "Next year you'll wait for this day, and that dove you loved—you'll take its garments and hide them. When she gets out of the pool and cannot find them, she will not be able to become a dove again and fly away, and she will stay with you and be yours."

Exactly one year passed.

The days were slow, the days were long, the days were cruel.

The forty rooms of the marble palace were forty tombs.

And then the day came.

When the doves appeared overhead, it was as if the sky was undulating. Again, they descended slowly, quietly, and landed on the rim of the pool, shook themselves off, shrugged off their garments, and became three beautiful girls. Disrobing, they entered the pool.

I hid Gevherengin's garments. They searched for them for a long time, and not finding them, her sisters flew up and away.

Gevherengin stayed.

Gevherengin stayed for me.

She begged and pleaded, but I wouldn't return her wings, her feathers, her dove shirt. I told her of my love, that I had been made to miss a whole year. I told her at length about my life. I wanted her to love me.

She loved me.

She truly loved me.

Shah Mürg formalized our betrothal in the bird sanctuary. After that, we set out on the road to return to my country, Gülistan, to my father's side, to my home.

Shah Mürg, taking leave of us, said, "Pray, do not return her wings lest she fly away. No matter how much she may love you, she will leave. Indeed, sometimes people leave because of their love. If you give her her wings, her heart will split in two. She will feel the need to make a choice, and she may choose them. Do not put her in a bind such as this! It could make you both unhappy. This could mean chancing a long and excruciating game. Don't trifle. Don't trifle with it. Don't give her the wings. Now go. May your road be open!"

We took flight on the back of one of Shah Mürg's birds. It was a long, colorful, sweeping journey, and we were full of delight.

And in the end we arrived.

Tahmur Shah, beholding me, his son, these years later, was joyful. Convening a grand assembly, and with a grand wedding and a magnificent ceremony, he crowned his happiness, our reunion, and my happiness. Gevherengin also looked to be happy.

Day after day imbibing this dense happiness made me rather drunk; it rather stupefied me. I spent the first night of our togetherness entirely beside myself, and I ended up leaving her dove shirt out in the open. When I woke in the morning, she was not next to me. Gevherengin must have grabbed her shirt, beat her wings, and become a dove. And there she was, perched on the roof of the opposite house.

"Ey, Jihan Shah! You tricked me away from my own home, my own kind, my own race. Yes, you loved me, I know that. You thought your love would suffice. You thought love solved everything. I won't deny it, I too loved you. But though I loved you, our circumstances were not equal. You gave me no other option but to love you. I wasn't able to make my own decision. Now I'll be able to think on my own, about whether or not I love you, about other things too . . . If you really love me, you will follow me. This is your country, you are among your own people, you shall certainly be happy here, but what am I to do? You never gave that a thought. Loving isn't easy, Jihan Shah. I'm going to return to my country, to my father's hearth. The name of my country is Kevher Engin. I shall await you there."

First she flew to my window and, bidding me farewell, she disappeared.

Now the sky was empty.

I spent the days looking at all this emptiness.

The entire palace learned of the truth at once. All the scientists, travelers, merchants, seers, geomancers, and dervish sages were called to the palace. The well traveled and the well read were gathered. No one knew the location of the country of Kevher Engin; they'd not even heard the name. I was despondent. Days, weeks, months passed. I stewed in my own passion; a thick hopelessness agonized in my arms. I needed to find this place. If I knew where it was, I wouldn't stay one more minute in my father's palace. But around me stretched a vast world in all four directions. The huge palace, like a lion's cage, barricaded me and bound my arms.

One day it occurred to me to go back to Nehrevan. But no one knew where Nehrevan was either. I'd go to Baghdad, and there, in that fabled city of the thousand and one nights, I'd find at least one person who knew. There was no other way, no other hope. I was going to live out my fate all over again and, arriving at the same point where I'd already been, this time I would behave differently and conquer my fate.

And so it was that I learned in Baghdad where Nehrevan was. To learn this took many days and nights, but I learned it. Forgetting my exhaustion, I set out directly on the road to Nehrevan. As soon as I reached its market, a barker was standing there shouting, "Win a beautiful bond maid and a thousand gold coins! Follow me!"

I followed him.

I followed my fate.

Everything was just like last time. The merchant didn't recognize me. He meets hundreds of youngsters every day, and, seducing each, he adds their fortune to his own, and yet all the faces and all the youngsters were the same to him.

We again reached the mountain, and I crawled inside the camel's belly; the eagles snatched up the carcass, and we climbed to the mountain peak. There I was deceived again, and I descended by the same path and reached the clearing. I found the marble palace and Shah Mürg, who said:

"My son, didn't I tell you not to give her the wings? The love between you had not yet been put to the test. The passion of your fairy tale has blinded your eyes, and you were naive. Beginning again anew isn't as easy a business as you'd thought. Besides, the doves never came back here after that day. You upset the balance of the sanctuary, and you made yourself unhappy. The exuberance of your feelings gave you no chance to experience what you truly felt. And no one here knows where her home is, her place. Perhaps in the months ahead the phoenix Zümrüdüanka will come. Only she knows. But it's unclear whether she will bring you there or not."

And so began the days of waiting, again.

My only hope now was Zümrüdüanka the phoenix.

She was the hope of all the heroes of all the stories.

Months later, when she came, I begged and begged. She was accustomed to passion and to passionate people; the worth of love and passion was clear to her. She had listened to so many stories. Carrying them on her back, she had grown old in so many stories. She understood me too, and agreed to take me on her back, though she only promised she would take me to the next closest hill; she could apparently go no further, fearful as she was of the fairy padishahs. That the mighty Zümrüdüanka had fears seemed foolish to me. On the way, we formed a good friendship, climbing Kaf Mountain, and she was willing to take me to that next closest hill. We passed over many a mountain, hill, plain, and nation. How different the world looks when seen from astride the great bird!

After one last ascent, we landed on the hill, and down below we saw a white palace gleaming bewilderingly. The winds were blinding with a whiteness I knew well. A sand-colored sky covered everything. That I was so very near the door of the palace of the country of Kevher Engin, with its constantly changing hues, became known to the fairies too. Zümrüdüanka had long since disappeared from view. Soon I was captured by the fairies, and I told them of my travails.

Gevherengin had been watching my journey for months.

I was taken directly to the fairy padishah.

This had been a test, and I had succeeded; here I was, at Gevherengin's doorstep.

I had reached Kaf Mountain, and behind it found the fairy castle with its tall towers that reached up to the rose-hued clouds. Gevherengin's face had been entirely erased from my eyes, and now I attempted to remember it. Whenever I tried, I saw a dove beat her wings and fly away, taking my beloved's face with her. The fairy padishah indeed believed that I loved his daughter. I don't know why he believed this, as I had done next to nothing to convince him. Perhaps he believed this due to the sheer ordeal I'd undergone. And so, we were betrothed there, surrounded by much rejoicing. I thought happy days awaited us. Gevherengin was beside me but I felt out of place. I was transient. Everything here was foreign to me: I had no memories in this country, nothing recalled my childhood. Day after day, I descended into a pale unhappiness, my gaze grew inattentive, my smiles meaningless. Gevherengin grasped it, my unhappiness, my restlessness, and the reason for them; she agonized over finding ways to help me, but nothing came of her efforts. For I was still an exile, though voluntarily so, and perfecting exile was a difficult task. In the end, she suggested returning together to my home. I knew this was a sacrifice. She wanted to compensate for my sacrifice. But she was going to undergo similar kinds of distress, similar suffering. In my homeland, she would feel foreign as I did here, experience the same loneliness that foreignness brings. When I tried explaining all this to her, she smiled and replied, "You are a man," she said. "You don't know how to change your own shirt. Whereas I am a woman, and I've no difficulty taking on your color. What you were not taught because you are a man was taught to me because I'm a woman. That's all."

I had no other hope than to believe her, to trust her. I knew this was the selfishness of a man, the selfishness of a lover. Soon we set out. The fairy padishah assigned us a company of daemons as our guardians. It was a slow journey with many stops; we endeavored to savor the journey, which consequently lasted quite a long time.

During one of our nighttime encampments, the daemons were sitting around absentmindedly, while I was stoking the fire so it wouldn't go out. Gevherengin was just a bit further on, resting in our tent. Just then a pack of leopards attacked us, and we didn't know where they'd come from or why they were coming for us in this silent forest. In the blink of an eye, they swarmed us and left behind Gevherengin torn into a thousand and one pieces. That red tent had beckoned death. I cannot find the words to describe my pain, I really cannot. Attack after attack, I remained unharmed. The pain of all those killed before my eyes—I survived time and again in order to carry this pain in me every day of my life. And this time it was Gevherengin . . . and in our most beautiful and happy period of our youth and our life . . . No leopards were ever seen again in this region . . . One of the daemons returned to the fairy padishah and explained what had happened. The padishah left at once and came to his dead daughter's side, and I begged of him, "O benevolent padishah! Permit me to bury my wife where she died, and I will wait at her grave till the end of my life. This is my last and only wish of you," I said. The padishah, who had believed in my love, now too believed in my pain.

"Doomed love, as they say, cannot be bloodless or without sacrifice," he said. "It doesn't fall to me to separate you, Jihan Shah. Do as you wish."

Alas, Belkıya! Since that day I've waited at this grave, waiting for my death. Nothing remains for me but to watch the seasons turn.

Jihan Shah came to the end of his story as Belkıya got to his feet.

"I know you will never again seek the company of human beings since a melancholy as deep as yours will yield to nothing. I only wish you peace of mind. I'll now be on my way."

Jihan Shah bid Belkıya farewell, and their fingertips once again touched. Their stories had been intertwined.

Yet again, Belkıya was fated for long journeys. One of the roads led to a garden. A garden! Again a garden! That feeling of a heaven lost! Belkıya hadn't yet stepped into the garden when an immense fan opened before him and covered up the view of the garden. This fan was even more beautiful than the charming multicolored garden itself because its extraordinary colors, form, and designs evoked a garden too.

The fan closed.

Now, before him stood the most magnificent and angelic Tavus-u Azam.

Belkıya called out, "O beautiful bird! O auspicious bird! Where are we now? Who are you then?"

"This is the garden of the Prophet Mohammad Aleyhisselam," the enchanting peacock replied. "I live here. They call me Tavus-u Azam. Together with the prophet Adam, I was banished from paradise."

Tavus-u Azam related to Belkıya how they'd been banished from paradise. His story was strange. Belkıya listened with amazement; what he heard made him question everything he'd ever learned previously.

"In any case," said Tavus-u Azam, "this is a topic for another story."

Belkıya asked, "O Tavus! Could you send me back to be among the humans, to my home?"

"This I cannot do," she said. "Wait for the Prophet Mohammad Aleyhisselam to come a little later, and if you tell him of your sorrows, perhaps he will send you back to your home."

The Prophet Mohammad Aleyhisselam listened to Belkıya. When Belkıya finished speaking, he said:

"Close your eyes." He took his hands, and Belkıya closed his eyes tight. When he opened them, he was in front of his castle.

Here, Shahmaran fell silent.

Jamsap was startled. Belkıya's return came quite suddenly for him.

"All this journeying ended with one blink of an eye, really?" said Jamsap.

"Life is like that," Shahmaran replied. "Life ends with one blink of an eye, doesn't it?"

Shahmaran was sad. They had come to the end of the tale. The sovereign knew that Jamsap would now go.

"I can't prolong the tale anymore," said Shahmaran. "Besides, it's already the end of the night of a thousand tales."

"Shall I close my eyes too, Shahmaran?" asked Jamsap.

Shahmaran replied, "I know you'll leave, I can't keep you here any longer. But I have one wish left for you. Once you're back home, never again go to the hammam, never again go bathing. For humans, once they have seen Shahmaran, will grow scales from the waist down when they bathe and betray the secret. And then it will be known that you've seen me, that you've been with me."

Jamsap once again took oaths upon oaths. He swore at length that he would say nothing to anyone, and he would not go to the hammam.

Shahmaran called on one of the daemons to take Jamsap to the gate, then turning to Jamsap, said, "Then go now. Don't dawdle, leave immediately!"

And then the sovereign cried for a long time behind him.

5.

And so Jamsap was back on the face of the earth.

The magic was over, the tale he'd listened to had reached its end. Shahmaran and the fairy-tale land were as if a faraway memory now. But it occurred to Jamsap that he was not happy. Returning home, being back on earth, reuniting with his mother and his people did not make him as happy as he'd thought. And yet he knew if he'd stayed in Shahmaran's land, he'd have felt the same. His was an unhappy exile, expelled from all lives, finding a place for himself neither below the surface nor on the surface. He missed Shahmaran, the delicate, beautiful face, those charming glances, those sweet words. Confident he would stay true to his vow, he felt a sense of inner peace. He would never say anything to anyone. And for years he did not.

When he reached the door of his house, stepping over the threshold, his mother was startled but her surprise soon turned to delight. Her son whom she'd not seen for a long time and had thought dead was standing before her alive and in high spirits. She smiled with her glittering eyes. Then they embraced, cried, shared their woes. His mother saw how her son had grown and sensed that it was not merely the intervening time that had led to this transformation.

The friends who had left Jamsap in the well had since grown up and become merchants. Their business prospered, their yields were high, and even if once in a while they went through a dry stretch, they still gave Jamsap's mother a few coins, sent her food, or wood for burning.

Jamsap did not want to see anyone. He felt he did not have the strength to make peace with them. Besides, it did not matter, in his eyes, whether or not he made peace with them. They could hand over the lion's share of their ill-gained fortunes in recompense for their betrayal and to keep Jamsap silent, but what would that change? Now they were all grown, and that carefree, disaffected adolescent circle of friends had long disappeared.

He was in a deep melancholy, a deep loneliness. He knew something no one else knew. He thought of his father Danyal and of Belkıya, and he understood how they had died lonely. He became one of those lonely ones stricken with the curse of knowing.

For many years, he kept his secret, and no one knew where or with whom he had been. He'd not been torn apart by tigers like they had told his mother and everyone else, but where had he been living for these years? With whom? No one else knew this, no one had found out. He lived, hiding behind his silence. Every day he saw to his daily business, worked, rested, read; at the same time, he remembered longingly the thousand nights of tales in Shahmaran's palace. He had experienced the kind of miracle that humans only experience once and never forget. After returning to earth, his life had grown colorless and dim. Passion, enthusiasm, even anger, all gone from his life. On one of his endless days, he came to the bitter realization that he was only living to finish out his life, and that, having seen Shahmaran once, he would never again be able to be the old Jamsap. Deep inside him, very deep, something was completely annihilated.

His secret separated him from people; he closed himself in his house, in his self.

For days, weeks, months, years, his life stayed the same. But then, one of those days, Keyhüsrev, the padishah of the land, fell into a grave and incurable illness. The many physicians, scientists, and charmers could not find a remedy. What's more, his condition was worsening with each passing day, as fatal wounds opened up in his body and he writhed in insufferable pain. It was a sickness like no other. His vizier, a geomancer skilled in magic, was named Shehmur. He was a vizier the people had never liked, the padishah's toady—calculating, opportunistic, villainous, and cruel. His geomancy always fixated on the devastation of others. His intellect was bent on cunning, deception, malice, and treason. Vizier Shehmur concluded from the padishah's symptoms that the only cure for his illness was the flesh of Shahmaran. If the padishah ate of Shahmaran's flesh, Shehmur said, he would be cured of his disease, the disorder in the country would abate, and the whole community would resume its normal, healthy life. His illness was the cause of all problems, sorrows, and distress. His recuperation, yes, his life, required Shahmaran's flesh. So, suddenly, a grand hunt for Shahmaran began throughout the country. Somehow everyone became an enemy of this Shahmaran they'd never met, never seen, and never known.

In truth, no one knew where Shahmaran was, but everyone tried to disprove anyone else who believed they'd seen Shahmaran or knew where the enchanted sovereign lived. No one trusted other people; everyone felt on edge, anxious, guilty—and worse, became each other's informant, murderer, executioner. Fathers became the enemies of their sons, masters the enemies of their apprentices, neighbors the enemies of their neighbors. These were the days of power-hungry men. The citizens, who had known nothing beneficial, favorable, or beautiful, wrought evil upon others, fed upon their fears, savored the positions they hoarded high and low, as if convinced this was the only way of being on the face of the earth. Oppression spread, houses were raided regularly, and people were rounded up in public squares and brought in groups to the baths to be washed and inspected for whether they were growing scaly below the waist and released when they passed this test. Human dignity and respect for people were trodden underfoot. Cruelty, oppression, and hardship quickly became the driving forces of life.

In his hut outside the city, Jamsap was living a colorless, airless life—narrow and out of reach. But the widening circle would absorb him too. The padishah's enforcers would be closing in on Jamsap's house. People had already fled the nearby villages, then the ones farther out. As the padishah's health worsened, the persecutions increased; there were fewer and fewer places left to hide as the widening circle ensnared everyone. Inevitably the day arrived when Jamsap was also taken in and sent to the baths. To that day, Jamsap had been true to Shahmaran and kept his oath never to go to the baths; he had preserved the secret of his body, but as soon as he was splashed with the first bowl of water, he saw the silvery scales spreading below the waist. Everyone else saw them too. (So many times he had seen this in his dreams—being forced into the baths, seeing his body growing scales and glistening below the waist, looking more and more like Shahmaran. In his own dreams, he became Shahmaran, that is, his own murderer.)

They seized Jamsap and brought him into the presence of the vizier. Jamsap insisted he had never seen, met, or known Shahmaran. They pressured him, and at first he kept to his story. But he convinced no one. All his denials came out sounding empty, and his scaly body betrayed everything, his body now its own enemy, quickly bringing about its own destruction. When he met all their questions without answer, all their insistence without response, they took him to be tortured. His scaly body became the target of the most gruesome assaults, the most embarrassing humiliations, the most unbearable agonies. Ultimately, he began to break down and quietly unravel. To bear himself up, to perform justly in his own eyes, to defend himself against everything else, he began to look for excuses and found them.

"I'll take them just to the mouth of the cave."

"Taking them to the mouth of the cave is not the same as showing them Shahmaran's place, not the same as betrayal."

"If I don't show them, someone else will anyway."

"Maybe there'll be some miracle and Shahmaran will elude them!"

And he said many other things. But somewhere inside him, he knew all the while that all of these were pitiful excuses.

And in the end, he brought Vizier Shehmur and his men, along with a group of others, to the mouth of the cave.

Jamsap fell back. The moment of shame had arrived. With his twitching finger, he pointed. "This is it!" he said.

He wanted the ground to shake, for the sky to rumble, for doomsday to break. The magician vizier Shehmur burned incense, cast spells, read out enchanted magic above the waters he poured at the mouth of the cave.

When its marble lid was lifted off, what appeared—in the midst of a thick smoke—was a daemon, its face covered with an ebony veil. Atop a silver tray it carried on its head was Shahmaran, with a look full of disappointment and ire. Vizier Shehmur, his hands shaking with excitement, reached out to seize Shahmaran, who, in turn, thought as though Ukap had returned: the same bulging eyes, quivering beard, the thin lips and slobbering mouth, the same face twitching from the strain of passion . . .

"Don't touch me!" said Shahmaran. "Don't even dare! Or I will sting you with my venom. Leave me. Let Jamsap take me, and I will leave this place on Jamsap's arms."

And then Shahmaran turned to Jamsap. "I told you, didn't I, Jamsap? Humans betray. Humans are powerless, feeble, capricious."

Jamsap turned away and hung his head.

"Just like Belkıya," said Shahmaran. "Yes, yes, how much you resemble Belkıya, never before did this occur to me."

Jamsap could not keep his composure; he fell to his knees and began to weep.

"Forgive me, beloved Shahmaran, forgive me," he said. "For years I kept your secret, for years my lips were sealed. And I fled and hid so long, believe me, but in the end, I was captured, and they tortured me for days, and I was defeated . . . I surrendered my heart and your secret along with it . . ."

"Crying suits you, dear Jamsap," said Shahmaran. "It seems men would be more beautiful if they could cry. But no matter, do not grieve. Who knows, maybe I prepared my own death. I readied the way from the very beginning; maybe I spent my whole life anticipating my own murderer, and I just thought I'd kept it secret: that from the start I had left my fate in the hands of others; fleeing and hiding from them, thinking I'd guarded the secret, thinking like a human while living like a serpent, falling prey to my feelings, awaiting the inevitable in my hideaway. All along, I must have been preparing the way for my death. Maybe my whole life has been one coy and lingering suicide. In any case, talking about this now benefits no one, but I do have just one more piece of advice for you, dear Jamsap, you know, just as I had one piece of advice for Belkıya. After I die, tell them to put me in a wide earthenware pot. Then, they should use the water from the baths they washed you in, and boil my body in that water. The first serving, don't drink it; let the vizier drink it, then you drink the second one. The first serving will carry my poison, the second my essence. As for the padishah, when he eats of my flesh, he will certainly regain his health, but he will not live long. How long do you think an empire that runs on cruelty can last? Soon enough it will collapse. My flesh, which is now a cure, will eventually turn poisonous. And this time, his body, owing to my venom coursing through it, will be covered with even worse wounds than before. Then, no one will be able to save him."

They headed back to the palace.

When they arrived and the wide gates opened, they saw that a large stove had been installed in the courtyard. A grand fire awaited sacrificial flesh. Around the four walls of the courtyard were wooden tables arrayed with food and golden goblets filled with drink; preparations for a great feast were underway, with lanterns and banners, games, dancers, jugglers, musicians playing instruments, magicians rehearsing their great demonstrations.

Hundreds of people watched Shahmaran's dismemberment.

As the boiling water in the earthenware pot foamed over, Shahmaran's body, cut into forty pieces, swirled among the bubbles, and as each piece floated up to the surface, it spoke in tongues and recited its cure.

That's also when Jamsap heard the news of Vizier Shehmur's death, who had taken the first serving of the potion. Shehmur gave up the ghost in a great struggle, writhing in the greatest of pain. Who knows, maybe his fate of wanting to be more of a padishah than the padishah meant dying before him.

Whereas, for the padishah, the serving he received brought him much peace.

A while later the fire went out, and the hearth died down.

Over the course of forty days, Jamsap fed the forty pieces of Shahmaran to the padishah. Every passing day his wounds healed ever more, his scabs diminished, his pain subsided. On the fortieth day, he was well enough to stand. He washed, dressed, perfumed and bejeweled himself, and held court.

But even before Jamsap could be summoned to appear before the padishah, he had already left the city, fated to venture over far mountain roads and deserts as a dervish.

After this no one saw Jamsap again.

But his name lived on eternally. His end is the source of various rumors.

It is said he was found suffocated in a hammam.

The hammam where he first washed.

When my master reached the end of Shahmaran's story, I was making preparations to move to the big city. A room-and-board scholarship I won would free me from him and Shahmaran making. A melancholy fell upon the both of us; we both averted our eyes from each other's. He described Shahmaran's end in a heartsick voice. It was clear I would not be able to follow his path, and so I would go. And yet, my craft had advanced a great deal. I'd become talented at both precise and speedy workmanship. Probably because of the boldness of my inexperience, I tried out bold colors. My master, who usually left me free with the work, would watch out for my expressiveness and intervene now and then when my courage spilled over into recklessness. He said, "What you've added to Shahmaran making is Shahmaran's face. Your Shahmarans don't just stare blankly, their faces express deep meaning, a dignified sorrow; in other words, you have been successful at this most difficult part. You are on a good path, your figures are not just symbols; they are living, suffering, feeling beings, aware of their actions, who are not reluctant to reveal emotions. That is the new thing for our craft. Your Shahmarans show what's inside them, because you have the power to see into people, my son!"

These words, these compliments—I didn't know how true they were and how much they were designed to give me strength of heart. I did draw fast and scrupulously. All of the Shahmaran plates I drew were admired, selling quickly. Before too long, everyone was keeping an eye on my progress, wondering about my future. My master boasted about me, and sometimes I got the feeling he was jealous of me—or acted in certain ways to make me think so. For a time, I was unable to discover whether those feelings were his or mine. But at one point my master said something that seemed to justify my suspicions. "Art is a business of rivalries," he said. "But the rivalry must not cause one to forget one's dignity." If being a master means training your own rival, it also means preparing the way for one's own death. Whatever struggle we've experienced, whatever its name may be, it spurred our creativity.

On the one hand, he clearly wanted me to tend the old hearth so he could pass on his art to me to carry forth. On the other hand, he knew I was going to leave. We never spoke about it, and he never said a thing. He knew I was going to abandon him. I was killing his future.

All the turmoil within me subsided.

All the negative feelings I held toward him disappeared bit by bit, and an intense love mixed with a bit of pity consumed my entire heart. I was leaving him.

I was at the age when I thought abandoning someone meant winning.

But when I went to kiss my master's hand before taking my leave, he said, "Shahmaran's legs are upon all the world's paths."

Years passed. I became known as a talented young writer. Around the time when my first book came out, I returned to that little provincial city, the place I was born and raised. I wanted to offer my first book to him. It was a belated office of the heart.

But my master, he'd died; I hadn't made it in time.

How long I'd thought about what I might say to him. I did want to tell him I was sorry that I'd left him out in the cold, heirless, without a son.

"I didn't betray you, my master," I would say. "Believe me, what I am doing now is also making Shahmarans. Didn't you once tell me, 'You have the power to see into people'?"

I wasn't able to say anything. Nothing.

After me, none of his apprentices had shown much promise.

His hearth was extinguished together with him.

I stood helpless now, just as I had before, at my grandmother's door, holding under my arm the first Shahmaran plate I'd drawn. Nothing was the same; the workshop wasn't even there. It had been demolished, and another structure was built in its place. Whenever we return, for whatever reason, don't we hope that everything will be exactly as we'd left it? Why is that? Standing in front of the ugly makeshift building that had gone up where my master's shop had been, I understood all of a sudden the melancholy of Belkıya's and Jamsap's returns. I closed my eyes without intending to. At the blink of an eye I wanted to be everywhere around the world. I recalled my master's words, about every path on earth where Shahmaran's legs have touched, and I decided to write them all. I had no other task left. I would write. I would write without stopping. My father had given me as an apprentice to the Shahmaran maker so I wouldn't become an empty-headed drifter. How could he have known that this apprenticeship adventure would make me a full-headed one . . .

I left that very day and wrote this story right afterward.

Master! Forgive me, it turns out I waited for your death to love you.

July–October 1983

Ökkeş and Jengaver

For Alpay İzharak

The Eastern Mediterranean, the mountain peaks, the sea's bosom.
Its sky is the province of birds (the sun doesn't singe their wings).
Its climate, like a charmed life.
Its thick forests aren't for everyone; some get turned around, miss their destination. To those unaware of its hideouts, death is a bird of prey. Its stars wreck caravans.
The nomads, they need big hearts. Thick wrists. Manly might.
People grow up with blood rites there.
They saddle up for unforeseen journeys with no return.
Only much later, they'll follow the lost hoof tracks.
But this time, life grants no passage through.

The Eastern Mediterranean's luminous blue is casting its light, the flame of its light, on a quiet wind. The mountain peaks are once again etching rage, pride, and love into the dawn.

Light and mist, morning and sun, love and rage, Ökkeş and Jengaver setting out on a tale . . .

It was the end of spring, the beginning of summer.

The earth was straining, reawakening with all the wild herbs and crops. Flowers were sulking no more.

(It was summertime. How many summers had passed since then? How many kinds of lives had we lived after it? And none of them had brought back a thing.

From the mountaintops you could see the sea. As if you could dip your fingers in and they'd get wet even though it was a day's ride on horseback to reach the sea.

Everything then was like a fable. Life carried with it a taste of the fable. The earth's mist rose into the trees, wrapped the trees with a fog that would not lift. The tree branches split the sun's light, framed the fog's secrets.

We understood; spring was done.

And it was, although how many summers had passed since? How many years? None of them brought back anything we'd lost. It is with those lost beauties, and with a suffocating nostalgia, that I remember that mountaintop. You. The birch trees.

Like a fairy tale . . .)

Mist and light, morning and sun, love and rage, Ökkeş and Jengaver.

In the evening dark, Ökkeş's eyes were glistening like two sparking ovens. Ökkeş's eyes. He lay sprawled out in a corner of the dark room as if nailed there. Wet and feverishly luminous, he couldn't close his eyes. At first, his mother thought it was from the pain. A few times she came up to his side and said quietly, in a tender voice, "Ökkeş," she said, "you should sleep a bit. You know you've got to gather your strength for tomorrow. You must, my son." Ökkeş said nothing. He was quietly pondering. Asking questions of his mind and heart. Weighing the custom. He'd never thought about the law or the justice of the custom. He just went along living according to what had been taught him. Now he was examining it in his mind. Now that his pain had subsided and the bed he lay in soothed his body, he was thinking through what he'd learned. "What is the wisdom of the custom?" he asked himself. The law of the custom is tested through pain, learned through pain. This was all he knew so far. His mother reached out to touch his hair. She wanted to alleviate his suffering. Each touch, she thought, might salve a wound.

"My soul isn't suffering, Mother," said Ökkeş, "nor is my flesh suffering."

His mother bowed her head with the gentle, affectionate expression of someone who has seen and undergone a great deal. They had experiences in common, she shared in his suffering, but Ökkeş still kept his distance from her. She took a long pull on her cigarette. She released all the smoke, thicker in the dark, from between her dry lips.

"Brothers-in-arms are tested through enmity, my son," she said. After that she fell quiet. Her words betrayed a doubt. She was trying to weigh what she would say next. Long ago, she grasped that she needed to approach Ökkeş with circumspection; he carried in him a different kind of heart. He was unlike his peers. This side of him made his mother afraid, but it also pleased her. Ökkeş was different, but there was no making him go back on his word. "This is what the custom commands. And tomorrow, you too . . ." Ökkeş's sparking-oven eyes, turned inward, cut through her words like a knife. These eyes were menacing, cruel.

"See, this is what I'm ashamed of," he said. "And tomorrow, you too. What does this all test, Mother? What is being tested?"

"Son, you speak as if you don't know our customs. Everything is tested with a custom. Its justice shows the way to the mind and to the heart. Shows the way of life to all. It tests your manhood too. Why do you look as though you don't understand? You're fifteen now. You have reached a man's age. It is time to test your manhood. If you can't withstand these two days of suffering, how will you withstand a lifetime of it?"

"If life is like these two days, I'm gone, Mother. Count me out."

"You're talking like a child, Ökkeş. You've been friends for many years; have you never battled Jengaver? Haven't you two ever wrestled? Why wrestle, if not to learn the game?"

"I don't know, Mother, I don't know. This isn't a game, it's cruelty!"

"Does it hurt a lot? Did he hit you hard?"

"My body doesn't hurt, Mother, my heart hurts."

"You've caused yourself so much trouble, Ökkeş! I had no idea you would cause yourself such anguish. This is a covenant, son, a second circumcision. There's no other way to prove your manhood to the clan."

His mother pressed ointment onto his wound. (She'd ground all the forest herbs in her palm.) Gently, mercifully, like a caress, her hand wound around Ökkeş's young body. "How can I ease your suffering? I wish I knew." Then she slowly stood up. She stopped at Ökkeş's feet, as if in prayer.

"You must sleep some," she said. "You must gather your strength for tomorrow. Your feet must be the feet of a deer, your fists birds of prey. In the morning I'll be making provisions for you to take along. They'll be drawing a wide circle from the peak of the mountain down to the bottom. At first, they'll let neither you nor Jengaver cross. That is the boundary of the ritual. Pray you don't let this slip your mind. It's the place the ritual begins. Then you will ride on horseback to the top of the Twin Ravines. They will bring the horse to you, so don't squander your strength there. That's when they will let Jengaver go. Then they will set you off behind him. For God's sake, don't take the wrong path. From dawn to dusk, keep good track of time. If Jengaver is one of your adversaries, so is time. Follow the sun's light, its angle. Jengaver is your peer, your age-mate. Where he goes, where he hides himself, where his heart's home is—you must be clear on these things. You'll need to know the habits of your age, the various aspects of the heart of a boy this age, the frightful domains of his soul. For God's sake, do not take the wrong path, son. Jengaver is your blood brother. He has a home in your heart, I know. But he will be your enemy for these two days. Whatever happens, don't return to the village empty-handed, son. Do not turn my face to the ground. Do not darken my brow. Do not make me a childless mother. Catch your prey, son. Erase Jengaver's affection from your heart. For two days, tie dark charms to your eyes, carry dark amulets in your heart. Think of Jengaver as your enemy. Think of him as the enemy of your soul. Think of him as a menacing bird of prey after your manhood. This is your second circumcision. Do not return to the village empty-handed. After that, Jengaver can be your brother-in-arms, your soulmate."

"It will never be as it once was, Mother. Now, no moment will be the way it used to be. That's where my fear comes from."

"Yes, it will, son, sure it will. Why would it not? In the end, it's two days of rivalry. Besides, it's what the custom demands. You can't be someone's true friend without fulfilling this custom. This is the rite of the age, this is how our ancestors proved their manhood at this age, how they advanced to manhood. It's a Sırat bridge, your Judgment Day, and you're going to sweat a bit. You'll feel the blazing face of fire and flame on your cheek. But you'll earn your manhood. You'll dwell in the country of man. Is that such a small source of gladness for you, my son?"

"Maybe I'll lose Jengaver. Maybe we'll lose each other. Maybe we'll lose each other and be neither comrades nor rivals, Mother."

"You have to keep your promise, dear son! If you're going to lose it, lose Jengaver, lose your friendship. But don't tarnish the honorable name of this house. Attend to the honor and repute of this hearth. After losing your father, you are my only hope, the only light of my soul. You are the only man of this house. Do not forget that! This is why I cannot knit darkness on my brow, this is why shame may not weigh down my heart, this is why I may not lose my child. This is my wish for you. You are my hope. You have from dawn to dusk. This is your life. Your whole life. Take a wrong step, make one mistake, accept one blemish, be even a little forgetful, it will lead you onto paths from which there is no return. For your whole life, you will not be able to raise your gaze from the ground. You cannot repeat your life, my son. You cannot repeat life. You will learn this when you are on the heels of your prey. Just don't forget this. From dawn to dusk, from the peak of the mountain to the Twin Ravines. You must search every place, inch by inch. This hunt isn't like hunting partridge or deer. This is a hunt where, if you return empty-handed, no clan will have you. Summer days are long, and time lingers, but summer days are like youth and pass quickly. Youth misleads man. Don't be fooled, son. And keep your heart far from Jengaver. Let your heart begrudge those open wounds in your body, let your rage swell until morning, until it no longer fits in your veins, and with the morning you'll put on your manhood like a weapon; you'll put it on like a weapon and give chase to your prey. When you trap him somewhere, you must beat him to the ground. The rule of the rite is that whoever is caught may not raise a hand to the hunter. He may not raise his hand to you. You must beat him until he cannot get up from the ground. Afterward, in the evening, the horsemen will come with torches burning in their hands. They will take you both from the battleground and throw you on the back of their horses, and when you reach the village, the drums will be beating. If I hear the beating of the drum, son, I will greet your honor and glory at the door. I will sing a *helhele* worthy of your valor, I will make a kerchief of my headscarf and dance a *halay*. But if with the sound of hooves I do not hear drums, it will be like lead pouring into my ears, and I will fall into a deep sleep if shame might let me. Your father ought to have been the one to tell you these things. But, sadly, there is only me. Your mother is a young widow. And this hearth has no other man but you. The smoke from this hearth will taunt the sky with your honor. Or our brow shall be ground into the earth our whole lives long. That's all I can say. Now you know how you must proceed. Jengaver is your prey now; nothing else matters. When they tied you to the tree, when he beat you in the name of his manhood, clearly he didn't question his heart. So now, don't listen to your heart, listen to your wounds instead. The wounds in your body point to Jengaver's heart, see whether they speak the way your heart does."

Silently his mother retreated into her corner. She opened her tobacco and rolled a new cigarette. She'd said all that needed to be said, she thought. For her part, her heart was quiet. But a flood was pressing on Ökkeş's heart, inundating it with different emotions, different forms of rage. His heart wouldn't be bridled. The rite's woeful tune wound itself through him like an ache. He wanted tomorrow to never come. He thought of today. He thought of it as a distant moment. Yet his wounds were fresh. He couldn't mislead his conscience. His mother spoke of the law. But this wasn't about just or unjust. This was about something else. Something. He sensed it. He felt it in his heart. Something was wrong here. And one had to play this wrongness like a game. Once again, Ökkeş examined his heart. His heart was tired. Every moment since the morning, every single moment since, he examined his heart, consulted it. His heart was tired now. He'd never encountered such questions, such interrogations, and he was bewildered. He thought of Jengaver. (Was he in a deep sleep on his mattress now? Was his heart pounding already like his fist?) Were they still comrades? Were they still brothers? He no longer knew. He didn't know anything anymore. It was a friendship that rested on so many years, so many tests. (Was it a friendship? Would they be able to withstand all the suffering to the end? Together?) Was custom testing this friendship too? But hadn't they already tested it themselves with their hearts together over these years? But now they weren't testing it, just losing it. Losing it flagrantly. He found the customs inconceivable. "Customs are like spells," his mother had said. "You don't reason with them, you follow their reason." His mother was a strong, resilient woman. He could not let her face be cast down to the ground. The endless blue of her eyes was like a cradle that comforted Ökkeş. His mother's eyes were like the far-off seas. (You had to climb down the mountain and traverse the plain; the sea was far away.)

The mattress pierced his wounds. Everything pierced his heart. He felt abandoned. Alone, utterly alone. An orphan moon grew in the sky. (Ah, summer nights . . . even then . . .) The moon passed over the windows, and its light shone on the humble furniture in the room. Outside, dogs howled. The smells of the mountain, the forest, the pines, the oaks, and the birch reached his nose. (The birch came last.)

He wanted to burn the whole forest down.

This battle had to end.

Today, he'd been tied to an enormous tree. ("Three sons burst forth from the same root, son. One is patience, the next is rage, the last is beauty. Beauty is also death." They had tethered him to the tree with seven loops. Tied up, he became feverish and turned red. A deluge descended onto his body. His feet could not carry his weight. It wasn't the pain in his soul that deterred him, nor the fear. (Jengaver frightened him.) Under the seven-strand rope, Ökkeş couldn't budge. His underclothes were sticking to his body. The first light of the sun rent the air of the mountain and the forest; a faint breeze grown tired from crossing the sea daubed a vague smell of moss into the air.

Jengaver was going to test his manhood in the eyes of the clan and its customs. Yet, it was Ökkeş who was testing Jengaver. (This was the wager of the inscrutable ceremony.) Whenever a thorn pierced Jengaver's sole, whenever the thorns of a rose scratched his fingers, Ökkeş used to feel the pain in his soul. His breath would quicken together with Jengaver's, his chest would heave and fall like the ironsmith's bellows. But now, would his friend's fists batter Ökkeş's face and make it unrecognizable? Would those fists open up wounds in his body that couldn't be healed? Each punch would open unhealable wounds in his heart. Everything would be over now, as if Ökkeş and Jengaver would have nothing to return to, nothing to return to.

First, the elder had taken them both side by side and gazed at both their faces for a long while. He was inspecting them, as if reading them. (He was reading their hearts in their faces.) The elder stood upon a hennaed rock. (His white garments went down to his feet. The boys used to scrape the rock and henna their little fingers.) Ökkeş and Jengaver remained down beneath, their shoulders touching. They were the same height. Their faces the same. Their eyes the same. Their ages. They were innocent. Innocent for the taking. The rough code of manhood was nowhere evident in the joyful glow of their eyes. With these same eyes they were looking at the elder's face. A damp kerchief had been tied around each of their necks, a red ball of silk hanging down from the knot. Their arms were pressed to their bodies on both sides. Their hands—or rather, their little fingers—touched. On the tips of their fingers shone a pale henna stain.) The elder, after thinking for a long while, had chosen Ökkeş as the one who would be bound, Jengaver as the unbound. (Whose fire, in whose heart, is known at the first spark? In whose heart was the true fire? Understanding this . . .

and after so many summers . . . maybe no time, once lived, can ever be recounted,

as for getting a story out of a fable, it is impossible.)

All of a sudden, he heard a *türkü* being sung, gently, deep in his ear: "And the friend's rose wounding me . . ." After the seven-strand rope was wound around his body, a last knot was tied. (Ökkeş's godfather tied the last knot.) Ökkeş was ready now. The clansmen mounted their horses. (His fate was now tied with that last knot.) For a while they sat still-faced and waited on horseback. Then they trotted around the tree and Jengaver a few times, their silent eyes marking the start of the ceremony. Soon they would begin to move away. Ökkeş and Jengaver would remain, utterly alone. They'd be alone. And they'd never be able to get back to what they'd been.

Once, while they were traversing the forest together on horseback, Jengaver reached for a tree, broke off a branch and gave it to Ökkeş. There were three buds at the end of it. They weren't quite yet flowers, as it was spring. "If you put them in water, Ökkeş, you'll have a branch with three flowers from me . . ." Ökkeş's heart took flight. Reaching out, he took the branch from Jengaver's hands. Their fingers touched, and it was as if the forest was coming into bloom. He saved the branch, as Jengaver told him to. And just when the pink-and-white flowers were about to bloom . . .

a feeling of hurt rattled around in Ökkeş's soul. Hurt without cause. He could never put a name to it, though it was always there. (A subtle melancholy is never known.) Enraged, he took the branch and threw it into the river. The river seized the branch with its three fresh, almost-flowering buds, and a pink-white joy lightened the face of the river. Even before the evening arrived, the two had already made up and embraced by the coffeehouse. Everything had been forgotten. They'd made peace. (But there'd been nothing to make peace about . . .) The branch Ökkeş had thrown in the river came to mind. Now regret rattled around in his heart. He went to the river.

The river flowed a long, long way.

It had swept away the spring branch with its three fresh almost-flowering buds, the spring branch with its three fresh almost-flowering buds was swept away . . .

Ökkeş couldn't forget it. But he didn't say a thing to Jengaver. He carried his rage around like a secret guilt within him. He tried not to let these bouts of baseless regret, this rage diminish his spirit. But he always, always remembered in some corner of his spirit the one spring branch he'd flung into the river. Now with his arms tied like this (the last knot had been tied over his hennaed little finger) that branch flooded back into his mind. That one branch the river swallowed. Now he didn't want the river to swallow anything. Just then, he felt the first punch to his belly. He lifted his head, and their eyes grazed each other. And that's when Ökkeş's eyes sparked.

And then that oven began to blaze. Jengaver's manhood hung in the air. (His punch hanging in the air.) His fingers loosened. Ökkeş's eyes made Jengaver forget the custom, manhood, everything. In Ökkeş's eyes it was not the suffering of the heart that he saw, Jengaver knew this most deeply. This was the first time these eyes were looking at him in this way. He understood that Ökkeş was no longer the man he'd struck. (This time the river swallowed Ökkeş.) Jengaver rescued his eyes back from Ökkeş. He bowed his head.

"I have to, Ökkeş," he said. "The custom, you know."

Ökkeş gazed with uncomprehending eyes. Eyes that could not be translated into any language. A silent shaft of light shone toward them, between the branches.

"I wish the elder had chosen me, Ökkeş," said Jengaver. "If only he'd chosen me instead. The one being tied to the tree has it easier. The one tied to the tree doesn't throw the first punch, he just waits. Believe me, Ökkeş, my lot is harder. I have to hit you. Even if my heart is scorched for it, even if my heart and mind are in a battle with each other, I'm obliged to give my fists over to the command of the rite. Forgive me! My manhood is at stake. And no one but me is there to protect it."

Ökkeş was quiet. Ökkeş didn't understand any of it. If Jengaver were the one tied to the tree, would he be able to hit him? So cutthroat, so pitiless, so hostile? Would he have been able to strike?

Jengaver was crying. Pleading. As if he'd been punching not Ökkeş but his own fists.

"I beg you, Ökkeş, curse me. Curse my mother, curse my father, curse my ancestors! Say whatever comes to your lips, whatever it is, Ökkeş. Don't leave me alone with my shame. Help me, don't withhold your help from me, Ökkeş! Say something, whatever comes to your lips, Ökkeş! Speak, Ökkeş! Speak! Speak! Speak! Don't break me like this, don't leave me hopeless like this, don't leave me alone! Do you hear me, Ökkeş?"

It was as though Ökkeş had left his soul and forgotten his body. He'd forgotten everything. The sound of the horsemen came from afar. A spray of sunlight fell on Ökkeş's face from between the trees, and he bowed his head.

Jengaver collapsed to the ground, panting. He waited for the horsemen. His fist was bleeding.

The horsemen untied Ökkeş. They coiled the rope and laid it at the base of the tree. They grabbed Ökkeş and sent him off on horseback.

Jengaver looked at the tree. The tree was blameless. He was alone.

Ökkeş's mother didn't speak for the rest of the night. Everything had been said. He'd been examining his mind. He was just waiting. Ökkeş knew his mother wasn't able to sleep. The moon spread across the window. An ambivalent, tense midnight, a despondent moon that filled the window of the village house. The poverty of the room was turbid, silver. The present was a summer tale.

Sleepless, Ökkeş listened to the devastation in his heart. The land of sleep was far off, and his eyes and heart offered no path there. The night was a long stretch of loneliness.

The horses had galloped down to the lower part of the Twin Ravines, scattering hoof sparks in the darkening hours. The ceremony was over. They were now outside the hallowed circle. Ökkeş's eyes were narrowed tight. Approaching the village, they could hear the twin drums beating. Jengaver had now entered his manhood. He had beaten Ökkeş until he could not raise himself from the ground nor open his eyes. Jengaver was a fearsome warrior with a mighty wrist. (Only those with the mighty wrist could carry the clan's spears.) And if tomorrow he eludes Ökkeş, he'd be twice the man. Both beating and eluding were expected of men, and he would be considered twice as manly. And if tomorrow Ökkeş couldn't find Jengaver, he would have to grind his face into the ground twice as much.

While the horses galloped, Ökkeş could hear Jengaver drawing near to him, clearly trying to take cover in the din of hoofbeats to avoid being noticed by the other horsemen. (He was guarding his manhood.) Ökkeş was unable to open his eyes, blood oozing down his face. The two rode apace with each other.

"Ökkeş, my brother," said Jengaver. "Ökkeş, are you listening to me? Ah, dear Ökkeş, the hangman's shame is worse than the suffering of the victim, I want to tell you this. Forgive me, my brother, I seek refuge in your heart! You know I love you. Believe me, tomorrow you will catch me. Catch me and crush me into the ground. I won't be a man twice, Ökkeş! One time at manhood was enough for my soul. Do you hear me, Ökkeş?"

In the evening, the elder kissed Jengaver on the forehead.

"Now you are a man, Jengaver," he said. "Ready yourself for tomorrow. Make your feet as swift as the deer. From sunup to sundown, stay far from the hunter's clutches. Do not lose your spirit for fear that summer days are long. Summer days are like a lifetime, they go quickly!"

Ökkeş's eyes couldn't open. Everyone thought this was the effect of the beating he had taken. Looking at Ökkeş, they marveled at Jengaver's punches. But Ökkeş couldn't open his eyes from shame. (He didn't want to look at the others.) He thought that, if he opened his eyes and came face-to-face with people, he'd be sharing in their shame . . . (They weren't aware of their shame.) He pressed his eyes shut as they brought him back to the house. He wanted to be outside of everything, to take refuge in a blackout oblivion that would keep him from bearing his share of this shame.

Jengaver had proven his manhood upon Ökkeş's young body. His manhood was as tough as the wounds he opened on Ökkeş's body. This was the meaning of these wounds, in everyone's eyes. All night long, his mother put ointment on them, salved them. (Ökkeş's body smelled like a forest.) She caressed the wounds gently, affectionately. She healed the wounds on his fifteen-year-old body quickly.

The night opened Ökkeş's eyes.

His eyes opened at night.

After everyone had left, in the dark . . .

They opened as if they'd never be able to shut again. He was following the tracks of a wrong now. His wounds, his bed, his pillow, all these had become hell. Was there a wrong? Something wrong? He was looking for it. He didn't want to hunt down Jengaver, just the wrong. His intellect, his knowledge, his upbringing weren't enough, neither for the hunt nor for being a hunter. Only his heart was on his side. He was alone.

This rite resembled neither wrestling nor playacting. Nor was it a matter of brute strength. Nor was it like a jereed feud. There was treason in this, perfidy.

There was a dagger behind this game.

This custom had something in it that harmed affection, friendship, comradeship.

Every custom claimed a part of you.

(If he knew when and why this custom had begun, maybe everything would be illuminated, resolved in his mind.)

"For so long, I shared the hunt with Jengaver. We'd shared ponies, shared the road, shared the work, shared the help—only we never shared a girl. We'd pined for the same girls, pursued the same girls, but changed our minds later. Girls were never shared. But the compass of our inexperienced hearts steered us toward the same girls. In the end, we both felt hopeless. And we both gave up. But in those days resentment didn't enter our hearts, nor did rage turn us against each other. On the contrary, our conversations deepened, and something we could not name drew us nearer to each other. We tested one another with rage, love, strife. What other custom did we need? Until today, we never raised a hand to one another. We even faked our wrestling. We both disrobed for defeat; we didn't really pull hard, and so our wrestling would last a long time. So that people would say:

"Manhood's garments are first tried on in childhood."

They would say, "Valor is known at seven."

They would say, "A newborn raised among wild horses learns how to kick."

They would say, "A child who has known pain will bear his manhood like a castle."

Why was it like this now, why?

"I'd known everything about you, Jengaver, I'd learned everything about you. But my heart had not tasted your fist."

The horsemen set off at dawn. The elder led the way, regaling the pack with his white garments. He heralded the morning with the silvery luster of his copious white beard. Jengaver's horse took up at the elder's side. Behind them were the other horsemen and Ökkeş. (His prey was up front.) For the entire journey, he couldn't see Jengaver's face. When they got to the Twin Ravines, Jengaver got down off his horse. He kissed the elder's hand. He turned and looked at Ökkeş for a long time. Their eyes touched each other. Jengaver's eyes looked with all that they could not say. Then he turned his head and crooked his neck like a child, dropped his shoulders. He was innocent. (Ökkeş wanted to cry. Wanted to howl through his tears.) Afterward, he walked to the upper part of the Twin Ravines and disappeared from sight. (It was as if Ökkeş would never see Jengaver again. Never see him again.) A little later they let Ökkeş loose after him. First, as was the custom, he kissed the elder's hand. Then he started walking, heavily. Jengaver was gone.

For a while, he halfheartedly followed Jengaver's tracks. He was supposed to get him to redeem his wounds. (To redeem their friendship.) The sun seeped gently through the trees, reaching the ground. Each shimmer of sunlight landed like a butterfly on the face of the forest. The earth, with its insects and bugs, stretched out in the sun. The land was reawakening. Amid the thick forest trees, he pushed through; a faint breeze wound around him. Both Ökkeş and Jengaver were riding the springtime of their lives. They were testing this springtime, at the start of a summer. This was the wager of spring. Now, fifteen was the age of adulthood. To enter into the company of men, to be accepted among the community of men, one had to pass through this circle, brave its justice. This is what Ökkeş was thinking along the way. He wanted to make himself believe in this custom. Belief—how much easier it would make everything. He knew it. His wounds needed to have meaning. There had to be something that Jengaver's punches were trying to teach him. Something that Ökkeş did not want to learn, nor see, at all. The thing that Jengaver's punches were trying to convey. And so, he was trying to understand it, and if he couldn't understand, then at least believe it. As he climbed the mountain, he began to see the intermittent sea among the thick trees, as in a fine landscape drawing. (He would beat Jengaver for his mother, not for himself.)

But would he find him?

Would he search for him?

He'd been thinking about this all night. Was he going to search or not? And what if he searched but didn't find him? This was also possible.

But even if he didn't find him, once he decided to search, there was no fooling himself about it. Because once he assented with his heart, he was bound to it. Failing to find him wouldn't make Ökkeş a hero, even in his own eyes. He wanted to stand watch over the friendship. Clearly, it was going to be a solitary watch. But if he began searching, what would this be a watch for? If after searching but failing to find him, would he still be able to persuade himself, let alone others, about standing watch over the friendship? It was impossible.

Thinking that everything was in the realm of possibility, the fact that reality was so much less reliable weighed upon Ökkeş's young heart. He missed the carefree days. How upside down everything had become. He sat for a while, aimlessly, at the foot of a tree. He fiddled with a chunk of earth in his hand. Inevitably, he thought of Jengaver. Where could he be now? What was he feeling? Was he afraid? Was he lying low? Was he running away? He couldn't reconcile any of this with Jengaver. Nor with himself.

All these trees were familiar. This forest, this mountain peak, this cluster of springs strewn around the water table. Just as they knew their childhoods inch by inch, so too did they know these parts. Every spot, here and there, as though it were in the palms of their hands. What were they to test here? What were they going to measure?

What had Ökkeş's mother said to him? "Where would Jengaver hide? This is the question that holds the key to your manhood. For years you have shared in his heart's journey. Now you'll follow his tracks on this very same path, you'll be the bird of prey! Let hawks take flight off your angry gaze! Let eagles alight on your claws. This is what becomes you. Steady the trigger of your gaze. Your mind's *qibla* must rest on Jengaver and Jengaver alone!"

These were secrets built over so many years of friendship, companionship. They had shared the path of companionship. This was the only way to share in a heart's secrets. Only friends opened their purse to each other. Now this coming up from behind, what was it if not treason against friendship? Those who invented this custom, what were they safeguarding by making enemies of friends?

On the narrow path toward the peak of the mountain, deep within a purplish rock formation are several nested caves. Inside, the caves are laden with a heavy darkness. They used to roam around these caves, without torches. Hand in hand, heart in heart. The insides of the caves are silent, cool. Even human breath finds its echo in those caves.

On the hermits' slope, where the birch trees wind around each other, there are three secret ravines. Hidden in the middle of the ravines are three wellsprings. The springs yield water for three brooks. The two friends had unwrapped many suppers up on that spot. If he went up there and found Jengaver at one of those springs, and threw him to the ground, would this not amount to plunging a dagger in the back of all those years? Would it not be treason? What would remain of their beauty untouched by human hands? He had no right to disturb them. To soil them.

He wouldn't go there. He was determined. If he wasn't going to safe-guard their friendship, he would at least safeguard their places, their young life . . . even if their young bodies had to crack under each other's punches, they had their young life; it would live on.

Nor would he go to the hennaed rocks where they'd laid down for ambush when hunting together. Jengaver was no deer, no dove. He was Jengaver. Ökkeş didn't want to find Jengaver in any place where they had memories. He wanted it to be an entirely different place. It should be a place they'd never camped at, where there would be no traces from the past. He wanted to be able to untie this gnarly knot without sullying any-thing. He wanted to protect their fifteen-year youth. He knew that if he went to their old hangouts, he wouldn't find just Jengaver but Jengaver and Ökkeş together. (He would share in the shame.) But he didn't want to. He didn't want his young life to fall into shadow.

He still held out hope of salvaging, smuggling away some things from this ritual circle.

He thought about Jengaver. (His face, his features, eluded him.)

"Ah, where are you, Jengaver?" he asked. "Where in this forest are you?"

Who knew where he could be? Was he running away? Was he hid-ing? Was he frightened? Was he wary? Jengaver couldn't be any of these things. He didn't want to predict what Jengaver would do. He couldn't vouch for Jengaver's heart. He couldn't vouch for him anymore. How painful this was. It wiped away the memory of all the pains his soul had endured. Ökkeş would stake a claim on his secrets, but he couldn't vouch for his heart. Was he a friend? An enemy? He didn't know. Since he had been able to clench his fists against Ökkeş, Jengaver was no longer the Jengaver of old. He didn't even want to think about what Jengaver would do, where he'd be able to go, where he'd be able to hide. In seeking to answer these questions, he'd lose parts of Jengaver, he'd betray some things. What was Jengaver even thinking about? Jengaver was a stranger to him now. He was hunting a stranger whose footprints he did not know. (Once he raised the first fist, Jengaver became a different person. When Ökkeş was being tied with the ropes, what he feared the most was that first punch. The last knot had been caught in his hennaed fingernail.)

Thinking about the past was of no use. If Jengaver had been the old Jen-gaver he'd never have plunged that fist into his belly. (He'd lost Jengaver.

He had to get used to it.) Now he didn't need to be wary of Jengaver, just of the past. (His young life.) Otherwise, he would never have lived it. He wouldn't be going back. Let him hide in one of those places. He wouldn't go. He'd already lost Jengaver, but he didn't want to lose everything. He didn't know what this new Jengaver was thinking, where he was hiding. Nor did he want to know. (Downhearted, his steady gaze strayed.) Ökkeş would look in other places, unvisited, entirely different places. (The forest was wide.) He wanted this new Jengaver to have found a new place.

"I too have my own custom," said Ökkeş. "My heart's custom."

(At that moment he sensed that a piece of his heart had gone missing. Jengaver had left.)

"So be it," he said. "So be it. My heart's custom will mend it." Then he said, "Jengaver, ah, Jengaver. How did you do this to me? How did you make yourself into such a stranger? How were you able to? How did you become my enemy? My enemy! I see now, the enemy who strikes your heart is your old friend. Ah, Jengaver!"

The sun was coming up. The summer heat filtered through the branches and the trees into the heart of the forest. The soil released its scent toward the sky. Ökkeş started to walk, softly. Yes, he would search, but not by thrusting a knife into Jengaver's secret core. He would search while safeguarding his young life. His feet refrained from the known places of the forest and the mountain. He would refrain. Ökkeş had laid out his heart in those places like landmines. No way he would tread on them. He couldn't decide whether or not he wanted to catch Jengaver. On one side stood his young life, on the other his mother. Each time he thought of the evening, the sound of the drum rang in his ears. His mother would be standing in the doorway. The drums had to sound. That was the custom. Their custom. His heart's custom had already lost the bid anyhow. He had to play the game according to their rules. (Likening it to the jereed, to wrestling, making it entertaining; twisting his pain into an absurd pleasure, into vainglory—there was no other way to withstand it, once he'd joined this game, once he'd fallen into this circle.) Custom had made him the sacrifice once; he wouldn't give in a second time. He would look for Jengaver. He would look in the places he didn't know.

Without thrusting a dagger into his secret core.

(The eyes of the sea, gazing from through the trees, grew wide.)

Ökkeş remembered some of the old fables. Godsent children, magic bodies, amulet eyes.

There once was a blessed child whose mother dipped him thrice in a river; a blessed child who couldn't be wounded. Alas, his mother had held him with her fingertips by the edge of his heel, and the edge of his heel did not touch the water. He could be wounded, just on that tiny finger-sized spot. No one knew this secret about the child. And so, they thought he couldn't die. One day, he told just one soulmate. He showed him his heel, and his soulmate struck him on it.

Then there was another blessed child whose body the mountains could not subdue. His strength equaled the giants, and everyone marveled at his God-given strength. One day he shared his secret with a soulmate. He said, "In my brow are three strands of hair. From there flows all of my power." At night, while he was sleeping, his comrade sidled up to him and extracted those three strands from his brow.

"May our tale not resemble those
in which one's secret is lost to treachery,"
is what he wished for,
and he forgot all of his mother's advice.

He began climbing straight up to the mountain peak. His wounds ached. Was he really going to find Jengaver? If he found him, would he beat him? Would he be able to beat him? Ah, how unknown everything was, how wide the human heart was. By the rules of the rite, he who is captured may not raise a hand. Jengaver would likewise be standing, as if his hands were tied. The one beaten the day before would now undo the wrong. To undo wrongs, to not let them go unanswered, were among the requisites of manhood. Would Ökkeş be able to strike him? To go at him pitilessly? He didn't know. This not knowing brought him further suffering. Would he be the hunter who tore his prey to shreds? Could he be that? Could he live up to this custom? Maybe he'd be able to decide in that moment. Exactly in that moment, everything would happen. Maybe very suddenly everything would happen, or maybe nothing would happen. This uncertainty distressed him to exhaustion. All of a sudden, he understood.

He needed to find his prey to allay the uncertainty.

To see what he would do, how he would behave in that moment. To see it for himself.

And this was the triumph of his heart's custom. Secretly, stealthily, it prevailed.

Ökkeş still couldn't see Jengaver as his prey.

This was true.

(There were other things he tested even while searching for him. It was as though a veil of mist had fallen upon this forest; parting this veil and advancing toward the prey, he worked also to part the veil that had fallen on the face of truth.)

This both gladdened and weakened him.

The climb lost its meaning.

Jengaver may have become a stranger to Ökkeş, but Ökkeş could not become a stranger to Jengaver. The winner was still Jengaver.

He didn't know if he would find him or not.

Not being able to find him would mean losing many things all at once.

Maybe he wouldn't be able to find him, and he wouldn't be able to test himself. To learn about himself. But still, within him, his heart's custom continued to rule.

He decided against climbing up to the summit. To look from that high up might not make his task easier, it might make it harder. (Indeed, wasn't he looking down from the peaks of his own heart at the village, at the clan, at the rite? Isn't that why, even at his young age, he felt like an outsider among them?) Nor could he see from the peaks into the foot of the thickly treed slopes. The highest peak did not render everything visible. (He was abandoned in this thickly treed forest. Everything began with abandonment. He would have to find his own path. In the spring, the flowers inundated the forest floor. You could not walk anywhere in the forest without stepping on a flower. People would be perplexed. They'd think up paths for their feet. It was as if the forest belonged to the flowers, as if they said, "You cannot pass without trampling us." The oleander inundated the forest now.)

Ökkeş squatted down by a tree. He had to be careful of the time. Time knows no mercy. He held his prayer beads. For a while he thought of a direction for himself. While he was wrestling with his questions—what was Jengaver thinking about? What was he planning? (Even thinking of his name exhausted him completely. While unable to bridle his own thoughts, it was impossible for him to intuit Jengaver's notions.) Was he also trying to guard his past, his young life? Or was he just running, trying, to hide as best he could? As he fled, was he a mirror of Ökkeş's secret, descending into the kindred darkness of Ökkeş's heart? Was he also being advised by his own mother? Did he feel a debt of honor to Ökkeş's secret core? Was he taking flight by way of the places they had traveled and wandered together, hunted prey, hunted fowl, hid and played games?

Which Jengaver was fleeing?

Was he also staying away from these places?

If he was staying away, was it to safeguard his young life or to be clever prey, bent as he was on proving his manhood a second time?

So, how was Ökkeş to figure this out? How was his wounded spirit to learn this?

(Yesterday when riding back to the village, he'd come up to him. "Tomorrow you will catch me," he'd said. He spoke of a "hangman's shame." He needed to find Jengaver. Maybe then he'd learn everything. Understand it all. Jengaver wasn't prey. He was truth.

Jengaver was a spirit bird now.)

Ökkeş forged ahead. His heart's custom had lost it once already. The drums must sound in the village tonight, and his mother must stand in the doorframe. It was only for his mother that he would not offer himself again as a sacrifice. His feet shuffled back and forth between opposing emotions.

His feet couldn't choose.

Couldn't decide on a direction.

His feet were perplexed.

His wounded body consumed his strength.

"Jengaver, ah, Jengaver," he said. "I can't follow your tracks at all. I don't know the bearing of your spirit. Now you are a stranger to me. Seven times a stranger. You are a spirit bird, I an errant bloody arrow. If you are Jengaver, if a part of the Jengaver I know remains in you, only then can I know your heart's intent, puzzle out your tracks."

Ökkeş roamed all day long, and dusk arrived.

Now the mountain peaks cut a purple-and-red flame. His mother's words came to mind: "Summer days are long, but do not waste your time. Summer days are like youth; they're quickly over."

(The summer evenings would descend slowly on the mountains. As though a sultanate were being built in the clouds. Evenings would begin like a bonfire. Days were long, nights deep, intense. One by one, each of the sun's seven colors would test itself—first its color, then its splendor, then its sovereignty. Then evening would fall. (The sea, a whisper behind the mountains.) Evening was like a rite too, like a ceremony.

When the day ended, people became melancholy as if they'd lived a charmed life. Ah, those incurable summer wounds!)

He would not be fooled. He would live every second like it was a whole life.

He understood. Life cannot be repeated.

"O my eccentric, clever son! O my clever Ökkeş! How many times already have you hidden the ore of your manhood in the secrecy of your heart? Do you think I don't understand? I know no one else has the heart that you do. I know your heart will not be tethered to custom. But son, do not forget, the biggest hearts are the most solitary ones. I beg you, son, do not drag my face to the ground. Do not make me live the rest of my life in shame. In the name of your mother's right, strike! Cast Jengaver into the ground. If your feet do not stamp out Jengaver, you will not find the road to manhood."

Dusk arrived.

Ökkeş did not betray his heart's custom. His feet stayed away from the places of his young life. Not even one of them did he visit. This was the honor of the secret core. He had laid down his heart like landmines in their old haunts. If Jengaver had gone back, shielded himself in one of those places, then let the river take him away from him like the spring branch. And with him, the land they had traveled together.

But if Jengaver stayed away from those hideouts, what would he do then?

Why would he stay away? Where would he go? Where would he stay? What spaces would he claim for himself?

Dusk arrived.

Time was narrowing for Ökkeş, for his questions.

Jengaver was still the spirit bird.

Knowing that it was so added his love's spell to his rage.

Jengaver was now the prey but not of the hunt. He was his heart's prey. He understood this now. Finding Jengaver would reveal his own heart to him.

This wasn't a hunt, it was a spell.

Then the sun began to set. He recalled his mother's words yet again: "Life cannot be repeated." He was now thinking more quickly. The places he had not explored were fewer and fewer. He thought about Jengaver. He thought of what was left of Jengaver to him.

"Before that, I have to find the direction of his heart," passed through his mind. "The direction of his heart will show me his tracks." He was thinking faster and faster. Faster, faster.

His steps scrambled about, his feet tripped on each other.

He forgot his wounds, his questions fell quiet, increasingly he sensed he was approaching the end. He was breathless.

Suddenly his feet steered him onto an unwanted course. Since the morning he had not thought about this. (Yet he had thought of so much.) Time was narrowing. "Soon the horsemen will be waiting at the head of the Twin Ravines," he thought.

He yielded to his feet.

(Nothing more remained for him to do.)

Yes, this was the last Jengaver now. There would be no other Jengaver.

Since the morning, an inexplicable feeling had kept him away from there. It had not even occurred to him to go there. (This meant that he had added to his young life even the last place they'd shared, as another place to be guarded. It meant his heart had claimed that place too, keeping it from him.)

He'd reached the top of the hill.

Three birch trees stood on the slope of the hill he was standing on.

The birch smell reached that far.

He walked down to where he had been tied the day before.

Beyond the three birch trees, behind the forest, the sun was setting heavily like a ball of fire.

When Ökkeş arrived, Jengaver got to his feet. He had his back turned to the birch tree in the middle. He'd been there since the morning without moving anywhere else, waiting for Ökkeş.

They looked into each other's eyes. Their eyes looked from a place where all languages ended.

If he ran to the river now, Ökkeş thought, he would be able to find that spring branch with the three flowers.

May–June 1981

Kasım and Nasır

What he saw was a plaque of the prophet Ali.

It was a faded plaque, gnawed and battered by time, hung in front of a greasy soot-darkened stove in a low-roofed village coffeehouse. For a while he couldn't take his eye off it. It was a miniature, reproduced from one of the wall tiles from the Kermanshah dervish lodge master's estate. It depicted the prophet Ali holding in his arms his son, a fallen martyr of Karbala. He had on a green gown, a yellow shirt underneath, a green turban, and a tulle veil as he leaned over the martyr. On the martyr's forehead was a bloody wound. All martyrs bled from the forehead.

A long, long time ago, during endless winter nights, storytellers, bards, and players with their pageant wagons would stop at village coffee-houses, whose frosted-over windows danced with the quivering flames from oil lamps . . . A storm could be tormenting the place, violent enough to threaten every coffeehouse in the world, but they would shake off all the snow, dry their thick woolen vests near the stove and, receiving the cups of coffee and share of tobacco offered to them, set about mending the torn gaps in the stories that adorned times past and are still remembered. They would dig out buried memories for people to remember, shake the desert dust off them, polish them, animate them, and recount them yet again. It isn't easy to get people to listen again about the people, stories, sagas, fables, heroes, and passions that have dispersed like the ashes of time, in full view of the giant stove's sparkling eyes, in winter coffeehouses with misty windows.

Yet again is never easy.

But the true yet again.

The story of Kasım and Nasır is one of these.

He had spent many years on horseback.

He had returned.

Faraway sounds reached his ears. At first he tried to recognize the sounds, then tried to discern where they were coming from. As he advanced toward his destination, the sounds grew louder, and he understood they were coming from the place he would be arriving at.

Many years spent on horseback.

Kasım Bey heard the drums the day he returned. He saw the festival fires, the piping-hot cauldrons, the poor people being cheered up by it all.

When he asked, they said:

"It's Sidar's circumcision. The celebrations are for him."

That's all they said, nothing else. He moved along with the crowd.

As he approached the fortress, the sounds grew. The gate was open. Passing through a cool, arched path, he came into a wide stone clearing inside the fortress. Pathways—short, long, narrow, wide, arched, uncovered—fanned out in all four directions. He stopped and looked long at all the paths. "Who is Sidar?" he asked. And that was when they told him.

"Nasır Bey's son," they said.

He thought: Nasır Bey is my brother; his festival is my festival too. This means that he married and became a father. He rejoiced. Fortune was winking at him, he thought, since his return coincided with this hallowed occasion. The missing uncle's homecoming had to be the best present for his nephew. And the happiness of his brother, his twin, would double.

"He's turned seven," they said.

"And who is Nasır Bey's wife?" Kasım asked.

"Suveyda, the wife of his deceased brother," they said.

That was how Kasım came to know.

No one had recognized Kasım. And until the end of the festivities, he did not introduce himself to anyone.

They are standing opposite one another right in the center of the wide circle drawn on the courtyard. They are now brothers and enemies. They stare at each other through the veils covering their faces. They lean over and kiss each other's left shoulder. Raising their heads, they again face each other, their stares sharp enough to pierce their veils. Something about their stare transcends all emotion. Something the veil's fabric and shadow cannot hide. Something driven, beyond all meaning, whose tracks remain inscrutable. Soon, they begin to circle like a hunter around prey . . . eyeing one another . . . eyeing for the kill . . . between them the law of brotherhood, the right of husbands . . . the kiss on the shoulder, the spell their lips have cast on each other, marking the start of the battle . . . Neither one of them will be able to leave this circle until one of them is dead.

When they'd turned fifteen, their father, Mustafa Bey, had armed his boys, and, on the trail of a deer, the two brothers had disappeared at full gallop into the forest. But an old curse had transformed their father into a deer, and it led the sons to kill him with their arrows. The twins had heard their father's screams but believed that it was the deer, which had seized their father's voice in order to escape certain death. So the twins, rabid with rage, showered the deer with their arrows. Then they cut off the deer's head, trying to release their father's voice. But once they'd decapitated the deer, the head changed into the head of their father. The twins were now holding their father's head. This the clan's elders attributed to the curse of the deer. To Judana's curse . . . Judana, who had forsaken her gazelle eyes so that she could give Mustafa Bey two sons.

Now the two sons circle around one another like leopards, perhaps thinking about the sin of the first blood they had committed. One of them will spill his brother's blood after having spilled his father's. The blood of the brother who had shared in the spilling of the father's blood. On that day, too, they'd been armed head to foot. They'd been given their first shave, a rite of passage into manhood, then they'd ridden on horseback through the forest, following the winding tracks in search of deer's blood. Everything had begun like a game, like a celebration. And now, it continued like a game, like a celebration.

They are inside the circle, with everyone around them.

Masked people appear on his path.

He passes through long stairways, narrow arcades, winding paths, berms, landings, and courtyards. He will arrive at the bride's room by way of a tight, half-lit corridor. From behind closed doors, from corners and bends, masked people hurtle toward him. Ambush him from all sides. They punch him in the back, trip him till he falls, and won't let go of his collar until they receive their reward from the money pouches he carries in the folds of his waistband. Reaching the bride's room is no easy task. Even on this last night, the groom must brave the trials set before him as part of a game, a tradition. He doesn't know who the masked people are, rather, he can't distinguish them. He knows they are his friends and relatives, but they wear frightful, smiling, vulgar masks or cover their faces with black tulle veils. This is their farewell as they release him from their company. They play their part with merciless mockery. With their masks on, they are strangers to him. Even though he knows it is a game, each trap behind a door or a corner still frightens him, conjuring up scenes from the nightmares he thought to have left in his past, in his childhood. He finally reaches the threshold of a half-open door. He stands in the light seeping out, takes a breath, then lightly pushes the door, which opens all the way. Suveyda stands there at the corner of the bed. The bridal veil over her face, her hands folded at her abdomen, her neck bowed, she waits for him. Nasır stands on the threshold of the open door, looking at Suveyda. Then, in a voice like a whisper, "From now on I am your husband," he tells her. With his hand behind him he gently closes the door. It's as if Kasım, now facing him inside the circle, has come out of that evening's dimly lit corridors and winding paths, to make the threat of that evening a reality. A gentle, mild breeze brushes the veil hiding Kasım's face.

Judana is seated in a high and solitary spot. Whatever her blind eyes are meant to see has come to her. Black shrouds envelop the place where she sits. She too is in black garments, with a red headband burning like a flame. A black tulle veil covers her face and eyes, and hides all her feelings . . . The others, the elders, the warriors, the notables, have gathered in rows surrounding the circle drawn on the ground. They are waiting. Waiting for someone's death. Judana now hates this crowd with an even more intense disgust. The crowd, and this crowd's black ceremony, will take her two sons from her. Will make one dead and the other a murderer. Will it be Kasım who dies, come home after fifteen years? The one she has not yet pressed against her bosom? The one she hasn't been able to talk with about the years when he was absent? Or will it be Nasır, in the springtime of manhood and chieftaincy? He, who'd waited exactly seven years for his brother's return? She doesn't know. She doesn't know anything. The one who knows is Mustafa Bey's severed head. And he doesn't speak. Ever.

They are waiting. Waiting for one of them to die.
They are watching, already confusing which one is Kasım and which one is Nasır, as the two brothers keep circling around one another. They are playing the game of their twin birth for the viewers. Their identical

clothes signal that they are two siblings of the same womb. Same size, same figure, same mold; one will live by way of the other's death. He will live exactly like the other. They spin. Like two tense tigers, free from the identities they hold in the onlookers' eyes. And soon, one of them charges forward . . .

They had returned from the forest with their father's severed head. They'd put it on a silver tray, and in the seven-level-deep darkness of the fortress, they deposited it in a damp subterranean chamber. The severed head, blood shimmering as it trickled out of the corner of its mouth, on a silver tray, on a table, with a fiery-colored silk covering. Even there, in the depths of the chamber, he is watching. Watching through his curse . . . Maybe he knew all this ahead of time. Most certainly he knew. Which is why he insisted on living in that head, in that dark, moist, humid chamber.

Judana thinks, "When I resolved to sacrifice my eyes to give him twin sons, to make him a man with sons, I only wanted to make him happy. Nothing else. This is what love's blindness must be. I considered no other feelings but his. Isn't this indeed love's shortcoming? Being unable to take anyone else's feelings into account but one's own? And yet, loving him to excess is what turned him cold toward me, made him hate me. Now here, in the middle of this courtyard inside this circle, it is my own eyes that are trying to blind each other. Even though I gave them up many years ago . . ."

Someone in the crowd recounted this.

(He was ancient. He knew stories that had long vanished. Times of drought, endless winters, great earthquakes, long wars, long migrations, ruthless chieftains, bloody passions, bloody chases, great hunts, and festivals that lasted forty days and forty nights. He remembered all of them.)

The storyteller was now among the crowd lining the circle. He stood outside of time and inside the crowd. While waiting on one death, he told the story of everyone. For one death was the story of everyone. They didn't believe what he told because they didn't believe what they saw either. People grow inconsolable when alone, but merciless in crowds. He kept telling, with patience and intent.

And in time, when one of the twins died, and he sprawled out dying on the ground, and everyone was curious about which one had died, and someone reached forth to grab and pull at his veil, and Judana sprang to her feet and commanded, "Do not unveil his face!," the storyteller reached the end of his story. The end of a story, the beginning of which everyone had long forgotten.

This is what he recounted:

"There was already a sign at the birth of these two sons that portended death . . . When Mustafa Bey, long deprived of sons, started feeling melancholy, stagnant, and ever so close to death, and Judana was in the throes of despair, that's when the enchantresses arrived . . ."

He told what they told:

"Falling in love can drag a man down. Loving is a woman's job. To men falls the job of guarding and protecting. A man of course loves, but he loves his family, his people, his horses, his weapons, his warring, and his blood shedding. He loves his enemy like an enemy. Some men love well-woven carpets, well-beaten copperware. A man must fill his heart with feelings like courage, valor, daring, and justice. Every man must give his heart over to the stories of heroism."

Hazer Bey's father had told this to Hazer Bey.

Those before him had told him this too. Hazer Bey told it to his sons as well.

The one who fell in love, rebelled, or violated the customs would also say the same things eventually. He would marry, make some children, and lay down his law. He would say, "Affection is a divisive feeling; it first separates the person from himself, then from others. So it's of no benefit to him either." And so, in the end, every man became everyman.

Hazer Bey had rebelled against his father.

He was one of the first chieftains to settle during the nomad times. Maybe this was the reason. He took a wife from a different clan, from a different tribe.

Hazer was an only son. His father wouldn't kill an only son. When his father died, the shadow of his ghost followed his son's tracks. A smoky-blue apparition, he roamed and wandered the smoking fires of the plain. He was seen on moonlit nights when the sounds of the river grew louder. He appeared to several people. He appeared most to Kureysha. Because she felt the most pain. He had never appeared to his son but awaited the day he would. Hazer Bey and his people carried the father's curse. Hazer Bey remained without a son for a long time. Kureysha's loins wouldn't take to his seed. As the mighty caravans and the songs of their bells echoed, the ghost settled in the house of the settler son.

He saw that the son's house was also afflicted with the deer's curse, a heavy, arduous curse! That's why he decided to stand along the edges of the curse, showing himself at times, then disappearing.

Suveyda's face was always downcast, hiding what she was feeling. In these parts, the thing people most needed to learn was how to present a face that does not reveal feelings. Suveyda's face was that kind of a face. One of the faces that's hard to draw. People look at each other with faces that are impossible to read. Looking into someone's face is like looking into the emptiness of a desert. The death angel—the one who would decide which of the twins would live to be Suveyda's husband—prowled around her. The ghost of Hazer Bey's father stood at the edge of the circle. People either didn't see him or thought he was an elderly villager. No one saw that he was a death angel. A cursed ghost sent to take the souls of his kin. Everyone was a death angel for the souls of their kin. As a kid, Hazer Bey had always thought he wanted to kill his father. Now Hazer Bey had also died. All his fears, his dreams died with him. His father's ghost no longer frightened him. Now nothing frightened him anymore.

Suveyda was now a sleeptalker. Everyone was a sleeptalker. THEY SLEEPTALKED ABOUT THEMSELVES AND THOSE WHO CAME BEFORE THEM. They were besieged. They were dressed as the ghosts of those who came before them. Their feelings rebelled. They wanted to be punished. To be held down, made smaller, constrained. Otherwise, they were afraid of themselves.

TO BE DEFINED, TO BE ASSIGNED
IS WHAT THEY WANTED

And what will/would be the end of sons with a ghost for a father? What is/was happening? The rains come down faster than in the old days . . . every day the sun is eclipsed . . . Hazer Bey and the sons of other ghosts are thinking all this, and more . . .

All the way down to Kasım and Nasır . . .

And everything, everything that had happened before these two! Once they become aware of the curse upon them, their ends are prepared for them. Foreordained. Who will untie the knot? Yes, who will untie the knot? Which son? FROM FATHER TO SON, FROM FATHER TO SON. They are waiting, waiting for someone's death . . . FROM FATHER TO SON. A whole crowd standing to the side. THE CROWD ALWAYS STANDS TO THE SIDE. They sing the song of the bystanders. THEY SING THE SONG OF THE BYSTANDERS. Just like now. JUST LIKE NOW. They never share in anyone's fate but always curse, judge, and condemn. This is the reason why they wear black, without and within. KUREYSHA TOO HAD SLEEPTALKED FOR MONTHS. Hers were the first. "I sense, I sense frightful, powerful things," she'd say. She had lived and died, proving her premonitions true. BUT SHE HASN'T DIED YET. The riverbanks where childless women walk are not far from the fortress. Wherever they may go, one hears their slow, faint laments. EVERYDAY JUDANA GOES TO VISIT HER HUSBAND, HIS SEVERED HEAD, IN HIS DARK VAULT. She asks about things to which she receives no answer. Like the childless women, the riverbanks keep wailing, the cliffs keep wailing, and Kureysha shuts her ears. She shuts her ears to all the sounds, no matter where. Her ears that can hear all the silences. If she were deaf, if she could be deaf, she'd be happy.

All the way down to Kasım and Nasır . . .

For this reason, now is not an end.

Lineages too have their secrets. FROM FATHER TO SON . . .

Let's take the story from the beginning, the very beginning: A place in the deep of the forest, in a secret part of it. Tracks are inscrutable, and secrets never revealed. This here is the deer's lair. Of all the deer in the world. This is what Kureysha said:

"Let us not make our home here."
(And said nothing else.)

She told them. THEY HELD FAST. She couldn't make them listen. "We will be cursed." THEY WERE CURSED. Hazer Bey did not listen. Dividing the tribe in two, dividing his father in two, dividing himself in two, he settled and made a home here. Once his path was marked by the curse, all fates onward would only darken this path further.

Before too long, Hazer Bey gave chase to a deer.

(On that day, that day of the hunt.)

He got caught in a deer's tracks.

(In that moment.)

His men were behind him. His past, his childhood, the angel of sin on his left shoulder, all of them were behind him.

(And so began the long fate and history of the curse.)

Since love is killing. You shall become your kill.

A blue tulle mist descended upon the forest . . . The forest green turned hazy, foggy . . . The early morning hour . . . shows everything differently . . . Humans appear, then disappear . . . Forms grow dim, flow from one into another and blend together . . . They take on each other's forms . . . Children hallucinate the fathers they'd killed or lost . . . WHERE AS HAZER BEY HALLUCINATES EVERYTHING EXCEPT HIS FATHER. The men advance in the forest . . . They will settle here . . . They move around the same place. WHERE NO ONE COMMANDS, HALLUCINATIONS BEGIN . . . Hazer Bey cannot part the fog; he shouts but cannot hear his voice; HIS VOICE HAS GROWN SMALL, OTHER, UNKNOWN TO HIM; neither he nor the clans before him, no one, could hear him. The arrow had already left the quiver. THE REBEL LIVES FOR THIS MOMENT. Holding on to the chieftain's flag, they move inside the forest, inside history. WAVES AND WAVES OF STORYTELLERS HAD PASSED THROUGH, RECOUNTING TALES THAT BELONGED TO OTHERS. People would listen to the tales they could not experience for themselves. He had taken a wife from another tribe. The rebel becomes his other . . . THE REBEL IS STARTLED WHEN THE MAGIC SPELL OF THE REBELLION IS OVER; HE LOSES HIS FOOTING. Knows not what to do. Neither do the storytellers. Nor the players. Nor the ghosts. Once he married, Hazer Bey became his own ghost. Now he had to spill a deer's blood. Customs demanded. Which customs? Caught, squeezed (which customs?) in between the old and the new . . . The arrow strays . . . off course . . . it will miss . . . it will miss its target . . .

Hazer Bey, you'll be lost in the forest!

There was more than one Hazer Bey. Which one then?

And which of them was shouting?

Everyone appears as another in the eyes of others.

In the forest they went hunting.

Who will hunt in the heights of the forest?
Some will hunt in the heart of the forest.

Bakır showed up hand in hand with his childhood. He was twenty-four, his childhood only seven. He felt gloomy and hopeless; he hadn't lived his childhood. HOW DOES ONE LIVE WHAT'S CALLED A CHILDHOOD? His mother, Suveyda, had been sitting in a corner and waiting. For seven years she had been waiting. (That is, you had to subtract from her time waiting as many years as his childhood lasted.) She was at her window. Always there. She had planted a flower in a pot and waited there for a sign. (She gave the flower the name Kasım.) Never withering, drying, or dying out, this flower kept her hope alive. It steeled her ability to wait, her belief that her husband hadn't died. (She hadn't cut her hair for seven years.) Yet, on the day Bakır's childhood had turned seven, it was her mother-in-law JUDANA who showed up. She was coming from SEVERED HEAD's chamber. As always. She had asked him about the past, the future, destiny. As always. And she had received no answers. As always. It had been exactly seven years. As always. She had to reach a decision, pronounce a verdict. She was the matriarch. (She'd lived long, experienced much, the mother of the Judi mountains.) The tribe waited, watching her lips.

Had Kasım died? Had he not died?

This was now the thing she most wanted to know on this earth.

Wherever the people go, the JINN OF VENGEANCE wander behind them, they watch their every movement, understand their every intention. They have the power to reveal and conceal everything.

Judana went and asked that day.

She asked SEVERED HEAD. She pleaded, cried, spoke of her death, her nightmares. BUT SEVERED HEAD DIDN'T UTTER A WORD. Judana said to him, "I'm back again, Mustafa!

"It never ends, never ends, never ends . . . this curse that afflicts our lineage never gives out! What dreadful vengeance this is, that so much sacrifice isn't enough, that so much blood won't suffice. All the labor, all the pain we've endured, nothing appeases its hatred . . . In time, even the oldest living volcanoes' breath gives out. And yet this wrath endures with the same rage. It doesn't end, doesn't end, doesn't end . . .

"Is there no way to expel this dark shadow from our lineage, Mustafa?

"You died, you retreated to death's silent country. You look at us from afar. Our sorrows do not touch you.

"The dark clouds in the sky over the fortress won't disperse, even for a moment. Our people are in endless mourning. After every folk song comes a lament, after every festival comes mourning. Our shoulders cannot bear this burden any longer. I am crushed under it. I have aged. Soon my death will arrive. I want a silent, unburdened death. How did I withstand this for so many years? I don't know. But now I am tired, Mustafa, I am old. My strength, my resilience, they are gone now. I want to die. I want to come be at your side. I know you are cross with me. Your silence is not death's silence. You died because my curse took hold. That's why you haven't forgiven me. That's why your severed head hasn't opened its mouth to utter a single word all these years.

"You buried your body headless in the earth so that you could see my death, see my deaths. But you may not need to wait long, it is near, Mustafa! I know, yes, yes, I know my death has drawn very near. I see dark dreams about myself, long nightmares . . . My tired heart cannot take any more. All the world's pain. You died, Kasım died, and why am I living, Mustafa? Why do I live?"

Silence.

Every time the play was staged, silences grew longer.

"You know Kasım didn't return. Kasım will not return. He sank into the waste of the desert with his unmourned body."

Silence.

"Kasım died, didn't he? You know the truth, tell me, I beg you! Don't make me do the wrong thing . . . You are not of this world, death had you retreat to a cold, faraway land. You see everything, you know everything. The only thing you do not know is your own end. For the only thing humans cannot know is their own end; even if they choose it for themselves, they don't know their end yet. What? Where? When?

"For so many generations, no one in our tribe has known a natural death. Did Kasım die? Did he not die? If only I knew! If I knew!

"My tired shoulders no longer want to feel the weight of any word from my mouth, any pronouncement I may make. I am tired, I am old, I am done. I cannot take part, cannot suffer what my sightless eyes have seen.

"The thread of our lineage points to black earth, always points to black earth . . . My fingers, pulling at the end of the thread, always point to black earth, always black earth.

"Black earth has been closing in on my face for so long.

"I'm decaying a slow decay, deep inside.

"And you, Mustafa? Have you nothing, nothing to say to me? One word? One sound? One sign? One . . . one . . . one thing?"

Silence.

"I understand that you want to leave me face-to-face with my judgment and my fate like I left you. Maybe you want to settle the score . . .

"I'm now going to Suveyda's side. I take it Kasım has died."

Slowly, gravely, she carried her body up the crypt's steps and disappeared.

After Judana left, Severed Head's eyes opened heavily. The only thing he could do was part his eyelids and speak. A narrow trickle of blood glinted in the corner of his mouth, dripping.

SEVERED HEAD SAID THIS TO US:

"Seven layers down in the earth, I am in the dungeon of a cursed fortress. How long have I been here? I don't know. Time matters little after death. When will my ordeal be over? When will I truly die? I don't know. The only thing I know is that everything will end when our curse ends.

"My father had this fortress built. It is said that, in nomad times, he was the first chieftain to settle. Chasing him were not just the enemy tribes but also his father's everlasting woe. That woe turned into a ghost and made its way all the way here. And the deer too . . . the deer.

"Did Kasım die? Did he not die?

"I do know the answer to this question.

"But knowing is no longer enough for our fate . . ."

Everything seemed like someone else's nightmare. As if we were seeing everything he had seen or was seeing.

Everyone in the crowd had been frightened by Severed Head.

Kureysha gave birth to her son. They named him Mustafa. Kureysha did not talk in her sleep anymore, nor did she see the ghost of Hazer Bey's father again. Kureysha lived without betraying the secret. If she'd betrayed it, she wouldn't have been able to live. It was enough to see Hazer Bey happy now that he was a father. THE HAPPINESS WOULD NOT LAST LONG. HAPPINESS OBTAINED THROUGH FATHERHOOD WOULD NOT PASS ON TO THE SONS. SONS WEREN'T BORN, FATHERS BECAME GHOSTS. The fortress walls reached higher and higher, hiding the people living inside. The opulence of the fortress cast a spell everywhere. THE FIRST BLOOD HAD AVENGED ITSELF, LEFT KUREYSHA PREGNANT, AND BROUGHT MUSTAFA INTO THE WORLD. On the day Mustafa Bey had his first shave, that is, when he turned fifteen, tradition had it that he would go hunting, hunting deer . . . the forest was again covered in fog . . . a blue tulle mist surrounded everything . . . the green of the forest turned blue . . . As if there were no deer living in this forest—this lair of the deer—as if there had never been any. It was a deserted and eerie place. Mustafa came upon just one deer, a deer enchanted with love's spell THAT IN FACT WOULD BECOME JUDANA,

THE MOTHER OF THE JUDI MOUNTAINS. He followed it into the darkest, most sheltered place in the forest WHAT DID HE LEAVE BEHIND WHEN HE FOLLOWED THAT DEER? and fell in love with his prey whose blood he would spill. THEIR BLOOD CALLED TO EACH OTHER. He couldn't take his eyes off her, couldn't for days . . . THEIR ORIGIN CALLED TO EACH OTHER.

It was around the same time when the enchantresses, those spell-casting women had arrived . . .

The barber who told us this story years later hadn't died yet. He hadn't succumbed to his jinn. He was still young then, young enough to wrestle his jinn.

Bakır and his childhood, wandering around the fortress, the ramparts, the lookout towers, the dark tunnels, courtyards, stone plazas, and narrow streets, were all of a sudden surrounded by the SEVEN JINN. They wore the seven colors of the sun. They approached whirling and whirling, taking on each other's colors, drowning everywhere in light and color.

The eyes of the past are dazzled.
The eyes of truth are dazzled.
Bakır shudders.

FIRST JINN: Kasım went to the wilderness for his people. For seven years he didn't return.

SECOND JINN: The wolves returned, the birds returned, Kasım didn't return.

THIRD JINN: Seven caravans had already traveled the same road Kasım took.

FOURTH JINN: They all returned, one by one. Kasım didn't return.

FIFTH JINN: Not days, not months, seven years.

SIXTH JINN: Easier said than done, easier told, easier imagined.

SEVENTH JINN: Seven years, exactly seven years.

ALL TOGETHER: Kasım didn't return.

Bakır frozen, alone with his childhood.

Later he found himself on the edge of that circle. Watching the feud. Which one of these was his father? He'd mixed them up. Like everyone else, he puzzled over who was who. Their veils and garments concealed them while exposing Bakır.

Night
The forest is whispering. Hazer Bey sleeps in his bed with his wife. Kureysha's face is turned toward the forest, deep inside. A silvery, cool summer
night filled with stars, the smell of botanicals, and the muttering of trees . . .
A wax candle shivering at their bedside casts their faces in shadow.

(THE PAGEANT WAGONS HAD COME TO THE PUBLIC SQUARE AFTER
SO MANY YEARS TO REENACT THEIR LIFE STORIES.)

At first a lone howl, a deer's howl, calling out to the forest, to us, maybe
to the savagery of the early ages before we knew speech, before we discovered fire. Images from those ages that we cannot remember stir in the dark
floors of our memory, stealthily accompany our movements, and come
out just for a moment, a very short moment, in the shape of a rage, the
cause of which we don't know, cannot know. THIS IS OUR SECOND SELF,
WHICH OUR INSTINCTS HAVE HIDDEN FROM US. TO AVOID FACING IT, WE
ESCAPE WITHIN OURSELVES. INTO OUR DARK INNER PATHS, NARROW
PATHS, WHERE, FROM TIME TO TIME, WE ACCOST OURSELVES WEARING
MASKS, WE FRIGHTEN OURSELVES AND STEAL AWAY FROM OURSELVES.
Then another deer's howl, as if responding to the one before, sono-
rous, husky, another howl to tear one's insides, and after it another, and
another; the howls multiply. Kureysha screams, screams in her bed . . .
She wakes up . . .
She wakes up facing us. She wakes up so we can see her.
Along with the forest and the interior.
Hazer Bey also wakes up from his wife's screams.
Maybe they wake up like this every night, or most nights. THE BARBER
DIDN'T TELL US ALL THIS. BECAUSE HE DIDN'T KNOW ALL THIS. THESE
SCENES, THEY HAD PLAYED THESE SCENES ON THE PAGEANT WAGONS
THAT HAD ARRIVED FROM THE MIDDLE AGES. OUR LIFE, OUR LIVES,
THE MORE THEY ARE TOLD AND RETOLD, THE LESS THEY BELONG TO
US. IN THE FORTRESS COURTYARD, MANY YEARS LATER . . . MANY YEARS
LATER THEY PLAYED THE SCENES THAT CAME BEFORE.
"Listen, they've started again," says Kureysha.
The actor playing the part of Kureysha says the same words.
Hazer Bey hasn't yet made it out of his sleep. They're still childless.
Kureysha is still singing lullabies into her lap, hallucinating. She thinks
no one will attest to what she is hearing.
Hazer Bey, wearied: "You exaggerate. You exaggerate everything,
Kureysha," he says. "The chieftain's wife ought to have a strong heart . . ."

Every night the deer howl below their window. They howl, always with one mouth, louder and louder, reaching up to their window, they howl, long and often . . .

"This was their home, we banished them from their homes, we took their homes from their hands," says Kureysha.

And they come, growing in number every evening . . .

"You shouldn't have shot that deer. You shouldn't have drawn first blood," says Kureysha.

"It's our custom," says Hazer Bey. "We spoke about this, you and me. Don't talk as if you don't know, Kureysha. If you don't take a sacrifice from the place you made your home, that place will be haram to you. You will be without law or order."

"It will still be haram. Still, we'll be without law and order. Because you took the sacrifice . . ."

When the clan sets an encampment, it is customary to go after a tough and spirited prey—which often happens to be a deer—THE CUSTOM CALLS FOR A SACRIFICE. IT WANTS TO DRAW BLOOD. The blood drawn is put into a bottle and hidden. It's seen as venom, the earth's venom. When the clan moves, the first blood is poured out on the earth, as the venom of the earth must be returned to the earth. Otherwise, the curse will follow you to a new encampment.

This is what the FIRST NARRATOR, stepping down from the first pageant wagon, told the spectators. He explained the ritual. To explain, to teach the custom to those who didn't know it. Though he was actually casting a spell with his words as he uttered them. Enchantment with words. Wasn't this what retelling was always about?

"Granted," said Kureysha. "This custom belongs to the nomad. Which means it belongs to the times when you roamed from place to place. Now that you, Hazer Bey, are intent on settling, on changing customs, why don't you let go of this custom from the old times?"

"Customs don't let go easily," said Hazer Bey. "Besides, we'll never bury this bottle," he said. "Will never pour it out. Because we are all here now. We will bury our dead in this very ground."

"And so, what will become of the venom's curse that is not given back to the earth?" asked Kureysha. "What if this unreleased curse takes hold of us? What if it does not unshackle us in this new place we've settled? Seeing that this place now is our first and last home. Our before and after is here. The fate of the bottle, its intended path, how will you honor it?"

Hazer Bey didn't respond to these words from his wife. He still didn't know the ways of reconciling old customs with new norms. This quandary, he thought, was also behind the ghosts that had been visiting his wife.

The ghost of Hazer Bey's father had first appeared to Kureysha. And then Kureysha attributed the curse of her barren loins to the first slain deer, to the first bloodletting.

"The deer you struck was laden. There was a child in her belly," she said. This was a sin. The bottle was still out in the open. Hazer Bey didn't know what he was going to do with that bottle. THE PLAYERS KEPT A LIGHT ABOVE THE BOTTLE.

"You can't think of anything else anymore," said Hazer Bey.

"Maybe because my own loins will not hold the seed, is that what you think, Hazer Bey? Is that what you want to say? Is it my childlessness that's turned me crazy? Is that what you want to say?"

Hazer Bey still couldn't get used to his wife's flare-ups, her taking offense at everything, resenting everything. "Why do you come out with these things? What all are you imagining?" he said.

"That deer was carrying. We are reaping the sin of it. There was a child in her belly," she said.

The actor playing Kureysha held her belly, her loins as she spoke.

"It's you who's accusing!" said Hazer Bey. "You blame our childlessness on my arrow."

The bottle of venom should have been buried so it wouldn't hold a curse for them in the next place they encamped. Place after place. Before and after. Because they decided to settle for good, all the times past, present, and future were mixed up.

"How could we have known?" asked Hazer Bey. "I only realized that she was carrying after I'd shot the arrow."

"Before I understood that she was carrying, my arrow had already left the quiver," said the actor playing Hazer Bey.

"I was too late."

All the forests' curse was below their windows now.

The endless howls let no one sleep.

"The others escaped, they were able to escape," said Kureysha. "But this deer was carrying; she could hardly leap. She was carrying a life in her belly. Dying, giving up her spirit, do you remember how she looked? I never forgot, never will forget."

Kureysha thought that no one had been hearing these sounds, that they were only pretending in order to keep Kureysha from recognizing her own madness. WHAT WAS MADNESS, HOW COULD THE MAD TELL THEY HAD GONE MAD? SHE WANTED TO KNOW. TO UNDERSTAND MADNESS.

The first blood was stored up in a high cupboard so that no one would make a mistake and drink it, knock it over and spill it.

"Would it kill if you drink it?" asked Kureysha.

"Yes, it certainly kills," Hazer Bey replied.

"Is this truth or belief?" said Kureysha.

"Are beliefs not true?" asked Hazer Bey.

"What strange customs you all have!" Kureysha said.

"It's true, you're an outsider. Our customs must come across as strange to you. But do you not have strange customs too? Everyone's customs seem strange to others," he said.

From one day to the next, her hallucinations grow, while she entreats Hazer Bey to migrate. And Hazer Bey's conversations with his wife become sparser each day. He dislikes the way she paces, how she speaks with the jinn, the way she keeps combing her hair.

"You, who love to trample on the customs," said Kureysha.

"I have some answers for you: I loved you, and this is why I married you. Because I could not persuade my heart, I persuaded my tribe. That's the first thing. Second, the time to settle had come. I've realized that the world was slowly changing . . ."

"This isn't our place; please, let's find another place and settle," Kureysha begged.

"If you look at it, no place belongs to anyone. Think about when we journeyed from encampment to encampment. The summer pastures, the winter shelters, all of nature was ours. But now it's our time to settle."

The actor who played the part of the narrator held in one hand a bottle full of red blood, and in the other a palmful of black earth. After showing both to the viewers at length, he dropped them from his hands. The bottle broke, the earth scattered. They mixed in with each other.

"The times mixed in with each other," he said.

Hazer Bey had no son and was alone. To understand his father, he had to have a son. How do you explain to a sonless man his father? How does the sonless man understand his father? He came and went in sanguine dreams, in sanguine hopelessness. Hazer Bey remained silent, while Kureysha had begun living a life close to death. They thought her cursed belly and loins were responsible for her dreams and visions . . . Now she's become a ghost, wandering up on the ramparts, the lookout towers, the dark dungeons. Behind her, THE JINN OF VENGEANCE hover about. SHE WAS WANDERING IN PLACE OF SOMEONE ELSE / IN PLACE OF OTHERS YET TO COME.

Then one day, Hazer Bey said, "I'm going to have a fortress built." He reasoned: inside an immense fortress, his people's feet would not touch the land, no deer's head or howl would be able to reach the windows, and he would be able to rescue Kureysha from the dark dreams and bloody ghosts that held her prisoner. He therefore engaged the region's greatest, most famous architects. Chief among them was a Hebrew. The First Narrator played the Hebrew architect. Hazer Bey had the fortress built. One like nothing that had ever been seen or would ever be seen.

Every passing day, the foundation went deeper, the walls got taller, the paths and corridors became more intricate . . . No one knew how many captives worked on the construction of the fortress.

One day the demolition men would arrive and say, 'The fortress walls were so strong that it took a hundred years to destroy them, they'd say, in a hundred years."

These words were repeated by the players playing in the fortress courtyard.

"I will have such a fortress built that you will see everything from above, and from afar. Neither the breath of the forest, nor the noise of the deer will touch you. Everyone who sees it will say that this fortress was stolen from a fairy tale . . ."

"Bury that bottle, Hazer. Bury it in the earth!"

This was the night when Kureysha woke up screaming.

Then they fell asleep again.

And they slept long and long.

The forest whispers. A silvery, cool summer night filled with stars, herbal scents, and the muttering of trees. Mustafa and Judana are on the same bed. A wax candle shivering at their bedside casts their faces in shadow.

Suddenly Judana wrenches herself out of the bed with a scream. And Mustafa after her.

"What happened? What's wrong, Judana?" asks Mustafa.

"Nothing! Nothing's wrong with me."

"What do you mean, 'Nothing's wrong with me'? You woke up screaming, screaming. You're covered in sweat . . ."

"I had a dream, a dark dream."

"May it come to good, may it come to good, God willing," Mustafa says. "What did you see that troubled you so?"

"In my dream, I saw your mother and your father."

"And . . ."

"Here, they were lying in this bed. But the fortress had not been built yet. And the deer were howling endlessly at the base of the windows." AFTER THE FORTRESS WAS FINISHED, HAZER BEY HAD HAD THE HEBREW ARCHITECT'S ARMS CUT OFF AT THE SHOULDERS. SO THAT HIS FORTRESS WOULD REMAIN WITHOUT EQUAL.

"The deer have always been there howling as long as I've known myself."

"But I too was there howling under the window . . . Don't you know, Mustafa, I always see myself as a deer in my dreams. This brings me suffering. Then, then I heard a child crying. The child cried for such a long time. That crying woke me up."

"All of your dreams latch onto a child."

"In my dream, your mother was childless too."

"Which means I hadn't been born yet . . ."

"I am childless too . . ."

"It's fine, Judana, you're still young, we have many years yet to live."

"My breasts keep swelling with milk, out of spite. I can't bear the weight, the pain of it . . . See, they were lying in this bed. You hadn't been born, and there I am howling at the window . . . My heart is bleeding . . . Your mother is slowly going mad . . ."

A ghost stepped out of a pageant wagon. Walked toward the ramparts. Acting the ghost of Hazer Bey's father. THE GHOST HAD THE FOLLOWING THINGS TO SAY:

"You divided my people in two, son

"You disobeyed your father

"You carved out a different path for yourself

"In my time of difficulty

"You left me sonless

"My curse is with you . . ."

Then the Ghost walked to the head of the bed. So did THE JINN OF VENGEANCE, dressed in the seven colors of the sun.

Startled, the ones in bed sprang up.

Out of their sleep.

Mustafa and his mother, Kureysha, had woken up with each other. They stared at one another with shock and fear. Kureysha looked for Hazer Bey in Mustafa's face; Mustafa looked for Judana in Kureysha. They woke up in the same bed, in the wrong beds. IN THE WRONG BEDS, FROM FATHER TO SON, FROM FATHER TO SON, IN THE WRONG BEDS. As though they were living in a netherworld. Mother and son kept staring at each other. Behind the pageant wagon, a fire was lit. Night was coming.

Outside, the deer howling.

The sound of a crying child.

Kureysha was in the throes of inconsolable pain and anguish; horsemen rode through her dreams, horses trampling her body. She watched the deer shot with arrows, and she shuddered. All the people of the clan wore pure white shrouds, and all were charging toward her. Now she understood that this was the curse, the vapor and venom wafting from the bottle that had remained unburied. SHE SEES THE CURSE AS A PLUME OF SMOKE, A THIN PLUME OF SMOKE. SHE SEES THE FOG DESCENDING INTO THE FOREST, THE BLUE TULLE MIST, EVERYTHING. A THOUGHT DARKENED BY HER HALLUCINATIONS TAKES HOLD OF HER MIND: if she killed herself with that venom in the bottle, drank it to the last drop, she could bring peace to her soul and to her people. With that, she locked all the doors. WHEN THE WRECKING CREW DUG INTO THE FORTRESS FOUNDATION, THEY FOUND THE PAIR OF ARMS THAT BELONGED TO THE HEBREW ARCHITECT. And she entrusted herself to the bottle's venom. And she set about to wait for death. Hazer Bey had told her: "It's poison, don't drink it by mistake, or you'll die." No, he hadn't said that much, he'd only said, "It's deadly," but she'd understood the rest. Because even as her husband was describing the poison, she had already become enamored of the idea of drinking that poison. Because she'd become enamored of her own death. SHE STRETCHES OUT ON THE BED FOR DAYS WITHOUT BUDGING, LYING THERE, NOT BUDGING. ACTING THE DEAD FOR THE PASSERSBY. IN HER ROOM, INCENSE IS BURNING AND THIN PLUMES OF SMOKE SEEP ACROSS THE TULLE CURTAINS, USHERING DEATH OUT, USHERING DEATH IN. She wanted her own death also to be at the hand of her husband. In this way, she would have punished her husband (punished he would have been). She wasn't deliberate in thinking these thoughts. They just flashed intermittently in her head, like lightning. Kureysha wanted to die; she did not want to go mad. No one could hold her back anymore, she was riding at full gallop. Behind her were the ghosts and the Jinn of Vengeance. She was running toward death. "Kureysha! Kureysha! Kureysha! Don't go, Kureysha! Don't go!" they said. Who said it? No one. Absolutely no one? No one. Maybe it was all just her. Everyone around her was just her. She has made up all of this to not go mad. This is why she only speaks with herself, in order to not go mad. She cried, she suffered, she suffered on everyone else's behalf. For everyone, more than everyone, she suffered on their behalf. SHE REPEATS ALL HER ACTIONS ONE MORE TIME SO THAT THE SPELL TAKES.

EACH REPETITION IS A SPELL, SHE THINKS. THE THREES THE SEV-
ENS THE FORTIES WATER WATER WATER WATER WATER WATER AGAIN
AGAIN AGAIN AGAIN AGAIN. She knew all, she had foreseen everything
already when the blue tulle mist descended into the forest and everyone
appeared as someone else to someone else. How did she understand?
She didn't know. She didn't know. She couldn't have known. She understood. She merely wanted not to go mad. And to bear a child. She was
seized with melancholy, deep, heavy. No matter what she did, it wouldn't
leave her, it wouldn't. She'd sing endless laments, whisper gentle lullabies along the riverbanks, at the edges of cliffs, she was afraid, she was
afraid, they were afraid. Here did not belong to them, it didn't. She wandered, repeated, spoke. Here did not belong to them, the riverbanks, the
deer's cliffheads. Each evening she would return home as the darkness
fell. Everyone looked at Kureysha as if she was a lost soul. That night too
she laid herself to bed early and began wrestling with her nightmares.

The bottle stood underneath a white covering (maybe a bedlinen). The
first blood.

She pulled on the sheet and lifted it. And when she did, she saw that
someone was under it. It was Mustafa Bey. Kureysha looked at him. She
winced but didn't recognize him.

"Who are you?" she asked. Mustafa Bey had not yet come back. He
had not yet come back to life.

"I am your son," he said.

"But you are not a fetus," she said.

"I am not," he said. "Because I shall never be."

Kureysha could not make sense of any of this; she thought she was in
a dream, in one of her nightmares.

"But you are a fully grown man. You even have a beard."

"Yes, I do, yes, I am a man. Still, it's you who will give birth to me."

They had shared these words in whispers. Someone is pounding the
door. They had been talking under the sheet. Her madness had died
down afterward. She remembers his face. She strains her memory, she
knows this face from somewhere. The pounding continues. This is the
man whom she'd woken up next to in her bed. Yes, yes, he. The man
in whose face she had looked for Hazer Bey. She'd forgotten him. The
Jinn had wrenched both of them out of their bed. "Open up, Kureysha,
open up!" her husband yells. She remembers she'd locked the door. She
was in the middle of getting ready. Her husband keeps yelling. She had
just grabbed the bottle where the first blood was waiting (her son disappears) and drank it to the last drop. NOW SHE THINKS DEATH WILL

COME QUICKLY AND TAKE HER AWAY. The bottle, the curse, both will be released at last. Yet the kicking sensations in her belly weren't a hallucination, she didn't . . . SHE WAS WITH CHILD . . . SHE DIDN'T DIE, SHE WAS PREGNANT . . . THE FIRST BLOOD . . . The Jinn of Vengeance are dancing the hora, stomping their feet, circling around the sheet. ANGELS OF MALICE, aware of the things to come, are singing. THEY SANG, THEIR VOICES LOUD. Kureysha is trying to get them to stop. They live for devastation, in the ruins of others. They are the most beautiful angels on the surface of the earth and the surface of the sky. The thundering in her belly increases. Hazer Bey is pounding on the door faster. His father's ghost wanders the interior of the room, smiling. Hazer Bey hollers from outside, he senses that wicked things are happening inside. He keeps pounding on the door. Her belly keeps pounding. Kureysha suddenly understands, understands mortally, that she'd become pregnant from the blood she'd drunk. Her son is lying in her bed, the son she encountered earlier under the sheet— THOUGH HE WAS IN DIFFERENT CLOTHES. "You will give birth to me in this bed," he says. Then he disappears. THEY DISAPPEAR . . .

The ghost of Hazer Bey's father opened the door for his son. Hazer Bey was seeing the ghost of his father for the first time. For the first time, his father's ghost revealed itself to his eyes. Kureysha's madness had ceased. For the first time, she could see that it had ceased. When the first blood became Mustafa Bey. When she became pregnant. For a woman . . . When Hazer Bey came face-to-face with his father, he hurled crazy screams. He hurled all the screams he'd amassed over these many years. Behind the ghost is his son, standing on his feet. LIKE HE HAD BEEN STANDING BEHIND THE DOOR. At first sight, Hazer Bey understands that this is his son. Standing on his feet and thirty years old. In truth, Hazer Bey isn't seeing his son, maybe will never get to see him, he will be long dead by the time his son turns thirty. And yet, there, from behind the shoulders of the ghost, his son appears to him. Cruelly, he appears. Hazer Bey's father steps to the side and makes way for the son. His son walks up to his son. Kureysha is holding the empty bottle of the first blood. She had gathered all the broken, scattered pieces of her being, made herself whole, ready with all the things she would say, all the rebukes she would deliver, and she is waiting for her husband (for her son). The expression on her face has changed, her gaze is charged, her body taut, arched.

Earlier: she is holding the bottle of the first blood in her hand.

"I cannot bear it anymore. How many more nights must I endure these howls, this crying . . . My childless loins throb with anguish. Ey,

Hazer Bey! Hazer Bey! (He is knocking on the door) Ey, Hazer Bey, now shaming his childless wife! Here is your first blood, here is your second sacrifice! This time the earth's venom will dowse your bride's belly. . . . This venom will take me and my barren womb to the earth's bosom."

She empties the bottle into her mouth, gulps it down, collapses. Then she begins writhing in anguish. THE SEVEN JINN are now spinning around her. Kureysha's belly swells and grows. She understands she's pregnant. The light cast on the bottle since the start of the play now gathers upon Kureysha's belly.

> HAZER: Who are you?
> MUSTAFA: I am your son.
> HAZER: How old are you?
> MUSTAFA: Thirty.
> HAZER: How old am I?
> MUSTAFA: You're dead.
> HAZER: Then how come I see you?
> MUSTAFA: Because I haven't been born yet.
> HAZER: When will you be born?
> MUSTAFA: Soon, very soon.

THE GHOST HAD DISAPPEARED WHILE FATHER AND SON WERE SPEAKING.

Hazer Bey saw the empty bottle in Kureysha's hand.

"What did you do with the first blood? What did you do? Where is it?" he demanded.

Kureysha didn't say, "I drank it." She couldn't say it. Because, since the moment she became pregnant, her dreams and nightmares had begun retreating, like a sea abandoning its shores . . . She wanted to live now.

"I—," she said, "I cast a spell with it."

"Magic?"

"Yes, magic."

Hazer Bey stopped, looked at his son, looked at his wife. He made out his son from his wife, his wife from his son.

"Yes, magic, and by evening I was pregnant. Look, if you want, at my belly, see how fast it's growing?"

Her belly kept swelling beneath Hazer Bey's hand. Kureysha said, "I will soon give birth! If not by tonight, certainly by morning, I will give birth."

"So, is this one speaking the truth?" he asked.

Kureysha nodded her head. "Yes, that is your son," she said.

And then MOTHER, FATHER, AND SON LIE IN BED TOGETHER. Mustafa lies in between them.

THE SEVEN JINN surround the bed.

The pageant wagon's cloth curtain slowly . . . They must be afraid . . . slowly comes down . . . afraid to touch one another . . . mother and father gently lean over their son . . . as the crowd gathered around the stone dais in the public square . . . they kiss him . . . row upon row of people at their feet . . . the light goes out . . . applause.

The bottle was completely empty . . . Kureysha had regained her calm, her equanimity. She lied when Hazer Bey asked about the bottle's contents. Now that she recovered, matured, she didn't have to tell the truth anymore. She was pregnant. She had scores to settle with the world. She understood the secret of her pregnancy; the road she had taken toward death had brought her back to life. Motherhood calms her madness . . . She has to remain silent, from now till her death: HAD SHE SPOKEN, HAD SHE FOUND THE COURAGE TO TELL EVERYTHING WHEN THE ENCHANTRESSES ARRIVED TO CAST THEIR SPELL ON MUSTAFA BEY, PERHAPS . . . Silence, now silence . . . The miracle had come true. Where miracles begin, so does truth. "I made magic with the first blood, and I got pregnant," she said. Hazer Bey didn't believe what he heard. Because he didn't believe what he saw either. Hazer Bey looked at his son, HE WAS FREED, FROM THE FIRST BLOOD, FROM THE BOTTLE HE DIDN'T KNOW WHAT TO DO WITH, as a ghost, he looked, AND HE HAD A SON. The moment stood still thirty-one years later. BUT WHOSE MEMORY WAS THIS NOW? Then, mother, father, and son, they lay in bed together, careful not to touch each other. EACH ONE KEEPING A SECRET FROM THE OTHERS. They were afraid of the others' incantations. A white sheet was laid out over them. The Jinn of Vengeance circled around them, the three could see none of them.

One of the players, appearing before the pageant wagon with the closed curtain, swept up the glass shards and the handful of earth, before disappearing behind the other pageant wagon.

So that's how Mustafa Bey was born.

No one knew that he was sired by a bottleful of blood, by a curse. Even his father didn't know. He was the child of the first blood. It would never again be buried in the ground, never could be. For this reason, when Kasım and Nasır cut off their father's head, they couldn't have known that their father would live on as a severed head, forever on a silver tray.

Mustafa Bey was unaware of his birth. He neither remembered this evening nor did he know the story behind it. THE BLOOD OF SACRIFICE, IT KEPT CALLING OUT FOR BLOOD. Thus began the deer's curse. Kureysha's ravings, the rising fortress walls had muffled the deer's howls, but neither could stop the blood oozing and flowing into the interior of the fortress. IT KEPT FLOWING INTO AND THROUGHOUT THE INTERIOR. IT SUSTAINED SEVERED HEAD; IT SUSTAINED THE ARCHITECT'S CUT-OFF ARMS. SUSTAINED THE CURSE, THE RAGE, THE VENGEANCE. HOW ELSE WOULD THE SOVEREIGN ENDURE? Years passed in the meantime. They would keep passing.

The players took a break for the night. They'd continue their play the next day. People made more and more fires throughout the courtyard, night descended, and stars inundated the sky.

Now they were in the middle of an age.

In the Middle Age.

When people talk about custom, name a custom, they become enslaved to its dark fate. It is a voluntary enslavement of sorts . . . It brings them massacres, death, untold suffering . . . And people come to need these things . . . Or they are made to need them . . . Many of the needs we think we need are like this: they are made into NECESSITIES. And so, people cannot do without them.

A while later, the pageant wagons and the players inside were left with the night's silence and solitude. The public square had emptied, and everyone had retreated into their homes.

Kureysha regained her senses. Her dreams and nightmares ended. She felt sure of herself. She was ready to be the matriarch. The ghost of Hazer Bey's father never returned again. And perhaps he gave the ghostly garment to Mustafa Bey. Whereas he had thought Hazer Bey would die, that he would die and leave with his father, his father's ghost, out the same door. But Kureysha lived together with that ghost every day, and it never died. Now it would. None of this happened. The ghost vanished, Mustafa Bey was born.

Hazer Bey's son Mustafa went hunting deer once he turned fifteen. Before the hunt, he was given a shave, as was the custom. (This is when the barber appeared.) But beforehand, the tribe was invited to a grand, very grand festival.

He had his first shave.

Later, the enchantresses would bring the white apron that had been tied around his neck and wrap it around the head of a deer to cast their spell. And he thus became enamored of the deer, the one he encountered during the hunt. Such that, for days, he gazed at the deer's eyes, deep into them.

ON THE SECOND DAY THE AREA WITH THE PAGEANT WAGONS WAS SURROUNDED ON ALL FOUR SIDES BY A WHITE CURTAIN THAT HUNG ABOVE THE GROUND. ALL THE SPECTATORS AND PLAYERS WERE TAKEN INTO THE CURTAINED AREA. WHAT WAS BEHIND THE CURTAIN BECAME THE FOREST.

Standing on a raised platform are the deer and Mustafa Bey's fifteen-year-old lovelorn self: two shadows on the curtain. The half-dropped curtain splits them in two right across the waist so that, below the curtain, the deer's body is revealed as that of a woman and Mustafa's body as that of a deer. Soon, a plume of smoke, incense, suffuses the area. Then the JINN OF VENGEANCE emerge. These are no actors; they are real jinn. They'd come to play.

FIRST JINN: He won't eat.
SECOND JINN: He won't drink.
THIRD JINN: He won't talk.
ALL TOGETHER: Won't eat, won't drink, won't talk.
FOURTH JINN: He just stands there, staring and staring at the deer.
FIFTH JINN: He has been like this for so long.
SIXTH JINN: So long since this black tulle mist descended on everybody.
SEVENTH JINN: It's a curse, this, the curse of the deer.
ALL TOGETHER: It's a curse, this, the curse of the deer.

FIRST JINN: Hajis.
SECOND JINN: Hojas.

THIRD JINN: Enchantresses.

ALL TOGETHER: None of any use.

FOURTH JINN: So much magic summoned.

FIFTH JINN: So many amulets inscribed.

SIXTH JINN: So many prayers recited.

ALL TOGETHER: None of any use, no use.

SEVENTH JINN: He stands before the deer, just stares and stares
like that; the tongue can't name it, but everyone knows.

ALL TOGETHER: It's love, nothing else.

THE JINN VANISH . . .

Later, Kureysha enters with Hazer Bey. They have become younger. And they're talking about what ought to be done for their sons.

Forty-one enchantresses ground the world's herbs in bronze mortars, boiled the stones and mountains in cauldrons, crushed the bones of auspicious, inauspicious animals. No matter what, no charm could unlock the boy's heart. Days passed.

He won't eat, he won't drink, he won't speak.

Then they said: let's make a spell, such a spell that will re-create the entire hunt. So that, we either kill the deer—WHICH MEANS ALSO KILL-ING YOUR SON SINCE HE WILL BE FOREVER LOST IN SEARCH OF THE DEER— or we'll change it into a woman, a beautiful, gazelle-like woman. Such a spell that re-creates the entire hunt and makes the play become real, magic become life, the deer a woman . . .

They, THE ENCHANTRESSES AND THE PLAYERS, re-created the entire hunt anew, including all its festivals and ceremonies. To spellbind reality, when they came to the spot where Mustafa Bey and the deer had first met—IN TWO SEPARATE WEDGES OF TIME—THE ENCHANTRESSES AND THE PLAYERS threw a sheet over them. (Kureysha had spoken with her son in whispers under the same sheet, before it was tied around his neck for his first shave.)

The only things to remain unchanged were/are the deer's eyes. SO IT WAS. Just the eyes, which enchant, intoxicate, lock down a person's heart, mind, and tongue. SO IT WAS.

And it happened just as it was foretold. Judana descended from the Judi Mountains where the deer prance on every cliff. Unshackled, Mus-tafa Bey married Judana. THEIR BLOOD HAD CALLED TO EACH OTHER. JUDANA DIDN'T RECALL HER PAST, HER DAYS IN THE FOREST, HER TIME AS A DEER. OTHERWISE SHE WOULDN'T BE ABLE TO LIVE. NO ONE COULD LIVE TWO LIVES AT ONCE. SHE HAD NO MEMORY, NO RECOLLEC-TIONS. So much so that, in time, Judana too left Mustafa sonless. And soon, Mustafa Bey lowered his head in shame. IN TRUTH, WHAT THEY WANTED WAS TO BRING ABOUT THEIR OWN BIRTH.

When the ruins of a rampart are illuminated, we see the DEAD AND VERY OLD Barber in gleaming white garments, white beard, and white hair. Also standing in the middle of the stage, his young self is shaving the fifteen-year-old Mustafa Bey. The old Barber addresses us:

"In those days, I was the bey's barber. Mustafa Bey's first shave was my hand's work. So was Hazer Bey's shave on his wedding day; I gave Mustafa Bey his first shave and his wedding-day shave also; Kasım and Nasır's first shaves and their wedding-day shaves. Bakır Bey's first shave was also my hand's work. I didn't make it to Sidar Bey. By the time he had his first shave I had been dead three years. Then my memory hit a sandstorm, but I still recall Mustafa Bey's first shave like it was yesterday. All of the past is in my memory like it was yesterday. My youth! O youth! Where are you?"

The Barber's youth is illuminated on the stage. The players have garlanded their heads with green branches, and behind the white, half-dropped curtain, they become a lush forest. They'll re-create one more time the enchantresses' spell, how their magic turned a deer into a woman. The enchantresses too had listened to the Barber's account of Mustafa Bey's first hunt, and this is how they were able to re-create the event. When the truth changes garments three times, it becomes something altogether different. And so it was.

They went and consulted the enchantresses again. The forty-first enchantress gazed into her gleaming copper vessel and read their fortune in the water. The people wagged their heads side to side, their faces dejected, their stares vacant.

The enchantresses said, "After all, she's not a woman, a real woman. We made her out of magic."

Judana looked at them long and intently.

They all looked back.

"Made from a deer, with a spell, a woman made out of magic, abducted from a fairy tale, a legend. Her eyes are of a deer. Her eyes are what remain of her deer nature. So long as her nature persists somewhere in her body, she cannot be a woman."

"Is there no possibility?" they asked. They searched for a possibility.

The forty-first enchantress told Judana, "You must give up your deer nature, that is, your eyes. From those two eyes, you will give Mustafa

Bey two sons, and you will spend the rest of what remains of your life as a blind woman."

Judana reeled as if struck by an arrow.

"If you are willing, we will begin the incantation now," they said.

Judana said, "Let me think at least." She looked, she waited, she thought.

She saw how, from one day to the next, Mustafa Bey was growing distant and, in time, might turn altogether cold, either take another wife or come to hate her.

That night, and the nights after, she thought long and patiently. Her eyes were her memory. Her childhood. But she loved Mustafa Bey and wanted to make him smile. And in the end, unable to forego her love for him, she went to the enchantresses and gave her consent.

At this point in the play, the half-dropped curtain shadowing Mustafa Bey and the deer parted in two directions like wings, and expanding far and wide, encircled the entire courtyard, taking everyone into its embrace. ALL THE PLAYERS AND THE SPECTATORS. Beyond the curtain was the forest, and the trees, the branches cast shadows on the curtain. The hunting festivities started being re-created once again.

WHO STOOD ALONGSIDE THE CIRCLE?

WHO STOOD ALONGSIDE THE CIRCLE FORMED BY THE CURTAIN?

The actors who played Hazer Bey and Kureysha waking up from a dream were the same actors who played Judana and Mustafa Bey waking up in the same bed from the same dream, and the spectators couldn't tell who was who.

PLAY AND DESTINY HAD JUST STARTED TAKING SHAPE IN THEIR HEADS.

After the first spell, she became pregnant with Kasım and Nasır. And, as she gave birth to them, both of her eyes went blind. From her two eyes she bore Mustafa Bey two sons. They would be her eyes into the world.

The chief enchantress concluded the enchantment, the play of enchantments, and she said, "Only her eyes remain of her old deer face . . . From now on, they will live on a woman's face, and now Mustafa Bey's can love her."

And Kureysha said, "O great god! Soon the deer will overtake the fortress. You alone know this, as does my poisoned heart," she said. And she could no longer speak, nor say anything more. But Mustafa Bey turned away from his wife.

"I loved those gazelle eyes of yours. But what else remains?" he asked and, turning his compass in the direction of his sons, began to love them. Judana seethed with envy and rage. Seizures took hold of her; she spewed blood and bitterness, she fainted, she shivered, she hallucinated.

She felt neglected, forgotten. Mustafa Bey was now enamored of his sons. ENAMORED OF HIS OWN IMPOTENCE. Once again, Judana ran to the enchantresses. "This is my quandary. What do I do now?" she asked.

In the meantime, the curtain began to draw in, gradually narrowing the circle, and gathered around the dais. Mustafa Bey and his two sons were each seen as shadows.

"You are going to sacrifice both your sons," they said.

Judana shuddered.

As if struck with an arrow.

"Then your eyes will see again, and again you will recover the light."

Agonizing pains, throbbing fits, conflicting feelings, she was back on the rack. Again the riverbanks, the cliffs. Resonant voices visited her. She was hearing what Kureysha had heard. Were they real? Was she in a dream? For days, she went back and forth, back and forth, back and forth. Twice she set out to sacrifice her two sons. She backed down both times. It was as if she was Kureysha again, then Judana again. Mustafa began to see his mother in Judana. His mother before he was born. This frightened Mustafa. He had a memory, a secret menacing memory, and no matter how hard he tried, he could not remember it.

The Hebrew architect had his severed arms buried in the foundation of the fortress.

He escaped into the forest, went hungry for days, and one day a deer came and began to suckle him. FOR DAYS, IT SUCKLED AND NOURISHED HIM. Later he married the deer and had half-deer, half-human children, and all the ones that snuck into the fortress were the children of the architect. THIS IS HOW ONE OF THE LEGENDS TELLS IT.

One day Judana changed course. She wanted her turmoil to end. She prayed a dark prayer: She said, "O Mustafa Bey, I want your death to be at the hands of your sons, at the hands of love, I want the hands of the sons you love to kill you." So that her curse would take, she made sacrificial offerings and prostrated herself at the ancestors' tombs.

And then on the fateful day, Kasım and Nasır returned to the fortress with Mustafa Bey's severed head. During the hunting rite they had set out to perform, the JINN OF VENGEANCE surprised them, showed the twins their father in the form of a deer, and Kasım and Nasır shot their father, thinking they were shooting a deer. That blue gauze descended upon the forest, the tree branches wove themselves into a snare and laid it over reality. KASIM AND NASIR fell into the snare.

THE SEVEN JINN DESCEND FROM THE PAGEANT WAGONS. THEY STRETCH A CURTAIN DEPICTING THE IMAGE OF A DEER IN FRONT OF MUSTAFA BEY. HE CANNOT ESCAPE. HE CANNOT SHOW HIS REAL FACE

TO HIS SONS. HE SCREAMS FROM BEHIND THE CURTAIN. BUT HIS CHIL-
DREN ONLY SEE THE IMAGE OF THE DEER ON THE CURTAIN. JUDGING
THE SCREAMS TO BE THE SPELL OF THE FOREST, THEY SHOOT THEIR
FATHER WITH THEIR ARROWS.

Judana feared her sons. She feared they may have sensed that she
once wanted to kill them. She used every occasion to treat them well,
ever better than well. She perceived her sons as two bloodthirsty killers.
Since childhood even, they loved spilling blood, loved violence and cruelty. It was impossible not to see their future. The nicer Judana behaved
toward them, the more enraged they became. THE PLAYERS GATHER UP
THE CLOTH, UNCOVERING MUSTAFA BEY.

The twins mercilessly oppressed the whole community that lived
inside the fortress. Since the day they started to walk and run, every
single day without fail they caused some trouble, smashed or spilled
something, destroyed something or hurt someone.

As they cut off the deer's head, what fell into their hands was their
father's head.

One day Kasım took a girl named Suveyda. The twins' paths parted
then. One year later they had a son. A son. A son that belonged to him
made Kasım gentler, but the steel in his eyes did not soften. Bakır was a
son without troubles, ceremony, or magic.

Kasım went to the wilderness, he went for the sake of his people and
did not return for seven years.

They said: he'll be back before a year.

They said: he'll be back before three years.

They said: he'll be back before five years.

They said: he'll be back before seven years.

He wasn't back.

He returned on the day of festivities surrounding Sidar's circumcision.

Gathered in the center, THE PAGEANT WAGONS were reenacting the
history of his people. He learned from them all that had happened in
his absence. He watched the future. How much of this was true, he did
not know.

There are many stories about what happened afterward.

The first version concludes in this way: after the festivities, he went to
console his mother. When the matriarch saw her son after fifteen years
in the wilderness, she was seized with terror. Suveyda went mad, caught
between two siblings, two husbands . . .

The clan's elders gathered and came to a decision.

They drew a circle: the Circle of Merit. Whoever died inside the circle
would die, and whoever lived would have the right to Suveyda and the

tribe's chieftaincy. Both brothers were handed sharp daggers. They both had their faces covered with veils, both were wrapped in green cloaks, pure-white shirts, and red belts.

Bakır and Sidar stood on the edge of the circle. One's father was the other's uncle, a father would kill, an uncle would die, and the boys were going to share a mother. Two sons, two sons with the same mother, stood by their fathers' sides. The ghosts of those who'd died before them also stood by, and so did the actors playing them . . . Soon, the daggers charged, the feud quickened, the spectators thirsted for blood and justice. THE THIRST FOR BLOOD AND JUSTICE, THAT IS, OF ALL THE TALES, OF ALL THE PLAYS . . .

One collapsed to the ground . . .

The other was left standing . . .

Once outside the circle, he would forget everything and rid himself of all guilt. For this reason, he wanted the dead one to be removed right away, the circle erased, and the play finished.

The elders, judges, patriarchs, and warriors rose to their feet. To see whom THE CIRCLE OF MERIT favored, they reached for the veil on the dead one's face, and as they reached, Judana sprang to her feet.

"Do not unveil his face," she said, "Do not unveil his face, it is Kasım who died, my right eye can see now."

So the one who died is the one who had returned. Nasır and Suveyda will carry on from where they left off. Nothing will change for Sidar, and maybe he'll remember today simply as his circumcision day. Only Bakır will emerge with a grave, unbearable wound. His brother's circumcision will be his second circumcision and covenant. Indeed, years later, when Bakır and Sidar battle each other . . .

Judana turned mad from grief, shaken to discover that the answer to her question, the answer she had been denied for years, was hidden in the dark hollows of her own eyes. It turns out, the strongest proof that Kasım hadn't died was her blindness, her continued blindness.

This is one of the stories. Maybe the most widely known. Most frequently told. Though, in the play performed by the players on pageant wagons, Kasım is not the one who dies, but Nasır. The reason they give for this version is some girl who was in love with Nasır.

This girl is an unnamed character. Her part consists of no more than three to five words. She had hoped to marry Nasır after Kasım married Suveyda, but when Kasım went to the wilderness, they decided to wait for his return. And when he did not return, it was Nasır's duty to marry Suveyda. This unnamed woman sealed her hopes inside her and began waiting, while all that hope gathered into venom inside her. She became her own curse. On the day Kasım returned and the Circle of Merit was drawn, she gave Nasır a fake knife. This is why, they say, it was Nasır who died, not Kasım.

The third, least-recounted version has Kasım coming back but leaving again without saying anything to anyone. As the story goes, he is melancholy and alone. In no state to tell anyone his truth, or any truth. He wants to rest, to sleep. He has killed many men. He's tired. He has seen many places, lived a great deal. The only person who knows that Kasım has returned is Judana. She knows because she starts seeing in one eye. She sends the tribesmen to search everywhere, but no one can find him. She climbs up to the ramparts, and looking out onto the plains, she sees Kasım heading off on horseback. OR THAT'S WHAT SHE THOUGHT. She calls after him but cannot make herself heard. Turning around and looking back to the public square, she sees the players have drawn out the Circle of Merit and are acting the scene after Kasım has returned . . . Is this really a play? Or a hallucination? Or has she alone not grasped the truth? She cannot tell. Just like she cannot tell why all of a sudden she can see out of her right eye . . .

"Human history, it seems, is rather like a history of enmities," thought the young journalist, looking at the plaque of prophet Ali. "There's always us and the others. There's always an AND in between. At the root of these enmities is the anguish that no one can ever be himself . . . A person who cannot be himself can be anything, can become anything . . ."

MAYBE IF THERE WERE WATER IN KARBALA, THEY WOULD HAVE BEEN ABLE TO WASH THEMSELVES OF THEIR SINS.

It was a habit from the old days, a custom. Players used to come and play at the feasts, the circumcisions. They portrayed themselves.

One day while the Prophet Mohammed was enjoying the company of his grandsons (Hasan and Hüseyin), Jebrail Aleyhisselam appeared. He said, Do you love them very much, o Resullullah? (He did love them very much.) And thereafter he said, they will be martyred (and he gave him a palmful of earth). This earth is the earth of Karbala on which your grandsons will be martyred. On the day they are martyred, this palmful of earth (it had to be kept in a glass bowl) will shed blood (on the day they were martyred, the earth in the glass bowl shed blood) and when Kasım died, they gathered his blood (for the Players, Nasır's blood) into a bottle that remained illuminated throughout the play. The day after this play ended, the fight between Bakir and Sidar would be retold. Sidar at seven—yet to be circumcised—and Bakır at fifteen, about to go on his first hunt . . . The storytellers asked, "How should we retell their fight?" They wanted to know the TERMS of their enmity. No one lives to see the battles waged in their name. NO ONE LIVES TO SEE THE BATTLES WAGED IN THEIR NAME. If Jesus had lived, would he have joined the Crusades? What was it that the Caliph Muawiyah and the prophet Ali couldn't have shared? And many questions yet to come . . . PEOPLE LIVE THEIR LIVES LIKE A FALSE CREED . . .

In the year nineteen seventy-eight, in the month of December, he arrived in Maraş as a young journalist. He saw a plaque of the prophet Ali. And then, in the remnants of an old, ruined coffeehouse, he listened to this rambling somniloquy that began with the story of this old plaque. He wanted to connect it to the age he was living in, to his present, to the events of his day. "Don't try too hard," said the storyteller. THE LAST NARRATOR. "There are gaps in the story, there are questions, see to it that you fill these in. That's the only way you can make your age beautiful. Else, what's all this got to do with us?"

April 1980
October 25–December 12, 1983

Binali and Temir

1.

Avar came up and sat by the dead man's head.

"I said so," he said. "I said so. But what good did it do? This too must be a lesson learned only at the price of death."

2.

He felt that sudden joy come checking on him when a spray of sunlight seeping through the bushy trees caught his face. (So there, he'd been caught.) The light caught him just when he knelt down (like absent-minded prey), just when he laid his head on his lap. Joy arriving with a touch of light. Even at the turn of the season, the giant trees' overgrown foliage doesn't allow the rays of the sun to fall to the ground so easily. Forest seasons last a long time, just like the outlaw season on the mountains. This was one of the forest's thickest, bushiest spots; the trees are endlessly entwined and the mountain permits no passage to its summit. Following tracks, spotting tracks is difficult here. Those who don't know the forest's language can find neither their way around nor the way to themselves.

When Temir found him, he was wounded.

He was lying (fallen, outspread) in the quiet of the forest.

So there, he had been caught. His heart was like newly tilled earth.

Temir smiled for a long time, for a reason he didn't know.

A piercing, feral glow flashed across his eyes.

And that hawk.

Toward the summit, the mountain casts off the forest, and there begin the rocky aeries of predatory birds, cliffs sharpened by the sun—their boundless territory. There, you don't play games with the sun. Nor with the steep falling cliffs. The sun catches humans like death does.

Try hide-and-seek, and the blind sun will always make you "it."

There, death is a glare.

The sloping, bare, rolling hills give way to squat trees at first, the evergreen maki trees, the grizzled heath, then the humble trees known for growing anywhere, then the giant, magnificent trees and lush leaves. The mountain grows and hides by adding to its splendor the secrets of the forest. Then that secret, deepened by the forest, finds its end at the naked and sharp cliffs stuck like a dagger in the mountain summit. Cliffs as naked and quiet as death. The sun rises to the east of that dagger and sets on its west. The plateau, this dagger-tipped death, marks every hour with sand on the clockface of the vast grassland. It starts from the foot of the mountain and extends, extends endlessly. In its desolateness, it shelters villages large and small, little encampments, and roads that never meet. With its steppe silence permeating everywhere, the plateau is like the borderland of the country of death. Its climate is nothing like the climate of the forest.

The rains had just begun.

A sudden downpour. Unexpected, it pockmarks the earth with holes and heaves (erasing all tracks), shaking branches, making everything green shine with its wetness, and then yields to bright, overpowering sunlight, a scorching noon, or a melancholy (purple, wistful, gauzy) evening.

In one day, the mountain lives through several seasons at a time.

In one day, the forest lives through several seasons at a time.

In one day, the person lives through several seasons at a time.

In this season, that is, as it is turning,

in this season when all seasons pass through each other, seasons that, in passing, multiply,

that is, at this time of seasons turning.

The mountain, the forest, and the person . . .

The earth's swollen bosom becomes inscrutable due to the handwriting of the rain; tracks wash into each other. For this reason, the most arduous hunts occur when the seasons are changing. The tense heart of the hunter overflows with the secret lust of aggression, the toxic pleasure of following the unknown, the unrecognized tracks.

The rains had just begun.

Yet the rain and the sun begin everything anew. Both the rain and the sun have the power to do so.

He was clearly injured. Maybe he would die. (Without being able to open his eyes, or speak, without explaining his troubles, without being able to.

Had he lost much blood? Without even giving his name. Without giving away who shot him. Had he lost much blood?) Why then? Why then, when he found him, did he feel this little, secret joy that didn't even alert the heart's owner to its cause? The secret illumination that caught his heart like that little spray of light that caught his face. Both had swooped in from some place and caught him in the quiet of the forest. Both lighting up at the same time.

He smiled for a long time, he didn't know why.

A piercing feral glow passed across his eyes, and the joy within him turned into a shiver. A wondrous shiver. He is a child of legends, their climate, who experienced in every new encounter an auspicious event. Raw and rough enough to sense the magic of this moment. (His wound throbs like a pulse. The reverberations of the forests!) He possessed one of those small but inspired lives that made him think that every event heralded another. His splendid melancholy brought on him by the mountain solitude suits very well his untamed childhood and the rumblings of the forest. For a long while he didn't even understand that it was joy he was feeling inside. He didn't recognize his emotions, didn't know their name. He'd never learned. They hadn't taught him. He couldn't understand.

What converged in the illumination of his face?

What overflowed from within him and what alighted on his face?

It was as if, in this forest darkened by sprouting leaves, the sun had lured him to its trap like an outlaw stealing through the impassable leaves and branches. This was a game he'd been playing with the sun for a long time, a pact between them. A game of hide-and-seek but played only on the mountain, in the forest. In the places closest to the sun, to hide from the sun. Who would beat whom? Is it ever clear in the forest who would beat whom? Who can beat whom? A question as old and as dark as the forest.

"I take refuge in the forest; you, however, are everywhere. So come and get me!"

Temir and the sun, their childhood days, their childhood battles would begin when he retreated into the most overgrown, most secluded areas of the forest.

Walking under the tree canopy, Temir could advance without being caught by the sun.

The injured person he found on the ground had made him forget the sun. Running to his side, he had knelt down and was caught.

He has never considered this. He never considered that when he found something, he would be caught, that he would lose the game.

The person was wounded; the sun was death.

As for the forest, it was the old forest. The oldest forest.

Now, on his lap was someone he didn't know—what's more, someone wounded. His fingertips part his thick hair; locks of dark, bushy hair run through his hands.

He carefully wraps his wound. At this moment, he wants only one thing on this earth to live: this hurt, unresponsive man whom he doesn't know, breathing fitfully under his hands, as if his entire fate seems to be tied to him. With all his strength and all his heart, he wants to take him and release him from the grip of death. He carefully wraps his wound, stopping the bleeding, at least for now. (He had lost a lot of blood, this much he knows.)

The hawk. Suddenly that hawk. Always that hawk.

From somewhere far off he vaguely hears the beating wings of some predatory bird. The very moment he found him wounded, he remembered that hawk. That owner of wings that had reached the mountain peaks. Lying in the shadow of a tree, it was breathing haltingly. It could not fly.

His eyelids opened, at first slowly, heavily. The spray of light that first illuminated his face now, as he lowered his head, fell on the face of the one in his lap. A tiny light rose up from the depths of his pupils—like a fish trying to reach the surface—and then suddenly, the eyelids closed again. He saw Temir. He had sensed him wrapping his wound. (Maybe his pain was subsiding, and that's why the fish was trying to get to the surface of the water.) His head was on someone's lap. He probably felt the calm of entrusting himself to a human. He was caught, but he wasn't dead. (Which would be better for him, anyway?) Caught but wasn't dead, he was thinking, and maybe taking solace in the fact. Who knows what a person thinks when they are this close to dying?

His copper-green face lit up for a second, just a second, as if he wanted to smile. Want as he might, his depleted strength couldn't even twitch the two furrows on his face, his dimples. After that, he became entirely languid and passed out, all of the light in his face fading away. (The sea grew dark. The fish returned to the depths.)

Much later Temir understood why he wanted him not to die. Much later. When he'd used all of his strength to bring him back to health and, later, the same strength to kill him.

He raised his head from the wound; he had wrapped the arm tightly and stopped the bleeding. Now he had to carry him to his lair. That was the safest place. He put the wounded one on his back and set out. With difficulty they advanced through the densely treed paths.

Mostly he thought about the hawk's wings.

Did they have wings too? Surely humans don't have wings. But, if nothing else, when they die, when their souls strain up to the sky, didn't they take wing? Like a hawk? Didn't they too glide up into the heights?

It had risen heavily, made a few rounds upward, downward, above Temir's head and then, to spite Temir, glided up and up, and higher, then even higher, and beating its wings, vanished.

Was death a country?

A country high up, even higher.

When they reached his lair, Temir was out of breath. Sweat poured down his back.

"Clearly someone is on his trail," was what he thought. "But even the devil couldn't find this place." He carried into the cave dry herbs, armfuls of herbs, twigs, and brushwood. Then he lit a fire. The smoke traveled into the depths of the cave and wafted out of a hole somewhere deep and far. No one would be able to figure out its origin. With the tip of his knife, heated up red-hot in the blazing fire, he extracted the bullet from the wound. (He suffered, howled, bit his lips.) He salved the wound full of ointment. He daubed the ointment with the essence of a thousand and one healing herbs, salved it into the wound as it oozed rot, and wrapped the arm and leg up tight.

Then the wounded one fell into a deep and long sleep. Writhing and howling, he shrank away from him, but as he slept, Temir loved him. He didn't think about this at the time, didn't even realize it.

Besides, who can recognize all the things that one is feeling?

From the mouth of the cave, Temir looked down. "The season descends from the mountain," he thought. The clouds heap up from the skirts of the mountain, the autumn's last caravans pass across the plain. Clouds waft by under their feet. There was little between them and evening. (Days have their evenings.) "If this man is an outlaw and the gendarmes are after him, he will be safe for the winter. Soon, no one will be able to brave this side of the mountain."

In the mountains, the season of the outlaws, too, was ending.

(Suddenly the thought crossed his mind that this may not be some notorious outlaw but rather a common thief. His mind clouded over.) Only the toughest mountains could and did harbor outlaws. But soon, surely, no mountain would shelter any outlaws at all. (He immediately banished this thought from his mind. The one he found wounded couldn't be just a villager or a common thief. He shouldn't be.) The one who knew this best was the one sleeping wounded.

The age of the tough mountain outlaw was ending. (Either he would have to put his tail between his legs and concede to spend fifteen years of his youth rotting in prison or prefer dying in these summits, like a legend.) It was time to come down to the plains, but how? Only the highest mountain summits remained, these last hideouts like unfallen castles. Now only the few remaining bands of outlaws make their home in those summits, in those inaccessible valleys, defying the mountain's dark history, where the soldiers, gendarmes, and armored vehicles won't reach.

A ruthless bloody war continued among them.

So what if you were an outlaw, if you couldn't be the mightiest, the most notorious one in these mountains? Now everyone knew outlaws no longer ruled the world.

After leaving jail, what's the use wandering the streets of the village and the town square like a captured and wounded lion? What remains of those tallest mountains, those harsh winds, those purple-veiled clouds? The wounded man he found would have rather died than surrender.

Still, the bosom of the mountains will always make room for its lovers. Songs steeped in longing, forget-me-not handkerchiefs, tobacco cases left behind by the outlaws, fugitives, and deserters, these songs still can roam the mountains. In the double-barreled silence of mountain nights, love and yearning can meander like a whistle. Even as the last of the outlaws fall one by one, a mountain legend is born every day, passing from mouth to mouth, echoing through the villages and the tribes.

Born and reborn as a legend.

Were it not for the outlaw sagas, no one would still believe in human strength and heart.

Temir was lost in thought, caught in the caravan of the autumn clouds.

"Maybe he isn't an outlaw but a lover," he mused. "His path, his heart might have fallen to a fatal love. Or maybe he has no one, maybe he is hungry, an outcast." He felt a kind of indifference toward him, mixed with pity. "If he's lovesick, he should have known better. What good is love to a helpless man? Isn't love itself helplessness?" He could not recall hearing people repeat this saying or similar ones. He'd heard most every saying he used from someone else. Which means he never had a saying of his own. He felt happy. "Love is helplessness" was his own saying.

Within him happiness, a whirl of the heart. He got up and tidied up the cave, and again carried herbs, sticks, twigs, and a few logs and bolstered the fire. (He is lying down in the corner.) He watched the shadows the fire made on the walls. This is something that always entertains him. And secretly it scares him too. He senses there are hidden and unknown things in these shadows. A secret, a talisman, a spell. (There was another person in his cave.) On lonely nights—in other words, every night—he'd watch the wall shadows at length. He'd make a world beyond out of them, from the shadows, from the flames of the fire. "Someone is after him," he said. (The flames accentuated the dampness of his forehead.) "Maybe several." (Stretched out on the mat, lying flat, he breathed in and out, deep in sleep.) "He made it this far. He must be strong. Tough. Certainly brave." (A first-time someone.) "Built like a rock. (Rock, rocks, cliffs. Hawk. The sun, its grassland rage. How it stings the eye. As if the sun is taking revenge on the world. A score it has been unable to settle since the world began.) Strong as strong gets. Like a mountain." (A first-time someone. The flames on his forehead. Solitude dissolving. He sleeps. Within him happiness, a whirl of the heart.) "I'll go check on the flock," he said. Descending the first hill, he found the flock where he had left it. Hulking sheepdogs surrounded the flock. They too were looking out for the evening.

The flock, spread out on a wide, pitched field, bore a melancholy that arrived with dusk. It bore the melancholy.

When he returns, he knows he will find him inside (waiting, sleeping) in his lair.

For the first time, the evening did not feel melancholy to him.

"This shepherd," said Avar. "He manages huge flocks all by himself. He makes his way up into the mountains with these flocks so big that you can't see where they begin or end. He's fifteen if a day. Barely the size of my hand, yet he defies the mountains, the wolves, the flocks. At this age he's already conquered all the mountains. A version of you, in other words. Another version of you. Big villages commend their flocks to his hand. In the mountains and the grasslands, he brings to pasture the flocks of so many of the greatest chieftains. He makes the sheep run as through wide prairies, all by himself. They say the forest animals all fear him. Not a single sheep, a single lamb in his care has ever been caught by the wolves or the birds of prey. At his age, he's become the mountains' most famous shepherd. They say that he doesn't play his kaval but bleeds it. If you ask me, don't go back, son, don't go!"

The sound of the kaval is vaguely audible. A gentle tune, sadness mixed with anger, a tune weeping inward, a gentle weeping tune. His eyes are closed, clearly; he is lost in the music, one can sense this, too.

He hears the faint sound now and again, then falls again into the well of sleep. This time he wasn't caught, he thinks, no one was able to catch him. He thinks this frightful hunt is over; this bloody pursuit has reached its end. He feels his wound, its stinging pain, and he is pleased. It is as if this pain makes it known to him that he is alive. As if he will soon bound back up onto his feet and say, "All the mountains are mine!" (Has he ever thought before that pain could give him pleasure? It is as if this gentle tune is accompanying the pain.)

If the outlaws retreat and leave the mountains' dark histories, he will be those mountains' last outlaw. The very last outlaw. He will live through the last sultanate of these purple mountains, these mournful purple mountains.

He'll die like an outlaw without losing to anyone, without surrendering to anyone, without falling into the hands of time. He thinks all this, along with the pain.

He lies unconscious.

Temir knows he will spend a while longer watching this silent wounded man like this, with helpless eyes.

He lies unconscious.

"Temir" he says. "My Temir! My brave one, open your eyes, my babe, my wounded gazelle, open your eyes! If you don't open them, I will die too! Open your eyes, you! Open them! Do you want me to die of sorrow? Open them, you dog's spawn!"

Temir does not open his eyes. He buries his black-coal hair, clumped with blood, under his arm, and in the hot and tender nest under his arm, he listens to him for the first time with a heart that's swollen with happiness. He listens as if he is unconscious, as if he'll never open his eyes again, never again. He takes pleasure in the sting of his wounds. He feels no pain.

"You know better than anyone what it means to conquer the mountains. You ought to know. You must have felt this stubbornness, this muteness of the heart, this resilience. You will not share this mountaintop with anyone. You certainly know best what it means to set your mind to being alone, to living up there on your own at the mountaintop; you know it with all your heart. Shepherding is this boy's job. What's called shepherding is a long captivity. Days of longing for a human face. Days that never end. Days one of a kind, braced by a sunrise and a sunset. They know fifty words if that. They even forget these from not speaking. This child overcame everything when he was just as tall as a hand. He grew accustomed to the mountain, to solitude, to the spell of living alone. This boy is terrifying. It seems to me he knows, he senses, many things we do not. Your heart quivers. What he feels, what he thinks, what passes through his mind, what passes through his heart, no one knows. I fear the man who can be silent for this long. I say, one must fear the man who can be silent for this long. If you ask me, don't go back, son, don't go!"

He lies unconscious.

He senses that he is going to die soon. Life is being drawn out of him. He senses it. Life drawing out, from his feet, from his legs, from his groin, from his torso, like water being drawn out of a well by a pump. He feels as though all of it will gather inside his head, inside his mouth, and all life will be emptied out with his last breath. He thinks about breathing, how his mind becomes lucid, his thinking clearer, while in this unconscious state. It seems breathing is keeping life alive, not the body. The body doesn't breathe. The life within us breathes. This must be what they call "last breath." Something that starts walking from our feet and our fingers and courses through our body toward our head and then abandons us in that last breath. Death. He is again in the dark arms of sleep, all his thoughts lose their clarity, become muddled. The kaval is no longer audible. Or he cannot hear it.

He doesn't move his head beneath his arm. Peaceful, safe. Unconscious. Hot. These are sensations he'd never tasted, never known. Things he was unfamiliar with. Can one yearn for things one has never known? Clearly, he can. He is plainly acting coy. Suddenly he feels his lips on his forehead. A few times he feels them.

"Temir! My son, open your eyes, poor lamb!"

It couldn't fly. (It would be caught.) Its wings were bloody. He remembered how a tiny spray of sunlight shining through the branches fell on one side of its wing and exposed its wound to the light, making it seem larger. The hawk could not fly. He was wrapping its wounds but also depriving the hawk of flight. Detaining it. Prolonging the hawk's captivity. He and the hawk lived together for a while. When all its wounds healed, he put the hawk in a cage, slowly killing it. He didn't think this was cruelty.

(Was he a hawk? Or, after all this time had passed, did it just please him to think that he was a hawk? In fact, sometimes Temir thinks that he didn't exist, never existed at all. It's true, he had come silently, left silently. Maybe he didn't exist. Had never been. Just like his mother and

father had never been. (Everything, everyone was silent.) He had imagined it one lonely, very lonely night when he couldn't sleep, probably
one of the stories he made up when he was trying to get to sleep.) A
wounded hawk story. Was it a hawk? Was it not? Not even this is clear.
He didn't trouble himself about it. Whatever it was, it was a big, gigantic
bird. It had fallen into his hands. Into his very hands. Fallen, wounded.
He had taken its fluttering heart between his hands, rubbed ointment
on its wound, cured its troubles, wiped the brown blood off its wings,
cleaned and wrapped them. He had looked after that hawk for days.
Cared for it, made it better. At first unwittingly but soon deliberately,
he inflicted pain on the poor bird. How does a living thing suffer? He
wanted to witness the suffering of a living being other than himself. How
does one experience pain? Is it something like seeing yourself, seeing
yourself in someone else? Like a dream fallen into water.

He couldn't leave the hawk alone. And the more he couldn't, the more
he hurt it.

One day, he forgot to close the cage door and found the hawk waiting
for him there at the opening. (He'd made a cage for the hawk while car-
ing for it. Built it with his own hands. He'd whittled down branches with
a knife, working meticulously, wanting to display all his carving skills as
he built the cage, as if he had something he wanted to hide for a lifetime.)
It was as if the hawk had waited for him. For his return. The noble lord
of the aeries had not wanted to fly off without taking its revenge, as if it
wanted to perform its escape while looking him in the eye. In its eyes—
eyes as sharp as the mouth of an abyss—was a night painted in black. A
black revenge. Temir never forgot that look from the hawk. He would
never forget it. A look of evil. A look of evildoing.

That was when he realized he'd always feared this hawk. This thought
licked past his brain like a switchblade.

Fear was shameful.

Now the one whose heart was fluttering was Temir. Just like that day.
That first day. Helpless, it lay down on the ground, some kind of a bird.
When he cupped his hands around its chest to pick it up from the
ground, he could feel the heart's fluttering ever faster in his palms. And
together with that quickening, it parted its eyelids. Slowly, it opened its
eyes. There was neither darkness nor the night in those eyes. It looked
into Temir's eyes. As if looking at death. As if aware that there was nothing left to save from the hands of death.

But now the hawk's eyes looked different. It was stronger now. Alone.
It had yanked away, freed its solitude from the hands of death. It could

fly. The cage bars couldn't hold its wings anymore. It could fly. It could return to the bosom of the cliffs, to its home on the edge of the abyss. With a noble rage, it was slowly flapping its wings, opening then closing them, clearly readying to take off. It had to have tested the power of its wings before. Before Temir arrived, before he returned. Maybe it had taken to the air, made a few rounds, and then returned to the cage to wait for Temir.

It would fly off while looking him in the eye and vanish.

It too would vanish then.

Like his mother, his father, his brothers. Again, Temir would be left alone. On his own with his mountain, his forest, his flock. He had no home other than his shepherd's cloak. That bristly felted shepherd's cloak was his home and his exile. Did home have wings too? Did exile?

For a moment, he wanted to say, "Don't fly."

He didn't say, he couldn't say, "Don't fly, don't go."

He would not go begging (I won't torment you anymore) of anyone, human or animal (I'll not torment you), or bird. Begging was the most disgraceful act. (You're not of this flock. You're a stranger. You can go.) Only dogs beg. For a morsel of bread, for a measly bone, the dogs. (Not one sheep, not one lamb did I lose to the wolves or birds, to this day. But you. Your wings.) Let it fly, let it go. (He didn't say. He couldn't say.)

As if it had never come. As if it had never been.

Back then he didn't know what he did was cruelty. Later, much later, when he himself was wounded, would he be able to name the few dark meanings he could tease out of his confused and frightening emotions: I won't torment you again, I won't make you suffer . . . His eyes were half-open. He was in pain. Insects, ants, bees were crawling on his body.

"I won't torment you again, I will not make you suffer, Temir. I know I was wrong, I made a mistake, I followed you, I let the devil tempt me. I was childish, it was unlike me, I know."

He undid, one by one, the ropes that tied Temir to the tree.

Temir collapsed on the ground.

He took him in his arms, carried him into his cave.

But you. Your wings. You are not of this flock, he thought. So be it, let it fly, let it go. He said nothing. He could say nothing.

Slowly, it had ascended slowly, circled high and low around Temir's head a few times, then, to spite Temir, soared up, high up, even higher up, spreading its wings, and vanished.

Was death a country?

A country way up high?

While all of this was happening, Temir couldn't even budge. Frozen in place. The hawk's talisman had frightened him. The cage couldn't safeguard it, couldn't hide it.

While circling above his head, its wings came between Temir and the sun. That wounded wing—the wound magnified by a spray of light—was now between Temir and the sun. Temir remained in its shadow.

Then, finally, the hawk pulled away into the summits that allowed no passage. It disappeared among the steep face of the rocks.

Temir was overcome from weeping all night.

During the night he looked at that shepherd's fire, glowing like a hawk's eye. Then he threw the cage into the fire. The cage burned and crackled and turned to ash. He knew it wouldn't return; he'd revived it, returned it from death, but he made it suffer. He had hurt it. Maybe it still would have left, even if he didn't make it suffer, who knows . . .

The flames grew as the cage crackled, and in the glow, he looked at the fire, at the forest, at the world, like a wounded hawk, he looked, looked, looked.

Then gently his eyelids closed, and he fell into sleep.

He knew that in the morning he would find neither the cage nor the hawk where they had been.

When they reached his cave, Temir was out of breath. Sweat running down his back. "Who might he be?" he thought. "Either he's following someone's tracks, or someone's following his." He looked long and carefully at the wounded man's face. Then he decided. "Clearly, someone's on his trail," he thought.

3.

The rains had just started.

His name was Binali.

The mountains were under siege.

So many rings of fire he had jumped through. He just couldn't die.

The bands of outlaws large and small who dwelled in the mountains were on his trail.

The outlaws followed tracks.

His own band had scattered (died, been wounded, escaped, were hidden) and was looking for him.

His band followed tracks.

All the gendarmes charged with bringing down all the outlaws in all the mountains were after him.

The gendarmes followed tracks.

For so long, he had kept Avar alive, looked after him and his belongings. They had helped one another in many ways, owed each other their lives. Avar and his men were on the trail.

Avar followed tracks.

He had to not die.

The rains had started recently. It made tracking harder. Binali's friends and foes alike despaired.

Temir still regarded him as wounded. A wounded one whom he looked after, watched over, protected. He just knew he was still alive. He knew that he breathed evenly though sometimes unevenly, that once in a while he tried to open his eyes, batted his eyelashes, and that his beard got longer. These things he could observe, watching them was in his power.

Temir felt confident.

Maybe for this reason he was seized by the thought that he could defend him against the entire world. He didn't give a hoot about all the people on his trail.

Besides, they wouldn't be able to find this place.

Binali was a formidable outlaw who—maybe for reasons of blood or honor, maybe of land, a cruel landlord or a love affair that sent him to prison, reasons that multiplied through countless rumors and tales and became harder and harder to name—had gone up and made these tough mountains his home, trapped and plundered some of the strongest bands of outlaws, and always come out on top in his struggle to become the most fearsome outlaw of the mountains.

Warrior songs lit up in his name, legends told in his honor traveled from hamlet to hamlet. (The day Temir found him, several small bands had formed an alliance and pushed him into a corner, but he had been able to break through the ambush and, later, just as he was about to fall into the gendarmes' hands, he had managed to elude them, too.)

The shadow of the flames accentuates his long dark face, his downturned moustache at night. For some time now, Temir has been watching Binali's face shimmer in the firelight rather than the shadows on the wall.

He wonders what kind of a man he is.

The rain outside. Long. The sound of the fire crackling.

Temir did not sleep for such a long time.

As if he were inside a well, as if awakened by the sound of the shepherd's kaval, as if heeding its call, his sleep is interrupted. But he cannot shake it

off and stand up, feeling keen aches in various parts of his body, and a little melody in his ears, as if death were playing blindman's bluff with him.

Temir has not been sleeping for very long.

The well in Binali's darkness and his struggles are because of the song
Temir plays on his kaval as he sings him a lullaby in his heavy, long, aching dreams, calling him into the world's wakeful dream.

Temir hangs on to his kaval for so long.

To its call, to its tune (without knowing it).

Maybe because it is something known for so many centuries to give
voice to the shepherd's heart, the power of the kaval and the kaval's call
appear more enchanted than ever to him.

"Water," he said. "Water!"

He didn't recognize his own voice. As if there were thornbushes
caught in his throat. Steppe flowers. The steppe inside him had bloomed
with flowers. His throat scarred and torn.

Temir leapt to his feet.

Leapt a thousand times.

How long had he waited for this? He tossed his kaval and bounded
straight toward him.

"Take it, ağam," he said, extending a bowl of water. (A round pewter
bowl, shining from the moonlight seeping into the cave.) Temir tried to
catch his eye; if he saw his eyes opened, he would believe he'd recovered,
only then he would believe it. (This was the first light of the world in
Binali's eyes.) As he tried to stand, to straighten up (an ice-cold bowl, an
entire life, in his eyes) his wound stung . . . (the cold between his hands
singed his palms, made them burn) and water drizzled from his lips to his
chin (and a thousand intimations ran between his fingers). Just then, as
when he felt pain, he understood for the first time that he was alive . . .

His wound stung, and he remembered the entire world and his past,
along with that wound.

"We were partridge hunting on that day.

"We'd reached a clearing where the forest thinned out, and suddenly
a gazelle appeared before me. I was at once afraid and enamored and
surprised; I didn't know what to do. My heart was like a cloudy puddle.
My feelings all mixed up; my mind clouded over. The animal stood close
to me. If I'd reached out, I could touch it, if I charged, I might have killed
it. We came eye to eye. We stayed eye to eye. Had I taken a step or two,
I'd have caught it. Unable to get over my surprise, or at least this was the
reason I presumed, I couldn't reach for my rifle. Partridge was what we'd

come out hunting for, and gazelles were far from my mind. But gazelles too get hunted for.

"Its movements were more agile than mine, it began to run away, and when it did, I shot it. A silence enveloped me, I couldn't rejoice, and my chest didn't swell at having added a gazelle to the countless partridge. Within me just that silence, as if my heart had emptied out and dry grassland had filled my ribcage. I'm not sure why I got so sad. My arms dropped, and I didn't dwell on it too long, inclined as I was to forget it. Back then I couldn't understand why."

"You don't know this bastard! He'll kill you; he won't let you live. If you're going to kill, then go. But if you say you're going to go talk, I say, don't go. You cannot talk with him. Language won't do. Language will come up short for talking. What is talking anyway? And what are you going to talk about with him? He may call water what we call water, herbs what we call herbs, but he lives in another universe. He may say *water*, may say *herb*, but he means a different kind of thing. How can I explain this to you? I'm helpless . . . Listen to me, this kid grew up with nobody. Imagine what it means to have no one . . . No one ever fooled this child, no one told him lies. Children like being fooled, they like to play games. This child played no games, no one played with him, no one ever fooled him. He has seen the world naked. Learned it naked. Try to think what that means for a bit. A man with nobody around turns feral, strange, animal—a wounded animal besides . . . His kind sinks his claws into the world's soil. Your outlaw spirit isn't enough to fight him, you'll lose in the end . . .

"What I'm saying isn't about your manhood. I know how strong you are, I know that better than anyone, but this kid lives in a different universe, speaks in a different language. If you lose, you'll lose for this reason, because you don't know him, you don't understand his heart and his language."

After giving him water to drink, Temir studied his face at length. (He felt things prowling inside him close to what he felt when the kaval was singing, things he didn't know, things he could never know.) So he had come back to life. He had spoken. His feet now pressed the soil of the world again. He had healed him, helped him recover. He responded to his call, to his tune. Yet Temir did not understand why it was that his initial joy quickly waned. As he came back to life, it seemed as though he had taken away half of Temir's strength. Temir was aimlessly feeling his way around his heart to understand why his joy was extinguished when his eyes were again caught in Binali's gaze.

A heavy, clammy air had descended upon the cave. For the first time, another person is living with him; Temir doesn't know what he is supposed to do. Living with a second person for the first time. The air becomes heavier, clammier.

Binali is eying his surroundings. Staking a claim on it as he does so.

Temir has lost all sense of peace.

The night's magic undone, its miracle vanished. Moonlight was just moonlight again. It hung dimly at the mouth of the cave.

As if Temir understands—these looks remind him of something, maybe a lot of things, that he doesn't like.

When Binali took his eyes off the surroundings and turned his head again to Temir, Temir suddenly understood that his joy too had died out. It was as though regaining his health, coming back to life had added burdens upon Binali's shoulders. Like a brief seasonal rain, he had been flushed with light, only to quickly darken again.

As if everything was better when he was wounded and lifeless.

Binali acts like it's his most natural right that Temir found and saved him, looked after him, and helped him heal. He behaves as if life is his right. Like all of life's blessings are his right. He acts like those people who feel no gratitude toward anyone, absolutely no one; as if he thinks, yes, I am happy to have recovered, but now it's time to take care of other tasks. He had experienced all his joy while drinking that bowl of water, and now all he felt was thirst. What Temir could not put a name to and would never be able to put a name to, was that thirst of his.

"Where are we?" he asked.

"In the slot canyons," said Temir and hushed. "Cliffs on four sides of us." He wanted him to feel unsafe. "Do you know this place?"

"I do."

"I found you in the bush of the forest. You'd lost a lot of blood."

"Thank you. Where's my rifle?"

"I saved it. It was in your lap. Don't worry, they won't find this place. Only the devil plays hide-and-seek in these caverns."

"Your name, what is it?"

He took a deep breath in and, releasing it, said "Temir." He checked his face. Not a line on his face twitched. He checked again. Which meant he hadn't heard the name. He wasn't even interested.

Temir was crestfallen.

"Has it been long?"

"Has what been long?"

"Since you brought me here?"

"Three days . . ."

"Alone?"

"Alone. Just me."

"No one saw . . ."

"No one. Else I'd have killed them."

"Who, the ones who saw?"

"Yes, the ones who saw."

Binali remained quiet for a while. The forest's reverberations winding around in his head. At a clearing in the forest, all sounds cease.

"Have you ever killed a man before?"

"Why do you ask?"

"Nothing! Just curious. You talked about killing as if it was really easy to do."

"Yeah, it's easy. Killing is the easiest."

"But you didn't answer my question."

"No, I never killed a man, but I can."

"And a gazelle? Did you ever shoot a gazelle?"

"You don't shoot gazelles. Else, you'd be cursed for life."

"What work do you do?"

"Did you not hear? A bit ago when you asked, I said my name is Temir. I'm a shepherd, there's no one who hasn't heard of me around here, my name is known in the grasslands and meadows . . . Why are you smiling sideways like that, did I say something strange?"

"You said there's no one who hasn't heard of you around here . . . ."

"Yes, I said that, what of it? It's true."

"Nothing, I just smiled is all."

"I don't like smiling, not at all, and I don't like those who smile. And can I say something to you? I don't like your looks either. You look like you own the whole world. I don't like that, didn't like that at all."

"Then one day I thought: I didn't go for the trigger after the animal started to escape. I'd lied to myself. I'd gone for the trigger earlier; maybe this was why it started to escape. I still don't know. But then why did I shoot it? Hunting gazelles was the furthest thing from my mind. If I had let it be, it would have been free, would have simply run away. We'd just met there in that forest clearing. Met each other, on the edge of that clearing. The forest behind me, the clearing ahead of the gazelle. Killing it didn't even cross my mind. Afterward I understood that, before he started to escape, when we were still eye to eye, its gaze had changed. For a second, a split second, it looked different. That's when I understood that it was going to escape next, that it would bolt and run. And once I recognized its changed gaze, I went for the trigger. As it was about to leap, I was ready to shoot. It had appeared before me unbidden but now it was trying to escape. This couldn't go unpunished. I wasn't even thinking when it appeared, caught me unawares, left me exposed. I could overcome my shock only by shooting it. Even so, I still can't tell the time between its changed gaze and my pulling the trigger."

Temir spent a hurt, crestfallen, sleepless night. He wanted him to get to his feet and leave at once. The heavy, clammy air that had settled inside the cave thickens with each passing day. Temir has difficulty breathing. Feels like he is constantly being watched.

All night he coughed, groaned, and talked in his sleep. Inside the cave, the disquiet was palpable.

Morning was hard.

(Mornings became hard.)

They came eye to eye while changing the dressing on the wound. His looks weren't as bad as last night, but they still carried something from last night in them.

Temir moves his hand around the wound as gently as he can to avoid giving him pain.

His first words were: "Where's my rifle?"

"Leave this place as soon as you feel better."

"I said, where's my rifle!"

"I told you I saved it! I told you, you're in a safe place."

Binali took a long breath. He stretched, and in his eyes was a withering look, perfectly clear to read.

"You didn't ask me who I am."

He hadn't asked who he was.

The thing he was most curious about.

It was as though he understood who he was as soon as he woke up. Or that he acted in a certain way that made immediately clear who he was.

Temir kept his cool, as if to suggest that he figured out who he was and didn't want to meddle and this was why he didn't ask. Besides, as soon as he woke, he'd made it so clear who he was that Temir didn't need to wonder. Because all of these thoughts freely crossed his mind without his bidding, without his even pausing to acknowledge them, Temir didn't dwell on any of them.

His voice, grown all the angrier and more imposing, thanks to his improving strength, rang throughout the cave:

"I am Binali," he said.

A deep wuthering silence followed.

His entire childhood came back to him, his broken-down childhood, his abandoned childhood, his despised, browbeaten, and crushed childhood. He heard from his mouth the name that aroused the admiration and hatred of every youth—Binali.

He'd known that this was someone who ruled over the mountains and the rocks with his power, had even wanted this to be true, but the thought hadn't even grazed a corner of his mind that this man could be Binali.

"Is that why you didn't recognize me?" he said. "Is it because you are Binali?"

Binali was now in a state of ease, having spoken his name. The rest would naturally follow. His name, that talismanic word had just fallen from his lips. (It had been years since he'd given in to the talisman of the words falling from his lips. Doubtlessly, his name was the most spellbinding of these words.) And when he uttered his name a moment earlier, Binali wanted to secure many things under his influence; he wanted Temir's wonder and fear.

He had always behaved as if the world and the mountains and people were his property. He had a right to these mountains, this world, like he'd won all of this world by the might of his wrist. He couldn't live, couldn't exist without feeling the force of the infinite and boundless power he commanded. The disquiet he felt until he spoke his name, until he said "I am Binali" was because of this need, as if a considerable weight had been lifted from his shoulders. He had armed himself with his name like arming himself with his weapon.

He was armed.

Binali.

A spellbinding name for him, and for others.

He couldn't deprive himself of his own spell. He had staked his entire life for this magic.

Never, under no circumstance would he give up his Binaliness. His Binaliness made him who he was.

Binali.

He took refuge in the power of the name now. The name was his most fortified castle. His own men, wherever they were, could stop the waters flowing just by saying, "We are Binali's men."

He took refuge in the power of the name now. He was a giant lying in his sickbed. A giant anew. Temir thought for a long while. How many times had he watched him lying in his sickbed, reached for his head while he was sleeping. Was this that person? Everyone is kin when sleeping. How many times, from how many people had he listened to Binali's stories, more than half of which had become lore . . . How many times had he listened like everyone else, and like everyone else how many times had he been entranced and brought to the same powerful hatred? There was something in the legend of Binali that instantly threatened and belittled the manhood of every youth. The stories of Binali completed what they lacked.

He treated Temir as if he was obliged to take care of him, as if he was one of the servants under his command, someone begging for food at his door. As if he wasn't even human. Something about Binali, even while he lay motionless in his sickbed, gradually took Temir in and wrestled him down. Even if Temir could neither name it nor size it, he felt and experienced all of it. He sensed that all of the disquiet he felt had something to do with Binali's Binaliness.

Binali was already a weight crushing his shoulders.

He wanted him to leave right this second.

Or he would always feel lacking, always wanting . . .

Being nothing like Binali.

A word remained in his ears, a thousand words, multiplying, multiplying, scattering across the night.

Being nothing like Binali.

So, what did he have?

You are either Binali or nothing.

What good is being a man if you weren't the best, the mightiest, the most powerful? In his sickbed, Binali doesn't lie like a sick person, he cannot, his legend doesn't let him rest, and his legend doesn't let Temir rest, something in his movements recall the legend, constantly recall it. Each time it revives his entire childhood again, his childhood magnified with the lore of Binali, his oppressed, despised, crushed childhood. As if Binali were the one responsible for Temir's childhood, for its privations, and this compounded his rage, his bitterness.

Never mind owing Temir his life, he doesn't even feel a debt of gratitude toward him. That's how it seems. As if, in his eyes, Temir had simply done his duty. And never mind even a debt of gratitude, he seems like he intends to scold Temir any second for doing his duty poorly.

He has given himself over to the spell of domination. As ever, he is everywhere in the habit of maintaining the glorious sultanate of his rule. Without knowing how else to act, he has always behaved like this toward the next person, his whole life through. Temir, for his part, has never been with another person. Now they are face-to-face in this dark cave.

With everything they've ever learned and everything they've never learned.

With what Binali has learned at the risk of death, and what Temir has learned secondhand.

Binali is aware that he cannot sink his teeth completely into Temir, and this upsets him. He is the kind of person who can only form relationships when he can sink his teeth into you. Then he can be your friend, your companion, if he can be anything at all. Testing his prey, circling around his prey, he sinks his teeth into it, maybe not killing it but certainly possessing it. He is accustomed to having the whole world and everyone and all the mountains in his teeth and claws.

He thinks Temir has not submitted to him completely, maybe because Binali is nailed motionless in bed.

Within him, deep down somewhere, he does feel a sense of gratitude (turning to anger and hatred) for having been saved. This feeling turns Binali crueler, as if, once he recovers, he will make Temir pay for his kindness.

Both of them spent that night wide awake.

Like there was something that had to be done, there and then. And because neither of them knew what this thing was, they were crushed under its weight. As if each was waiting for the other to make the first move. The heavy, noxious air stuffing that cave thickened, grew heavier, and left them utterly breathless. They couldn't bear this strain, this weight anymore. This filthy, clammy, suffocating air was now too much for both of them.

He milked a bowl of milk in the morning.

In the same pewter bowl . . . He took out a jar of blackberry sherbet. When he returned, he found Binali straightened up on his elbows in the bed, checking around him, whichever places his hands could reach. Temir understood he was looking for his rifle. His anger grew, and he was gripped with the feeling that he'd been double-crossed. He felt like he had been betrayed.

Nothing had changed on Binali's face though. Rather than someone caught guilty in the act, it had the expression of a patient angry at a nurse for failing at his task, for being late and neglectful, a patient irritated that he had to exert himself while doing the work that the other should have done.

Temir's anger swelled. He went and took the rifle from the place he'd hidden it.

"Is this what's you're looking for, Binali ağam?" he asked.

His voice was harsh, exacting, and forceful. There was something in his voice that tore through, dispersed the tense air—its dense heaviness, its sinister, wearying tenseness that had settled in the cave for days—and the dreary clouds weighed with rain. Something reckless, something defiant, spiteful, something of a show of force.

Binali noticed the veiled threat in Temir's voice, and it irked him. With an equally harsh and commanding voice, he shouted, "Give it to me!"

"I will, just wait," said Temir. Slowly he undid his belt, lowered his pants down his thighs. Binali was startled, tried to figure out what Temir was doing.

"Is this not your weapon, Binali ağam?" he asked.

Now Binali made no sound. For the first time he looked at Temir's face carefully, as if he wanted to understand, to know. As if he was seeing him for the first time.

"The rifle of the great Binali, the most notorious and fearsome outlaw in the mountains, whose name makes villages tremble? The rifle that makes Binali Binali!"

Temir lowered his underpants. Taking his long, slender reed into his hand—hair had just begun to grow around it—he held it over the weapon and began pissing on it. His eyes gleamed, his face full of light.

His old face was back.

The clouds in his eyes vanished, the air of the cave grew less heavy.

Looking like he'd taken a bullet, Binali let out a long scream, after he'd steadied himself from the surprise. As if he was lowing. Between his black, downturned moustache and his beard, which had been growing for days, this lowing that sounded like a sharp howl turned into a lion's roar. He reeled with a sharp pain, aware that he could not move from his bed. The overwhelming weight of being dependent on someone, being captive to someone, overtook him. He was hopeless, and he'd never thought of himself this way. If, in this moment, he could've gotten to his feet and torn this bastard to pieces, hacked his flesh bit by bit, drunk his blood bowl after bowl, he would have.

After finishing his piss, Temir shook his reed a few more times, drizzling the barrel with the last few drops.

He turned to Binali, who was frothing at the mouth, shaking from rage.

"Still want your weapon?" he repeated.

Binali looked at Temir with his bloodshot eyes, as if ready to eviscerate him. Temir then tossed the rifle at him.

The battle had begun. He had indeed started the battle. Now a faint, gentle wind was blowing through the cave.

Temir felt like his old self, solitary and strong.

He took the bowl of milk and put it on the bedside.

"Milk," he said. "I milked it for you. So you won't worry: I didn't piss in it."

That day he didn't wrap the wound. Late at night, he came back in. Without looking, he knew that he wasn't sleeping.

"All these things I'm telling you, I didn't think them in a day. They gradually resolved in my head, on their own. I came to understand them, while dying, and killing. They came to me in the blind, at the trigger, while hiding, while escaping and giving chase. After shooting that gazelle, the desert I'd squeezed deep into myself wouldn't leave me, wouldn't show me any mercy. The emptiness that filled my being now stood between me and the trigger. Surely, if that day I'd gone out to hunt gazelles and not partridge and I'd come upon that same gazelle in that same spot, I wouldn't have thought about it so long. Wouldn't have thought about killing. About what killing and dying meant. About that blink of an eye. Everything that happened then. Everything happens and passes within that blink of an eye. Before you know it, you have killed. I've shot lots of men. Lots of traitors, turncoats, deserters. I've assassinated many. But none have made me experience the emptiness I felt when I shot the gazelle. I thought nothing about any of them, didn't think twice. Killing means feeling no remorse, ever. In that space where the forest gently opened up, in that clearing, on that even plain, this gazelle suddenly came to me, came into my life that I thought was an invincible castle, and changed something in me that I still cannot name. It wrenched something from me. Now I couldn't be that old Binali anymore. Now I became someone who couldn't shoot men without blinking. Shoot I did, but now I had to think for a blink of an eye. My trigger finger started hesitating. If I die one day, I'll die for this reason: because I've now learned what it means to kill. Outlaws always live on the trigger, live on the boundary of death. They live as if death will come calling through the gaps between trees, from behind every bush that stirs. Every shadow finds the face of death, you shoot into every darkness. That's how I always waited for death. I didn't know, I couldn't know that death would come to me in the face of a gazelle. And I didn't know I was going to kill death."

Walking the cliffs, along the precipice, and being the closest to death, Binali would feel the same way. His body would drain away, his balls quiver. Heights had always frightened him. Yet he was destined to heights, retreating to higher, ever higher places. On the edge of the precipice and looking down at the cliffs and rocks, he felt nauseated, his balls tensed and ached, and in such moments, he pushed his legs tight together. He didn't show his fear to anyone else, didn't let them sense it.

Even after climbing such heights, what business did this fear have in his heart? What was it for? It was as if that spirit within us, that spirit that does not belong to our body, kept flickering, like a votive candle almost going out.

Just a bit ago, when Temir was pissing on the weapon, that's how it felt too. Just like when he would reach those sharp-edged precipices. When he was pissing on the weapon, Binali's eyes were stuck on Temir's crotch. He was seething with rage, trying to straighten up from the bed where he lay, thrashing about. He could feel the hair on his balls twitching, his muscles tight and tired from pressing his legs together.

Temir came to exist for Binali only as he pissed on his weapon. It was then that he first saw him. Temir occurred to him just then. It just then dawned on him that he wasn't one of those working under his command, that he was someone else. He was a man of his own. Only when someone stood up to Binali, when someone defied him, did he notice them. Does this mean that, in his eyes, the only form of existence in the world is defiance? Is this an outlaw sensibility? Can an outlaw not think any other way, not behave any other way? Is this why he hadn't noticed the little bands of outlaws that from one day to the next became dangerous enemies, why he hadn't taken them seriously, hadn't sensed their constantly growing clandestine hatred? Was that why from the beginning he had been oblivious to their threat? He never could be bothered with them, he had even scorned them, he had overlooked their quiet progression. It wasn't until they were right under his nose, standing on their own two feet, defying him with weapons drawn, that he noticed them. As if he were seeing them for the first time. Binali learned through violence. Knew through violence. Until that moment, that is, until that moment of violence, everything stood, everything happened as if behind a gauze, a mist, a fog.

This little squirt Temir, no bigger than your hand, had suddenly defied him, and all at once he became a man in his eyes. That's when he understood that he had a face, eyes, hands, rage. (What a long reed a fifteen-year-old bastard like that had.) Only at that point was he a man of his own . . .

For Binali, people only come to exist when they're enemies.

That's why he's in the mountains.

That's why he's an outlaw.

That heavy, clammy air in the cave dissipated for Binali too.

Now they were outright enemies, two enemies thirsting for each other's blood. The impassioned violence of enmity seized them and burned in their blood. They hated each other with all their might.

The battle had begun.

The next day, while he was wrapping the wound, they avoided each other's eyes.

A secret shame gnawed at Binali's heart. Having to rely on this bastard diminished his name, his power, his honor. His voice carried a trace of this anger.

"Why are you helping me? Why are you hiding me?"

Temir responded without raising his head. "I don't know."

He thought for a bit, then he said, "There's a lot I don't know."

"I didn't forget what you did to me," said Binali.

Temir raised his head and asked, "What do you mean? That I saved you, or that I pissed on your gun?"

Binali paused, winced. There was something in this child that made him wince, he noticed. Something unexpected that caught him unawares.

"Both," he said. His voice turned softer, even frightened.

That's right; someone like Binali would not forget either one. He wasn't one to forget either one, but when he'd just said "I didn't forget what you did to me," he'd only meant the second one. The veiled and cautious threat in his voice was due to this.

"Don't forget," said Temir. "Look, Binali ağam, I fear no one but Allah. And not even him sometimes. Don't forget this either," he said. His voice came out like he was spitting. He pulled the end of the cloth he'd bandaged the wound with. Binali let out a scream that sounded like a howl.

"Your wound is in my hands, you are in my hands, don't forget it, don't you ever forget this!"

"You dog's spawn! Are you threatening me? Who do you think you are to threaten the mighty Binali . . ."

"I am the Köroğlu of these mountains."

Binali shot out an ill-tempered laugh, more like a roar, full of loathing. "Köroğlu, huh? Look, it's Köroğlu, at last! Köroğlu! Köroğlu!"

Mustering all his strength, Temir lands a back-handed slap across Binali's face. Binali reels. The middle of Binali's face is a mess now. Binali is dumbfounded. Dazed not so much from the slap itself than from the fact that someone can slap him, has slapped him at all.

"Don't laugh again! Don't laugh, I said!"

Binali understands that laughter is a weapon he can use against Temir.

"I'm not going to see you laugh again! You won't laugh. You'll never laugh again!"

The open wound on him throbbing, he is powerless and hopeless. Aware that he has to submit to him, he grows angrier, burns with the same indignation that had always struck others. Binali seethes with rage.

Rage. Unadulterated, manly rage. Outlaw rage, blind rage, a rage synonymous with death, relentless, unstoppable. A rage that had kept him up on the mountain, kept him an outlaw for these many years.

But the throbbing wound overpowers his rage.

His rage subsides, as does his voice. "What is your intention, Temir?"

"I don't have any intentions or whatever, just that you don't laugh anymore, that's it."

Binali cannot figure out what to do. He is in a constant state of surprise. That a little squirt of a kid can make him this helpless, that cannot be! This is the first time, the first time in his life that he feels this desperate.

He doesn't have his strength back, he can't get up from the bed. Even though he is getting better, his wounds keep him down.

He doesn't have his rifle with him. His five-hundred-meter marksmanship is worth nothing here.

Nor can he make his fists do the talking.

None of his men, who would kill, who would die at his command, is anywhere around.

And he has no idea what to do in such a quandary; he's never had to think about anything like this till today. Such a possibility didn't even graze the edge of his mind. Whatever tough knot he'd had to unravel, he'd undo it with his manhood, with his fists. But this time he is faced with a different knot. Nothing he knows will undo it. Binali always lived on his strength, his manhood, his greatness, his name.

He's never thought what he'd do when stuck in this kind of situation, never has he been in such a situation. He is stripped of all his weapons now, every one of them taken from his hands.

He feels so helpless in the face of something so unknown to him that he is afraid he'd do anything this little bastard wants. In times like these, a person cannot know where to stand.

When someone who's never been defeated, someone who's defended his life always with his weapon, his fist, his manhood, finds himself one day completely disarmed, trapped in a closed space, for instance, a cave, and is facing a cruel and power-hungry adversary who himself doesn't know what he wants, that someone will not, cannot, know what to do. That's why, because he thinks even losing once means losing everything, he cannot know where to stand.

Without realizing it himself, he wants to lose all of it, everything, everyone.

Just once, to be defeated just once, is death in his eyes. And he thinks, only by losing everything does one deserve death.

Because he sees his own defeat as the end of the world.

Because he thinks his own defeat is the end of an era, the decisive loss of a cause.

These are Binali's thoughts now.

The violence in his rage stems from his feeling—for the first time ever—so insecure about himself and the person facing him.

His insecurity, in turn, again and again reawakens his wish to kill, his desire to destroy.

Temir suddenly makes a move for Binali's pants. Binali is startled.

"What you doing?" he shouted.

"I'm going to see yours."

"What are you going to do when you see it?"

"Nothing. Just see. You saw mine while I was pissing. I'm going to see yours too."

Quickly he loosens his pants and slips off his underwear.

Then he gets to his feet, laughing.

"Mine is bigger than yours!"

"Mine is bigger than Binali's, the mountains' greatest."

"What happened to you not liking laughter?"

Temir is confused. His laughter dies down.

"Right . . . I never used to like it . . ."

"Are you in pain?" Temir asked.

"Some, a little," said Binali.

Temir pressed his finger a little harder around the wound. Then he asked again, "Now?"

"Now a bit more."

And then Temir pressed his finger harder.

"And now?"

Raising his head, Binali looked at Temir's face carefully. He thought he was examining his wound, but this bastard was just having fun with him, and he felt like a dog with a tin can tied to its tail. He wanted to spit in his face that second, spit in his face with all the vengeance that filled him. Then he changed his mind, using all his strength to change his mind. He'd never bridled his disdain until today, never quelled his indignation. But now he didn't feel strong enough to let his disdain flow freely. For the first time he felt like a different person, and he tried to behave accordingly. But inside him, the disdain was gathering and resurfacing again, the saliva gathering in his mouth, on his tongue, below his tongue, roamed around his mouth. He couldn't decide. His wound was in his hands. Until he recovered, until he could stand up, he had to stay away from this child, say nothing, not mess with him.

How to speak with this child?

How should he?

What should he say to keep him at arm's length, when he is still in need of him? Still helpless, with his hands and arms tied?

For the first time in his life, he is looking for a third way between killing and dying, a path across life.

"If you have any honor, if you have a shred of manhood, shoot me. Shoot me and free yourself! You and me, free us both."

Better to be this naked shepherd's prey than being hunted by those on his trail. If nothing else, he wouldn't become bait for those backstabbers in the mountains, a reward for the gendarmes. He'd die and vanish without a sound.

His worst fear is getting ambushed here. No one should reap anything from his death—fame, money, nothing. He doesn't want anyone to stake their legacy on his name, on his death. No outlaw in these mountains should gain honor or status by treading on his death. But, on the other hand, there is the honor of the outlaw: submitting to a nameless shepherd like this would stain his name and overshadow his glory. That is, after all, giving people reason to say, some little squirt no bigger than a hand had knocked off the great Binali.

His death has honor too.

His death has the most honor.

His own death will pave other people's destinies, he knows this. This is the reason everyone is on his trail.

Everyone knows that whoever shoots Binali will lay claim to all of Binali's fame throughout these mountains. Sometimes fame is passed from enemy to enemy like it's passed from father to son.

More than being alive, Binali wants to own his death.

He now toils to defend the honor of his death.

But he has torn through the grave cloth, he will recover somehow, get on his feet somehow, grab his rifle, his trigger, his glory. That's when, see, that's when . . .

He decides against surrendering his life over to the naked shepherd after all, decides against begging, "If you have any honor, if you have a shred of manhood . . ."

"Does it hurt here?" Temir asks.

Binali swallows the saliva pooling in his mouth.

"After shooting that gazelle, I could no longer be the old me. Because I killed death . . . that's how I came to know death."

"Are you in love?" said Temir.

"I'm not," said Binali. "Why do you ask?"

"You explained death like it was love, is all . . . I always wonder, this death they talk about, is it a male or a female?"

"It has to be male," said Binali. "Like Allah, like the devil, it too has to be male."

"Why did you tell me all this?" asked Temir.

"Earlier, when you were looking at me, you looked like that gazelle," said Binali. "I mean, you looked with that look it had right before escaping."

"So, if I had given you your rifle, would you have shot me too? Like you shot the gazelle?"

"I don't know," said Binali. "I can't know."

Binali recounted all of this on the last night.

But he didn't know himself that it was the last night.

He heard for a while the reassuring sound of the kaval, heard it fitfully. He felt the tune, its intense cry, in his wound. Once in a while he feels like he is about to fall from one of the cliff rocks, like he is going to tumble down the precipice. His balls tighten; he starts shivering in his dream, then he wakes up trembling. A sharp light briefly illuminates his consciousness, and he hears himself and the kaval. Then he rolls back into sleep, into that deep well of darkness. There he stays, in that deep well, occasionally hearing the kaval's voice calling him, until he begins thrashing about.

This time, he stays awake for a long while.

He was pretty much awake when he heard the kaval for the last time. He opened his eyes, blinked. His eyes adjusted to the darkness of the cave, he quickly moved from one darkness to the other darkness. He saw Temir at the mouth of the cave, and behind him the night, the stars and the moon veiled with clouds. Hunched over his kaval, ecstatic, he was lost in a long tune. Sounds of little bells were heard behind him; clearly there was a herd somewhere nearby. For a while he stopped and listened to the kaval, this time listening without pause or interruption. He was now convinced he had come back to himself. He had been saved. He was thankful for being saved, thankful for not getting caught. He thought about where he was, how long he'd been here, and with whom. Then:

"Water," he said. "Water!"

He didn't recognize his own voice. As if there were thornbushes caught in his throat. Steppe flowers. The steppe inside him had flowered. Thorny stem after thorny stem.

Temir leapt to his feet.

"Take it, ağam" he said, extending a bowl of water. As he tried to straighten up, his wound stung . . . It was painful. Just then, when he felt pain, he understood for the first time that he was alive . . .

4.

"So, tell me, whose mountains are these?"

"They're yours."

"In full! Else, I'd pour it out and make you lick the ground."

"It's yours, ağam."

"Ha, so it is."

"It is, ağam."

"Who is the mightiest of these mountains?"

"You, ağam."

"Who knows these mountains?"

"You, ağam."

"Who is the sovereign of these mountains?"

"You, ağam."

"Will I not kill you if I wish?"

"You will kill, ağam."

"When I kill you will I not chop up your body into morsels?"

"You will chop it up, ağam."

"When I chop it up, will I not put your carcass out for the wolves and the birds?"

"You will, ağam."

"Will I not throw your carcass to the dogs?"

"You will throw it, ağam."

"Will you not kiss my hand and my foot?"

"I will kiss, ağam."

"Will you not beg like a dog at my door?"

"I will beg, ağam."

"The bloodiest of tyrants, the peer of the poor, look at me: Who is the greatest of these mountains? Binali or Temir?"

"Temir, ağam."

"If Temir wants, will he not lay Binali's carcass on the ground?"

"He will, ağam."

"Ha, just like that, take this bowl of milk, this scrap of meat, dog!"

"I am a dog, ağam."

Binali sloshed the milk around his parched mouth; for two days nothing had passed his craw. His tongue and palate had dried, he lost strength, and this weakened his hopes of saving himself.

Temir watched Binali attacking what had been given him like a hungry wolf. Binali was beside himself. Temir watched each huge bite he swallowed as it went down his throat; his dark face darkening even more as he ate the food, looking even more like a dog as he did so, he thought.

"When I found you, your face was like the face of a baby," said Temir. "As you recover, you look more like a dog!"

Binali pauses for a moment, then resumes chewing the morsel.

"It was easy to bark orders when your stomach's full, was it not, Binali ağam? Giving orders when your stomach's rumbling is tough, isn't it?"

He was now in the boundless country of malice.

This bastard shepherd was capable of a malice as wide as his imagination. He couldn't make a sound, wouldn't be able to make a sound.

He came to understand. After all the effort and toil, he came to understand this: he was a captive. Each passing day drained him of strength. Each passing day made his defeat more complete. Temir had vanquished him, and all the weapons were on his side. There was no other hope but to shush and submit. He was hungry, wounded, and weak. He was in his hands; he'd fallen into his hands.

He kept repeating this to himself so he would believe it, so he would accept that he was in his hands.

Besides, he knows that someday he will fully recover and sneak away from this place. That he will make Temir pay fourfold for what he had done to him. He will crush him like a dog under his feet.

Quietly he gathers vengeance. In the depths of his heart's rage, the venom of vengeance thickens.

Suddenly Binali understands the silence.

The silence he hasn't been able to understand for so many years.

The power of that silence.

What accumulates in that silence.

He now understands the silence of those who hated him, those who were his enemies, he understands the difficulty he's had in understanding them. While he is helpless, while he is like them: the long and secret feeling of vengeance, of enslavement . . .

Every which thing a person who lords over others hasn't understood for years, he suddenly understands. Even the people who, unprovoked, become his enemy, everything, everybody, he understands all of it.

For the first time he sees his crushing power from the eyes of others.

He'd decided long ago: he would do everything Temir said.

Even before making this decision, he'd already started obeying his every command.

He was someone who'd never been defeated, and for the first time he tasted defeat. He didn't know where to stand. He doesn't know the limits of his honor, didn't know it even when he was the master.

Both were the same thing anyway.

The one who gives orders and the slave who obeys, they share the same dishonor. Everywhere, every time.

How many days since:

He is wallowing in sundry feelings.

His straw mattress becomes a bed of thorns against his wounded body. The nights linger treacherously, his eyes can't bear sleep. Temir grows crueler by the day. His throat dries from swallowing his own spit.

He keeps silent, he keeps silent and swallows.

Temir, for his part, has noticed that every passing day Binali withdraws, and he keeps pushing him. He wants to scale his limits. To reach them. But he doesn't know that he himself has no limits. And that Binali too dwelled in desperate limitlessness like him.

Those who learn by violence, live by violence, exist by violence have no limits. Once the battle begins, their violence exceeds the battle.

What fueled Temir's cruelty is how Binali's face has for quite a long time erased itself. Binali succeeds at hiding his thoughts, his feelings, behind his face. Captivity taught him this. His gaze has changed, concealed itself. The domineering expression early on and the one of surprise and anger later left in their wake a lifeless emptiness. This frightful vagueness, a scary vacancy, makes Temir altogether ill-tempered. For a while now he hasn't been able to decipher Binali's feelings, his thoughts, his reactions. He can't sense what he will do. Binali has retreated into the hollow of his face, hidden himself in its vacancy. He takes refuge there, protects himself.

Binali's face is a second cave inside the cave. They search for each other and hunt each other: Binali in Temir's cave, Temir in Binali's cave. A balance is attained, one that deepens the mystery of the battle.

It infuriates Temir that the mighty Binali is like a wounded animal in his hands, that he fulfills his every wish. And this time, it is Binali's weakness that threatens Temir's manhood. That greatness can be such an easy thing to bring down, that a legend can so easily crumble and spoil in the isolation of a cave offends his own manhood. He wants Binali to show his Binaliness, if just a little. Otherwise, he will come to believe that everything is empty, completely empty, like Binali's face.

This feels like the end of most everything.

As for Binali, he is in his dark corner of the cave, immersed in his thoughts, his calculations. He is thinking, dreaming, devising paths to his freedom.

He is trying to swallow his humiliation, his defeat.

And he is thinking: only two people know about what is going on between them. He and the other one know about the battle between them. Only the two of them know that Binali had to beg for hours for a bowl of sherbet, a shred of meat, a piece of bread, how he demeaned himself, destroyed his honor. Besides, the other, Temir that is, will die, will absolutely die without saying anything, without being able to say anything, to anyone, he will be dust and vanish. He must. Even if he talks, who will believe him? If he attempts to recount what happened, they will laugh at him, deride him, no one will believe a word of it. To this day, nothing like this has ever happened. They'll think he'd lost his mind. Who will believe that mighty Binali, who for years made the rocks and cliffs tremble, begged and pleaded before a wee spat shepherd no bigger than a hand? Even Binali's carcass could choke Temir's neck, take all the life out of him. It's not for nothing that he is called Binali. Certainly that's how everyone would think of it. That's how they have to think. It's as clear as day too that this secret between two people will be buried together with Temir's carcass in the dark history of these mountains. Let him do as he wishes, say what he wishes, inflict whatever torture strikes his fancy, until I recover, until I get on my feet, but once I'm free, the mountains will tremble ever more gravely before me. Until now I didn't know the wrath of an outlaw who has tasted defeat. I ought to die like a man. Like an outlaw. My death deserves honor, a legend, a great elegy. It must. I must be mourned with great ceremony. After I break the jaws of all those marauding bands, after I crunch them like bugs, after I say, "I don't die easily," only then should I be killed. Like the mountains' last outlaw. Lawlessness must end with my sultanate, if it must, if these mountains will no longer harbor the outlaw.

The last word of the outlaw ought to be my death.

I ought to die like a man. So what if I pleaded here like a bitch whore? No one knows, no one sees, not even a third person has heard one word I have said. It will all be settled when I slaughter him. This is an enclosed, dark, remote lair; so what if I begged to a half-wit? He doesn't even count as a man. He's a shepherd. Like every other kaval-playing shepherd. He thinks he's Köroğlu, thinks he's the padishah of the mountains, thinks he owns them. And soon he will croak and disappear.

"Say, let me serve you, ağam."

"Let me serve you, ağam."

"Say, let me be your dog waiting at your door, ağam."

"Let me be your dog waiting at your door, ağam."

"Say, let me be the sacrifice at your altar, ağam."

"Let me be the sacrifice at your altar, ağam."

"And then, and then, say, I am the bitch dog you feed. If you didn't care for me, I would croak and vanish."

His voice comes out affectless and monotone. No anger, no rush, no feeling in his voice. As if just carrying out his chores.

And then he sets about eating the meat roll Temir had left for him.

After the meal, Temir redressed his wounds, refreshed the ointment. The scabbing had thickened, and it itched slightly, sweetly around the wounds. Binali's face brightened; to hide the brightening of his face, Binali shielded his head from Temir.

Lying down to sleep, Temir said, "Binali."

It was the late hours of the night, the hours when the fire is going out and the rain quickens again.

"The feast of sacrifice is coming."

A shiver passed between Binali's legs.

"It's as if I'm watching over all the sacrificial lambs."

The silhouette at the mouth of the cave brought his heart to his throat. At first Binali thought it was Temir, Temir returning home earlier than usual. But Temir didn't enter this way. Whoever was coming was taking timid and ginger steps and trying to adjust his eyes to the dark. It had to be someone else. The light seeping in from the mouth of the cave marked out the silhouette but concealed the face. Binali was totally trapped and believed there was no hope remaining for him. Then others appeared at the mouth of the cave. They were armed. Clearly, they were tracking someone. Maybe they would not stay long, maybe they just wanted to stop by and have a look around. Binali shrank into the corner where he'd squeezed himself. Yes, maybe a routine duty call, they'd just have a look, peek inside and leave. In the tar-black darkness of the cave, they couldn't even see each other's eyes anyway, and the fires had died out hours ago. But the one in front seemed determined, he was walking straight ahead with decisive steps, as if he intended to reach the end of the cave. Binali suddenly thought about Temir and wanted him to be there at that moment. He remembered him with a strange sense of friendship, with longing. He didn't understand it himself. The eyes of the one who'd entered first had adjusted to the darkness, and he found Binali squeezed in his corner. For a time, he examined him, then came closer. Suddenly he recognized him and, being certain, lit a match. Yes, it was him.

"Binali," he said, "I knew it, I knew I'd find you!"

"You're a man, isn't that so, Binali? The mightiest in these mountains, isn't that so?"

He came in with a bowl of milk and bread stuffed with meat. He came and sat across from him.

"Isn't that so, Binali?"

His manners are strange.

"The bloodiest of tyrants, the peer of the poor, the greatest outlaw of these mountains, Binali, let's start from the beginning."

Binali worn out. Binali spent.

"Let's see. Whose mountains are these?"

"Yours."

"Say it in full. Or else I'll pour it on the ground and make you lick it up."

"Yours, ağam."

"Ha! Just like that."

"Who is the mightiest of these mountains?"

"You, ağam."

5.

The stream flows like a sharp ache.

The sky is inundated with stars. The mountain winds lullaby the trees to sleep. Everywhere the rustling of leaves, and when the winds cease, the absolute silence of darkness. The night frost, not yet fully condensed, works its way into the human interior.

He had left a piece of it there, where that tree was. Half of his mind is there now. Ponderous, daydreaming, holding his head between his hands, he hums to himself. As the wind dies down, he listens to the faint, languorous sound of the stream.

In his heart the reverberating forest . . .

"I must be getting old," he thinks to himself. "I'm getting old. Did I used to be like this? I used to do whatever I felt like, and afterward I didn't just sit down like a dove and ponder. Now every move I make drives me to contemplation. My own hands are always around my throat. And so I fear for my life. Thinking a lot isn't good, it makes a man listless. Nails him to his seat. It won't let him budge, it quietly hollows him out where he's stuck and eats him away. I must be getting old. All the heaviness of this heart is due to that. I'm defeated, yes, yes, I'm defeated. It's over now."

His men are scattered around, some sleeping where they'd dug in, some on lookout. He listens to the night breathing. The pulse of the forest, the mountains.

"Where else shall I climb to?" passes through his mind. "The other side of the summit is death . . ." If they left him, he'd pull back into his little corner, go plant his fields, watch his lands, live, and vanish. But now it is very late for everything. He is tired, weary.

He's come upon one of the narrow streams that descend into the rocky wells, and he listens to the sounds of the cicadas. He's given himself over to the evening, tired, worn out, twinged with pain. He's never felt this tired before, his shoulders collapsed, his knees loose, and what he's been doing hasn't calmed him, hasn't loosened the tangled yarn inside him; rather, it has caused it to tangle even worse.

He is confused, ponderous, tense.

He can't recognize himself, and this in turn drags him all the more into panic. He wants to be the Binali he's known, was used to, was familiar with. He is a stranger to himself.

He feels his heart. It hasn't grown cold. On the contrary, it has flared up all the worse, though this time his anger isn't only for Temir but also for himself, it scorches him from within.

"This baby's seen quite a few beatings. He grew up with beatings, whackings, insults. He lay down and woke in stables that belonged to strangers. He has known no loving bosom. People either pitied him or beat him. He came to know people from their slaps, their kicks, their curses. You can't defeat him that way. You can't teach him anything by beatings and cursing. Besides, he already knows everything. Nothing will work. Since you want to go find him, kill him and be off as soon as you find him. This boy's going to be trouble for those mountains. Being another dull shepherd is not for him. Wait till he grows up a bit more, ripens, and these mountains will be no match for him, he'll be a curse upon everyone, a curse; kill him now and be done with him. There is no end to testing his strength. Since he's defying you now, he'll do worse later. He has no intention of dying without becoming a legend. He'll want a name, he'll want fame. Absolutely want them. It's people like him that want fame the most. He'll want to attain something no one had given them. Since no one has given him anything, he'll be all the crueler in taking it. Claiming the world by the strength of your wrist is no easy task, you know that. If I were you, Binali, I would skin his corpse on the ground where I found him, you'd save yourself and everyone else. This child is going to take a lot out of the world, a lot."

The evening frost hardens.

He thinks about the wind under that tree.

The night becomes a poison for him to drink. In his mouth, a noxious tobacco taste.

He spits on the ground.

And then he spits again.

Back in the forest, he said, "My battle is actually beginning just now." He was standing up on his feet, all of his wounds healed. His rage and greed for vengeance had healed him fast. He stood facing the mountain now, like an oath. This was his life's greatest hunt.

When he found Temir, his heart was beating madly. To this day, no hunt had excited him as much. He had spent the past few days living together with his phantasm. He recalled over and over what he'd gone through (what Temir had made him go through) and kept his rage blazing in him, kept his hatred and hunger for vengeance alive. He'd freed himself from his cruelty, but not from him and the phantasm of him.

They had accounts yet to settle between them.

Accounts yet to settle.

And as long as he didn't find Temir, didn't find him and take his vengeance, they would remain unsettled.

"I cannot live with this defeat! This secret shame! I'd be gnawing at myself, and in the end they'd find my dried-up corpse by a tree. Temir must meet his punishment, experience his punishment. There's no other way, none. These mountains, this forest would be haram to me, they'd be my dungeon."

The tracks covered up by decayed leaves make the trackers' job all the harder. Each new leaf that falls from its limb covers a footprint. In the last moments of the season, tree limbs, leaves gently fall onto the ground.

All of Binali's men assembled, they had been looking up and down for Temir.

"Hey, Köroğlu of the mountains! Look here!"

Turning around slowly, Temir's face was white as chalk. He was standing on a slope where the forest thinned and opened onto a clearing. (Death does give humans wings.) He knows that he is caught. That is certain. That pounding of the heart is now over. (He wants to spread his wings and fly, without anyone touching him, without coming face-to-face with anyone.)

Now they were face-to-face.

Binali and Temir.

Face-to-face for Binali's battle.

Before his eyes are the wings of that hawk, circling. The world is turning. Temir wants to be a tree, a bird, earth, nothing.

He shakes with joy like a tree caught in the wind, shivering where he stands. His own joy frightens him, he feels how this joy exceeds him. He cannot keep up with the beating of his heart. Whereas Temir's face is a fistful of ash . . . as if a mountain wind had erased everything from his face. This lime-white face adds to Binali's joy; he is all the more pleased that his prey has fallen into his trap. He slowly raises his rifle and begins shooting bullets in the direction of Temir. Bullets fall around Temir from all sides. Bullets pelt the ground at his feet. Temir keeps skipping. Bullets ricochet to the left and right (death has come right up to his face) breaking off branches, tree bark, rocks. A thick smell of gunpowder mixes in with the smells of the trees, flowers, wet herbs, and dried leaves.

Binali is grinning with satisfaction at the grand beginning of his battle, and a wet, sticky smile settles ear to ear on his face. Seized with the lust of the torture about the start, his eyes are blind to everything else. As if a long-held dream of his is coming true. His prey already writhing in his claws, he is drunk with his own power.

Killing Temir slowly is his life's only meaning now. His nostrils flare and contract incessantly, his breath isn't enough to catch his racing heart . . . His body keeps twitching.

"Alright, let's get this going, Temir ağam," he says. "Right from the beginning. I'm going to do to you exactly what you did to me. You'll learn what payback means. Where shall we begin, would you say? At which part? Shall I first wound you and then save you from death? Or do you want to start begging already?"

A few more bullets zip past his feet, and Temir hops around again.

"Where shall I wound you? Where would you like your wound? We'll still heal your wound gently afterward, we'll wrap it up nicely. Where shall I stick the bullet? Come on, you choose the spot, you choose where you'll receive the wound. I can do you this much favor. After all, we have our shared past, you and I."

He shoots another bullet into the air.

"Now my battle begins in earnest, Temir. Watch and see how to make a man beg, how to take vengeance. Watch and see . . . I'll do a thousand times to you what you've done to me . . . You won't die with a single bullet, no way, but like the dogs, dragging your carcass. I'll kill you bit by bit. So, let's have you start begging, let's hear how you beg . . ."

Holding his head up, he looked right into Binali's eyes

"I'll never beg for my life. Shoot and be done with it," said Temir.

Binali was taken aback. This was something he'd never expected, never thought of, never crossed his mind, something he'd never reckoned with. Drunk with his rage, he had thought everything was going to be how he'd dreamed it. Binali was one of those who thought that life consisted entirely of his dreams.

"What do you mean you won't beg, man? You will beg! You will beg like a dog, and how you will beg!"

"I won't beg," said Temir. "It's just one life. You can take it . . . That's all."

Binali doesn't move.

All of his thoughts about humans and valor, everything he knew, he thinks them over.

He shoots another bullet.

All people, no matter who they are, beg, plead, go low when they fall into a hopeless situation, don't they? Humans are like that. They ought to be. But this child, this hand-sized child, why is he so stubborn? Why is he resisting? What is he so confident about?

He shoots another bullet while he's thinking all this.

"Beg, man! Plead! Cry! Do something!"

The bullet skips right between his two feet, and as he bounces back, he falls on the ground.

So why did I beg? Why did I plead so much? Why didn't I say, kill me and spare me the trouble? Why couldn't I say that? I who am Binali?

Another bullet just as he tries to get up.

Maybe because he trusts nothing, never could trust anything. I who am Binali . . . Still, he has a life. Life is sacred, it's easy to give it away. Maybe it's valor, true valor.

Another bullet. Because this thought is driving Binali mad.

This time he manages to get to his feet. His face is still pale white but not from fear this time; before the whiteness of his face was from fear, but this time he has clearly gone beyond fear. It's willingness to die, the whiteness of his face is preparation for the journey. The last and long journey.

With every bullet, Binali begins thinking more.

With every bullet, the coiled spring of his consciousness loosens a bit more.

If he doesn't beg, if he can't make this bastard beg, he'll be devastated, he won't be able to quell his rage, take his revenge. He knows that killing won't be enough. Killing will not save Binali's honor; rather, it will diminish it. If he loses to his rage and kills him, this bastard and his corpse will take away from Binali something more; he will take it and carry it away, together with his corpse. Never to return it.

Suddenly the answer to that question . . . Now Binali can give the answer. Now he's able to find the answer.

"No," he says inwardly. "No, I wouldn't have been able to shoot him. Back there, when I said, 'I don't know,' I really did not know. But now I know. Turns out, I wouldn't have been able to shoot. Even if he'd put my weapon into my hand, I wouldn't. A person cannot kill death twice."

Binali looks into Temir's eyes.

Temir does not look as if he wants to escape.

Temir needs to beg, plead, whine, grovel. If he doesn't, Temir will be the winner of this battle. Even if he dies, the battle will extend into the other side of death.

"Ah! I understand," said Binali. "You don't believe it, do you? That I'm going to chop you up in pieces. You don't believe I'll feed your carcass to the dogs. That's why your head is so high, your brow so tough."

If Temir begs and grovels, he will be justified in his own eyes, in his own eyes he will come out clean. He will be less ashamed of himself. He will be at peace, believing that this is just the way of being human.

But Temir just stands there. A vacancy on his face. A great vacancy.

As if, in a moment, he will spread his wings and fly.

Like he's ready to die.

"You wait," said Binali. "You wait, this is nothing; I haven't even hurt you yet; all this is to put fear in your eyes. Your blood hasn't spilled yet, your flesh hasn't been minced. Watch how you will beg like a dog, how you'll grovel. Watch and see."

He walks up to Temir.

Temir stands before him like a mountain, unyielding.

Binali's first punch comes down on his face.

Blood comes gushing.

The wind ceases, the sound of the stream grows in his ears. The night grows. Silence. Cold. The steppe inside him. Everything grows. Ever since he was rescued from that cave, he's spent every night thinking of Temir. He's stayed awake with the dream of the moment he would find him. How many nights his eyes would bear no sleep. He's lived with the spellbinding violence of it. Now, that is, the first night he found him, he is still thinking of him. He couldn't free himself from him. Under a tree, a bit ahead. In the first clearing, beyond that elevation there.

Binali's insistence is something Temir cannot understand . . . Temir cannot understand the thing he wants to bend and twist in him by making him beg, by making him plead, by humiliating him. He thinks Binali's doing all this out of an ordinary vengeance. Just to cool his heart, to take away the injustice. But Binali is intent on redeeming himself, his powerlessness. What he wants to snatch away from Temir is something different; something that entirely belongs to him.

Temir of course cannot understand this.

He is self-possessed, resilient, defiant.

In this battle, too, they misunderstand each other. Whatever it is that motivates each continues to elude the other. Two people who have been this close, when the punches and kicks of one have mangled and bloodied the other's face and body, they still cannot explain what it is that they want from each other. Enmity alone resolves nothing. They each lay the wrong kind of claim on the other, each carrying out the wrong kind of attack. Neither side knows how to explain himself to the other. In no way do they know, nor can they explain.

He keeps longing for that pair of wings. To go where the hawk and the others fly off to.

When Temir couldn't find him in his spot, it was like he understood everything. Somehow, he felt his absence with longing. A wistfulness, a loneliness overcame him. "Why didn't I kill him?" he said. "Why didn't I kill him? But if I killed him, I would have missed him even more. Now he won't let me live." His days were spent oscillating between escaping (to where? how?) and staying.

When Binali found him, he was on the run.

He'd made his decision.

"Wait, this is nothing, Temir ağam. We're going to have a lot more fun together. Don't start moaning like that with the first punch. The first punch is nothing, its pain short-lived . . ."

Binali seized Temir on the ground. The second punch descended on his flank. While Temir was bent double, writhing in twice as much pain, Binali undid his belt with a sudden movement and began lashing him. The belt kept cracking down on his back like lightning, over and over. With each lash, Temir writhed all the more. The punches and the kicks followed one after the other.

"So you're not going to beg, huh, dog?"

Temir raises his head. His eyes aflame with hatred . . . As though the beating he'd taken had no effect on him, isn't having any. With a voice drowning in saliva, he says, "I'm not like you, Binali. I won't beg for any life, never mind a wretched life. I'll beg to no one. Men don't beg, only dogs beg."

Binali is livid.

He can feel his powerlessness from head to toe. He can sense that there is no settling accounts with this child, no possibility of it.

He's alone, utterly alone.

He cannot bring himself to believe what has happened.

This means that not everyone caught in this situation behaves the same. Despair doesn't explain everything. This means Binali is alone, utterly alone, on his own. Or that Binali is not the one who's alone, but rather Temir. He is the one who is truly alone. Binali acted like everyone else, like all the other people. Temir is the one who does not resemble the others. This is not something that beatings, curses, torture, or death can overcome.

Maybe his strength is in his solitude.

The thought that Temir's strength is of a kind that Binali cannot overcome, can never overcome, drives him mad. It's as if he's not warring with a dull, scrawny shepherd but with an invisible giant.

He cuts into the shirt and pants, and with the tip of his knife, swiftly pulls them off, discarding them. A thin streak of blood is running over Temir's body.

"Come on, beg, dog! Come on, say, spare me, let me supplicate at your feet, beg for peace, grovel, repent. Who do you think you are, man? Did you think everything you did would go unpunished?"

The evening nears.

(Days have evenings.)

The tired sun prepares to retreat behind the mountains. The leaves and limbs are not as sheltering as before. The season is passing. Time passing. Now it is the ghazal season. The rains lean hard on the clouds. Now it is the rainy season.

Temir raises his head from where he was crouched.

One knife strike takes his underclothes from his legs. A lean streak of light almost catches his face, the emptiness in it. Then it withdraws.

He is now the blind man caught by the sun.

He doesn't see, he doesn't look.

He remembers his game, his game with the sun from far off, as if a childhood memory.

Binali undoes his pants, pulls out his reed. Walking toward Temir crouched on the ground, he begins to piss on him. Piss oozes down from the back of his neck, from his strands of hair to his shoulders, his back. Temir thrashes about with his hands, tries to escape, only to be kicked again and again. The sun lights up Binali's urine with a yellow-gold spray of light . . . After the last few drops drip down, he ties up his pants again.

Then, grabbing Temir by the hair, he throws him to the ground.

Temir thrashes about, fighting the dried branches, herbs, and thorns sticking to his body, tearing his skin, piercing into his wounds.

He carries him to the base of a giant tree. In the middle of a clearing. He lifts Temir to his feet. He presses his face against the tree, and with a thick cord from around his waist, he ties him tightly to the tree. Holding his arms up above his head, he presses his whole body to the tree. Then he wraps the cord round and round. He finishes with a heavy knot.

Temir shivers, not just from the evening winds that start blowing. Temir wants to cry, shaking uncontrollably.

He recalls his childhood.

All of his childhood.

His loneliness has never caused him this much pain. And just when he feels like an adult. The moment when he realizes how much of an adult he has become.

When he is tied naked to a tree, covered in blood, piss, wounds, and bruises.

Binali pours a bowl of milk, a bowl of sherbet, over him.

"All the ants, the bees, the insects are going to crawl all over you. Here, till morning, in the forest frost, at the base of this tree. The winds' teeth will bite your flesh, and inch by inch, you will become fodder for the insects. Go ahead and don't beg, go ahead and resist, defend your valor, claim your manhood as much as you can. However much you resist, what will your strength get you? You're in my hands, until the end, in my hands.

"The entire night is yours, Temir. The insects of the dark are yours. And before we forget, let's fashion you a wound. So that blood oozes from some part of you until morning."

He presses the sharp point of the knife against his back. Temir's back shudders. The knife wanders around on his back. Then it moves down-ward, first looking for a spot around his waist, then deciding on the round of his buttocks; there is a large, black birthmark on his right but-tock, and the knife tip thrusts a few centimeters into it. Binali wriggles the knife inside. The tree shakes from Temir's scream.

"We'll see each other tomorrow, Temir," he says. "If you survive till morning, we'll see each other."

Temir turns his head to the other side, facing right. (He can only move his head.) The sun, the last sun . . . suddenly catches Temir in the eyes. And that is when he starts crying, shaking uncontrollably . . .

When the sun too catches him.

In the distance, birds he doesn't know . . . Cicadas . . . It occurs to him that he could never learn the names of flowers and birds. The night songs of the forest, one ends, the other begins. The dark, its abundance. Binali keeps feeling out his heart. He finds no peace in it.

"I'm defeated," he said. "This battle has ended. He won. He's got valor, valor to the bone. Goes to show that some people can withstand every kind of cruelty. And why did I lose? Why did I beg and plead? Why did I sink down? But you wait, this is just his first day; by the third day his neck will bend too . . . No, no, it won't. There is fire blazing in this bastard's eyes. He's got more valor than us, is what it means, it means he's got more heart. He won't beg, that kid, he won't beg even if he's dying. How much longer can this last anyway? How much longer can I endure this torture I'm inflicting? How much can he endure? Instead of enjoying the sleep of Binali who inflicted on him all that torture back there, does it make any sense that he is sitting here and thinking long and hard like this? Am I the same man I was during the day? (Days have evenings.) Why did I do all of this? (Such emptiness in his face . . . he'd die before he begged.) And my heart is still ill at ease! That silence, that emptiness, is always in me, like it will echo if I shout. My heart is no heart but a carbuncle. It pains me. So why did he think I deserved such torment, such humiliation, such torture? When he was by himself, did he also think about all he'd done? (I can't know, I can't know at all. Nor can he. No one can know anyone when they are alone.) Did he fight with himself? We never talked about it, never talked . . . What was between us that robbed us of humanity? Since I opened my eyes to the world again, we always wrestled, tested each other. But I don't know him, and he doesn't know me."

Binali aches inside. The frost grows dense, expands through the forests, blankets the whole mountain. The rustling of the leaves intensifies; the sound of the stream turns indistinct. Binali dwells inside a desolate sorrow.

He feels as though his men are now far away from him, far away.

"It turns out I wasn't brave. Not as brave as I thought. I made two kinds of mistakes. I was wrong then just as now. Mine is not a tested valor, not a tried-and-true valor. That hand-size kid, that half-wit of a peasant, does he deserve such torture? Now I understand—that child was playing with me, plain and simple . . . And what did I do? I saw fit to inflict on him unspeakable torment, as if I'd captured a fierce enemy. I must have lost my men's respect, certainly. They must not have been able to fathom why I had chased this child for so long, tied him to a tree and abandoned him to the night's frost. They couldn't make sense of my enmity. How was he my match? They know it well. Enmity too has its own value. You don't feel it for nothing. You shouldn't. My chasing down this nameless shepherd, my hating him this much—that they would not understand, of course. They must have seen that it was beneath me. I'm sure they must have even started to think that there is some other business underneath this business.

"But how could it have been otherwise? How else would I have made him pay for all he did to me? How could I have left him unpunished? If I had begged and pleaded, there must have been something I cherished, something I was hiding, protecting. I put my name, my honor, my manhood out there. Just to live a little longer, I gave them up in the darkness of that cave. As for him, he has nothing. Nothing. Or maybe he does have something. More than any of us. And that's why he can defy death so much. Why he can cross over to the other side, go beyond death.

"I can no longer catch up to him. We're not even on the same road."

Binali wrestled with conflicted feelings all night long. Torn in two, he tried to mend his self.

"The second desert," he said. "This is the second desert in me . . . My strength, my power now only brings me loneliness. I'm sensing something like regret. For everything. For everyone. These must have been all that I wanted to possess, all that I fought for. Turns out a single bullet, a single night can change a human life this much."

Now he is ashamed of himself even more, much more than before.

"If only he had begged once! If he had said, 'Don't hit! Don't kick! Don't!' he wouldn't have left me this lonely. Nothing would have bothered me as much. Look at me, as if I am about to go beg him, beg him to beg to me. I'm going to beg again."

Daybreak. Binali hasn't slept. The gleam of dawn.

Binali gets to his feet, feeling the morning frost in his bones. He thinks he is even late in getting up. The night hasn't helped resolve anything, everything remains the same. He can't stomach anything that has happened.

"It's now that I've truly lost the Binali I used to be," he said. "Not when I was weak, but when I was powerful." This is what the night has taught him.

"While I was weak, it wasn't in my hands to protect him (not as much as I thought), but when I was powerful it was in my hands, it was, until the very end. But the powerful errs the most. I was drunk with power, and that drunkenness made me forget everything. There's less of me now. The battle is over. I was beaten. That's all."

He walked away from the place he'd been sitting all night, toward the elevation, and when he climbed up, a bit farther ahead in the middle of a clearing, he saw the giant tree, and Temir's naked body strapped to the tree.

Slowly he climbed down.

Heavily, he started to approach Temir.

Temir's body lay lifeless.

"He's dead," he said. He didn't recognize his own voice. As if there were nettles stuck in his throat. Steppe flowers. . . . His throat was torn. His voice was bleeding.

"He's dead," he said.

His head hangs to one side. As if he is now part of the tree. Part of the tree, of the earth, the forest. Of absence.

Inside Binali a desert, sharp as a whistle.

He approaches Temir.

All of his body is covered with insects, bugs; swollen, it looks like a drowned corpse. The blood seeping from his hips had dried on his legs. Insects whose names he didn't know—like birds, like flowers—wandered around on the dried blood.

A faint twitching in Temir's body, he is breathing slowly, very slowly, fitfully.

A mad joy overtakes him.

As if a flood inundates the forest.

Rain from the mountains.

Washing his being.

For the first time, Binali does not feel like a murderer.

Day is breaking.

"I will never badger you again, I will not torment you."

One by one he undoes the ropes tying Temir to the tree.

"I know I made a mistake, I made an error. I let you get inside my head, I listened to the devil, I was childish, it didn't become me, I know it."

Temir collapsed at the base of the tree.

He lay unconscious.

"Temir!," he says, "my Temir! My brave one, open your eyes, my babe, my wounded gazelle, open your eyes! If you don't open them, I will die too! Open your eyes, you! Open them! Do you want me to die of sorrow? Open them, you bitch's spawn!"

Temir does not open his eyes. He buries his black-coal hair clumped with blood under his arm, and in the hot and tender nest under his arm, he is this happy for the first time, for the first time he listens to him with a heart swollen with joy. He listens as if unconscious, as if he'd never open his eyes again, never again. He feels the pain in his wounds with pleasure. They give him no trouble.

Binali kisses his hair.

He smells his own piss on Temir's hair. He is ashamed, he wants to forget what happened.

And then he bends down and lifts him off the ground.

In his arms, he carried him back to his cave.

"The battle is over," he said.

6.

This is the afterward.

The afterward as described in the language of lore:

For days, he cared for Temir. Washed his body, rubbed it, anointed it, healed its wounds. Like a father would. Now they were two people.

Temir knew love for the first time.

For the first time he knew compassion.

Though he didn't know it himself, his eyes started to look pleadingly at Binali. When asking for something, when asking a question, when seeking his advice, for the first time. He was reliving his belated childhood without knowing it. The steel in his eyes softened. He no longer looked at the world with hate.

Long afterward, one day, the devil of manhood that never sleeps gave Binali a nudge.

Temir's submissive innocence nudged him.

Nursing his grudge, he said inwardly: "The battle begins again, Temir," he said. "We waged war on one another with a weapon you know well, very well; you beat me. Your hatred was charged. No hatred, no resolve could match yours. You were the mountain. But no matter how tall, a mountain always grants passage. And I found the passage just now. I found how you will be defeated. This is a weapon you have never known. You don't even know it's a weapon. I didn't even know it until the moment I realized I would beat you with it. You see? I am in your debt even for having learned this. You see how much we owe each other, and people who are in each other's debt other cannot be friends, Temir.

"Love is this weapon. You never knew love. This is why the battle begins again.

"You will die little by little, without even knowing it. Every day a little more."

For a while Temir didn't even think this was a battle. He saw he was dying slowly. Slowly being killed. He saw Binali changing from day to day, coming to resemble a crafty fox with his looks, his smiles, his friendship. He saw that Binali was not the Binali he used to be. But just as before, his name overshadowed everyone. The name Binali was like a seal stamped on everyone's manhood.

Later he understood that, unbeknownst to him, Binali had resumed their battle. And he also understood that the thing called love that he was being taught was no different from the thing he knew all along: violence. Experienced in the same way. That's why, when Binali caught him alone in the quiet of the forest and went for his rifle, he did not hesitate to pull the trigger.

This was something he'd always believed in.

He'd returned to the thing he'd always believed in.

That's why he didn't hesitate.

Yet Binali did.

When Temir yelled, "Hey look here, Binali ağam," and he turned around and saw the emptiness in Temir's face, he understood everything.

His face was blank, just as it had been on that other day; an emptiness white as death had come and settled on his face.

For a moment, Binali thought for less than a moment. Just a blink of an eye . . . His trigger finger frozen.

"Now we are two people no longer," said Temir. "I am one." And he pulled the trigger, saying nothing else.

Inside him, the long, old desert, sharp as a whistle, came to an end.

He was entirely empty inside. Binali's face was entirely empty.

Lifting his head, he looked at the branches, the naked branches, the trees.

There was no sun, no hide-and-seek now. The blind sky was emptier than empty. Or it was covered with masses of balled-up clouds, which means the same. The season had come to an end.

When Avar found him, he was dead.

He was lying in a corner of the forest (toppled, outstretched).

"I've told this story a lot," he said. "So many times, without tiring, without growing weary. Don't go, I said. I did not get him to listen. Kill him, I said. I did not get him to listen. Since the day I found him in that cave and helped him escape, we always talked about that boy. Binali was sonless, Temir was fatherless. They hungered for each other's death."

Avar came and stood at the head of the dead man.

"I said so," he said. "I said so. But what good did it do? This too must be one of the lessons learned at the price of death."

March 12–June 12, 1983, Ankara

Ensar and Jivan

At that noon hour, when they stood on opposing sides of the river and kept playing, they didn't know each other yet.

The angry sun in a cloudless sky erases all shadows, making everything turn to tiny specks of dust and a honey-colored desolation. It blankets every hot surface, hides it, buries it; nothing else but the sun itself is tangible. Time yields to the lassitude of summer. Everything is suspended in air; everything conjures the solitude of hell . . . dead hours. Not a peep in the village. (Not a peep in the villages.) Everywhere seems deserted, as if buried. Like old ruins, half buried in the ground—without memory, color, smell, or movement. Tired dogs, their tongues halfway out and laboring to breathe, have scrambled for shade under the few trees they could find, or in the hand's-width refuge by the walls under the eaves. Small children, oblivious of the saliva drooling from their half-open mouths or the flies landing on their faces, lie on straw mats or low sofas, sleeping a sleep akin to coma.

The overheated ground smolders.

He can see this from the spot where he is crouched, gazing at the opposite bank . . . He sees the ground smoldering and sundry images of a scorched summer; he sees dreams bewildered by the heat.

These were the days when the riverbed nearly dried up, when the river barely flowed.

Was this the same river that, at the end of the summer, swelled and overflowed with the arrival of the rains? This same river that, in the winter, brimmed over, seethed, raged, then froze into ice—the river that hereafter would always remind him of Jivan—and allowed neither rafts nor bridges across its rushes. So many times it had claimed so many lives. So many songs, so many elegies given over to its killing power, its rage, its wrath.

Along the villages,

and the mothers who gave their sons to this river
it kept flowing like a silent snake

165

and flows still.
It allows no one to forget their pain
Because it is always here, by everyone's side . . .
The same river?

The sun falling on the river ripples in swirls and crumbles, it shimmers and shifts places . . . The water in the eddies grows docile; it flows and flows. It gives people confidence, as if nothing would happen, nothing could happen. But it carries a deep ache in its heart.

All the foul currents of his heart wash his face.

Wasn't he supposed to never return? He had promised to never return.

He had missed the river.

Truly missed it.

His was a colicky, sick, aching longing, but it was longing.

Blood lures, the killer returns to the scene of the crime, or one does not enter the same river twice.

One and the same, one and the same, now everything is one and the same.

He wants the waters to part and take him, to sing him lullabies till eternity. Guilt ties us to the past. If only people could be rid of memories.

From where he is sitting crouched, he can see the earth smoldering from the heat and everything else, just as he did on that other day. Again, he sees the child on the other side of the river.

The water, the sun, the child, and a mischievous little puppy.

On a day when the lashing tongue of the sands keeps everyone indoors, what business do these two children have on the two shores of the river, crouching in the water up to their ankles, at this mad noon hour?

On the two shores of one destiny.

Holding the river by its two edges, they are waiting. For their destiny, or for other things. Waiting for everything that hasn't happened (everything that would disturb this eternal calm), waiting without knowing, without understanding. Everything that the oppressive heat, the suffocating boredom at those changeless, blistering noon hours makes you think or doesn't let you think, everything . . .

Holding the river by its two edges, they are gazing at each other. (They had caught each other's gaze when they lifted their heads up from the water they had been stirring with excited hands. They were startled by each other's presence, and happy.)

The one across waves his hand, calls the other to his side. After all, they are two of them: he and his dog.

That's how they first met.

Sunbeams break and scatter, the water's surface fills with shards and splinters of light. They pierce into his heart; he winces. Thousands of splinters reflected in the ripples scatter and break in the prism of the years past that visit him again, gradually dissolving. Now he sees nothing but water, just water . . .

Ensar crouches back down in his spot, just like back then. He wants for nothing to have changed in the years since. Didn't he return here to say, "Just like back then"?

A silhouette suddenly appears on the other shore.

A gleaming white silhouette, or a silhouette in white. A man. A young man. A thirty-year-old dead man. He almost recognizes him, straining his memory. Parting the images flitting before his eyes, he opens the path to the past. He looks, squinting, shielding his eyes from the sun with his hand. It's an angel of death. If it isn't a game the sun plays often around here, or a heat-induced illusion, although in the distance there is a bridge that disrupts all illusions, that no longer allows any—it wasn't there back then—or if it isn't a new trick of the dreams that try his memory, that strain his eyes; or maybe the jinn, that is, if all the jinn of Mesopotamia haven't overtaken the place, then it is Jivan he is seeing here. Waiting for me on the opposite shore after so many years, had he been alive . . .

This is the lot of humans. As at Elsinore Castle, after midnight, appearing when the moon hides behind a cloud—only a prolonged nightmare is left to me, from all I've read—here, in the raging heat, at noon, when the torrid sunlight erases all the shadows, he emerges.

In the climate of our souls, the only thing that changes is the dial on our watches.

And yet around here they still use the hourglass,
   its face the length of a spear,
     and the shadow of the spear
       wound unto death . . .

I am a physician now, a healer. Yet it does me no good. I thought that it would bring me peace. I want to get to the other side of the river.

How many days, how many noon hours they had shared the river's two banks, made a friendship from afar. In the evenings, they'd return to their homes, their voices cracking, worn out from calling out to one another . . .

In a few days, the river would dry up, the waters would recede—maybe waist-high or knee-high. Then they would be able to get across, to touch each other, to play together.

Their friends in their own villages weren't enough for either of them.

That summer the river didn't run low.

Ensar was fourteen, Jivan was fifteen years old.

Grownup kids now.

Winter's darkness had separated them. Two solitudes on the two banks of the river.

"Till spring then," Jivan had said.

"Till spring then," Ensar had said.

They spent the whole winter separately, stayed in their own villages, with their own friends, playing their own games. Some nights they looked over at the village across the river, the lights of the village, trying to find each other's light, each other's window. Those were starless nights.

How many times the river overflowed during those winters, shackling both sides with ice, freezing it solid in places. Masses of ice floated on the water. If only the river would freeze completely. At least it would grant passage then, and one could walk across to the other side. This was the hope, but now . . .

Some days, Ensar went down to the edge of the river with the hope of finding Jivan on the other side.

Jivan wasn't there.

Calling out was for naught, no one would hear . . .

In that sharp cold, that parching frost, on the edge of raging, head-high waves, he paced around for hours, and then turned back to his house, his hearth.

On nights like this, bad things came to Ensar's mind, like death or separation.

They listened in their beds to the sound of the wind in the village night's solitude, each sharing his solitude with the other's solitude.

The next day, this time, Jivan would go down to the water's edge, and this time Jivan's eyes looked for Ensar on the other bank. He, too, went up and down the length of the river, calling out, shouting, shivering.

But all winter long the river and the wind ground down their voices.

All winter, they were able to meet only once.

On the same day,

at the same hour, they both had come down

In both their hearts a crazy gladness, a jittery pledge, the overexcitement of their adolescence . . . All the winter stories they listened to as they sat by their hearths . . . They shouted out to one another until it became a cry, but the boorish voice of the river pressed their two voices down, smothered them. They drew circles in the air with their hands and arms, but they couldn't understand what the other wanted to say. Still, ever so happy, they bounced around all day long without reaching each other.

Like the heroes of old legends retold each spring, they postponed their meeting till spring.

But on that winter day, with that sharp frost and the knife blade of the frozen river standing between them, they understood that they were buddies, friends, brothers, and that winter would not make them forget each other. Their hearts had not been buried under the snow. Whether they go away to a foreign land or to the military, they would not forget each other. The fire of their friendship ignited their young hearts, their pale faces. Neither the river nor the cold would extinguish their resolve.

But on the first day of spring, they stood as enemies on the open plain.

As the last pathfinders of a tradition in decline, whose majesty had been lost, fallen into disrepair, they stood straight up on the back of two unsaddled horses, two rivals holding jereeds in the name of their villages.

Sounds of drums and tambourines coming from faraway villages— faraway pageants, faraway tidings. Some nights, just the sound of the kaval along the river sufficed to get people's blood simmering.

Spring had arrived.

Nature reviving itself, stretching gently, turning its soft, brown, warm belly toward the sun, toward abundance.

All the folks from neighboring villages had swarmed the plain. Entire villages had set out on the road that day, reaching the upper flanks of the river, then, from there, crossing to the other side on rafts. With the spring ice melting and the arrival of rains, the river had swelled and, though docile along the upper banks, created turbulent waves, threatening the rafts and the log bridges spanning the currents. So many beasts of burden made their way across, with their colorful trimmings, saddlecloths, and pots and pans on their backs. The journey turned into a play, a ceremony, a jubilee. Villages that had been buried in the snows of a long winter, people buried in their houses, shook off the winter sleep with the arrival of warm weather, and descended on that endless plain that stretched to the right of the river. Gleaming white tents were set up everywhere, colorful rugs spread out on the ground, kilims unrolled, bonfires lit, cauldrons set asimmer. For days, the river carried men on its back. With the arrival of the crowds, the plain seemed smaller. Children, newly of age, showed up, trained for the jereed. Those already skilled at riding and the jereed paced around bareback, while for those who were green, younger, newer, the horses were donned with saddlecloths.

The crowd, a sea of bodies, finally settled down. The flat plain was parceled, foursquare. The crowds of spectators arranged themselves along the two sides of the plain, leaving a large, very large empty field in the middle, with rows and rows of warriors on horseback lining the other two sides, waiting.

Silence, wide and seamless, descended upon the plain. Were it not for the occasional rustling of a tent flap in the gentle wind, nothing moved. Silence was something tangible now. One could hear the pulse of spring rising from the depths of the earth.

Horses are lined up next to each other, heroes lined up next to each other, their ears pricked. Something in this silence cleanses a man, purifies him, gives him strength. The two sides are like two enemy armies facing each other, silent, dark, inscrutable, motionless.

This was my first jereed meet. My first at a festival like this. For a long time I had been trained by skillful hands, and now I was waiting excitedly for my turn. Each rider, in his turn, would charge forth into the arena, pushing his horse to run, hurling his jereed at his opponent, giving it all his effort to topple him off his horse. If a contender got into serious trouble but managed to escape his opponent, he would retreat into the safe zone reserved for him. This was an out-of-bounds space for exhausted riders to rest, regather their strength, and avoid danger. The rider, raring to thrust his jereed, lifted his butt off the saddle, which required that he squeeze the horse's rump tightly with his legs to keep his body straight and carry his whole weight. Our opponents were from the village across the river. As the games got under way, the crowd, heretofore silent, came alive, burgeoned. Wave after wave, voices reverberated across the plain. While the contestants were caught up in the tension of the game, the spectators still experienced it as a festivity . . . With each signal, two horsemen from the opposing sides charged the middle. When it was my turn, I also charged like the others, thinking about nothing else but winning. Back at that age, winning is more important than anything. Everything looks to a teenager's eye like a race . . . My rival was coming straight at me on the back of a chestnut horse. I tried to make out his face, his body, from a distance. I wanted to observe him, see his face, understand his inward self. That was necessary for me to predict how he might play the match. I couldn't be an enemy to a person whose face I hadn't seen, whose gaze I didn't know, whose inward self I didn't understand. I couldn't defend myself from him or strike at the right time. After all, every race was a game of enmity. He ran with such speed right toward me, and as I looked carefully through my squinting eyes, I grasped that it was Jivan approaching. He saw me too, recognized me. We both approached the skirmish line drawn out at the center, where, as rivals, we would meet for the first time.

In this sense, our first jereed match was a defeat for both of us.

Our faces glowed when we saw each other.

But we were in the middle of a match and could not behave differently.

We didn't know what to do and, surprised, started circling around each other. The spectators had little difficulty understanding that our moves were not those of hunters circling around their prey, and they must have chalked up our confusion to inexperience. Yet we were trying to look at each other, size each other up, grasp each other's intentions. We had never been this close to each other before. As if I could hear the sound of the river flowing between us.

Impatient voices forced us to make a move.

I delivered the first hit.

(Before we had even touched one another, we got to taste each other's fury.) Jivan staggered. He stared at me as if betrayed, as if hurt.

"This is a match," I whispered to him. "What can we do, meeting like this in the middle of a match?" The second hit came from him. The feud was on. We were both inexperienced and also excited. Several emotions spurred us on at once. What surpassed all the others was doubtlessly the excitement of meeting each other. We both played an awkward, clumsy match, full of errors. The spectators gave up hope for us. I couldn't savor my first jereed, I'd dreamed of an eye-for-an-eye, tooth-for-a-tooth match, but here we stood, floundering on bareback horses with rough saddlecloth. And yet, that safety zone where contenders could take refuge when they got into trouble, we didn't use it even once.

In the end, I toppled Jivan. I had won.

We spent that summer together.

When the river ran low, we swam together, went hunting, chopped wood. We visited shrines, made oaths, wished wishes, became blood brothers, played *lorke*, wrote odes to girls, gave each other colorful *puşi*s and *agal*s, smoked cigarettes in the shade. I brought him a silver tobacco box, and he brought me amber prayer beads with a silver tassel. He brought me a cigarette holder, I brought him a lighter, we carved our names on our rifle stocks. We helped each other refresh the kohl lines on our eyes painted with a quill from a bird of prey, to look bold and daring. Jivan's mischievous dog had grown and kept us company. Days came and went, crops began to turn yellow and the sky began to fill with patches of clouds. That great summer was a happy game. It was ending. We also played at jereed. To learn and teach the intricacies of a game takes a lot of time; besides, Jivan wasn't as serious about jereed as I was, or let's say he didn't particularly care for the rivalry of it. It was only a game to him. Back then, I'd assumed he thought that way because he wasn't bold enough, but much later I realized that it was because he understood life better.

Toward the end of summer Jivan started showing up less often. His dog had disappeared. He went looking for him for days. He was sad. Preparations for the winter now kept us apart, and we started to meet only on rare occasions. The swelling river had again swept the bridge away, and for a while I couldn't cross over to the other side. He didn't cross over to this side either. As my chores multiplied, I thought that he couldn't take himself away from work either. The field, the soil, the tasks at home, there was so much to do anyway, and you never knew when the winter, the frost, would come. Still, I felt a wide and deep disquiet that left me breathless. My heart was like the earth swelling, my pulse like a newly aroused river. I was full of aches and sighs I could not explain. That morning I walked to the river's upper bank. If the hanging bridge was repaired, I would cross over to the other side, or else I would just take someone's raft.

But before I even reached the upper bank, a raft came into view, rocking and tottering left and right. Flowing downstream, it was moving in my direction. At first, I thought no one was on the raft, but as it approached, I noticed a silhouette pressed against the raft's floor. Why wasn't the raft moving toward the opposite bank, why was it going straight down with the currents? Particularly in this season? Had I not seen the silhouette on it, I would have thought the waves had seized the raft and were sweeping it away. But there was a silhouette with its head buried on the raft's floor, it was struggling, shielding its face . . . I stood there, shocked, trying to understand what was happening. A little later, a few more rafts appeared at regular intervals behind this raft. They were tied to each other with thick ropes. I became very curious. The wayward raft came so close that I recognized Jivan. He was shouting, crying, screaming out. No sooner had I recognized him than I took off my jacket and threw myself in the river. Swimming like a lunatic, I gashed through the bosom of the river. My world turned black, my eyes could see nothing. In the end, I reached the raft. I was panting. Jivan was stuck in a corner, thrashing about. I climbed onto the raft. I called to Jivan. He seemed like he couldn't hear. Shrunk in his corner, he was shaking. As I moved closer, he raised his head and looked. I was aghast, I couldn't recognize him. This wasn't Jivan. This wasn't Jivan's face. It was someone else. The devil I had burned. As if I were possessed by the jinn, there was nothing like it. Couldn't be. My eyes wide open, I was living a nightmare, a hallucination. He didn't see me, couldn't move his pupils. He was drooling from the corner of his mouth; his head, his body kept shaking. This was not Jivan. It couldn't be. It must not be. The thing I feared most since childhood had happened. Someone I knew and loved had transformed into another, become someone else. The other rafts caught up to us, paddling faster, aided by the down currents. There were several men. They called out to me.

"Hey, son! Did they run off with your mind? Get off that! Why'd you throw yourself into the middle of a raging river?"

I understood nothing and stared at them bewildered. Jivan was writhing and moaning.

"Don't touch him!" they said. "Beware, don't touch each other!"

"What's with Jivan?" I said. "What's wrong with him?" I said. The ones on the rafts were from his village.

"The water jinn got into him!" they said. "Sending him down the river, we're trying to chase the jinn out of him!"

A voice came from every head, the sound of the crowd mixing in with the noise of the river and fading.

Another man from another raft called out:

"The dog bit him, that's how the jinn got into him . . ."

I understood.

I had to not touch him. He had retreated into another realm. He'd become something else. Someone else. I remembered the harvest games we'd played in my childhood. Before my eyes came my father, out from behind the devil mask that had delighted everyone, made everyone smile, even me. How scared I was of him, how ashamed. No one had the right to become someone else.

Now Jivan lunged upon me from his corner, I grabbed the oar and, holding it crosswise, tried to push him off and protect myself. I knew this was our last jereed. The devil mask I stole and burned so that my father would never again become the devil, that mask returned, and just as I was in the crook of death, it came back to me in the face of the one I loved the most. Jivan tried to bite me, scratch me, tear into me; he was afraid of the water and the sun. For my part, I tried to protect my body from him, and him from the water; and I struggled to keep the sun behind me, and him in my shadow. The oar between us kept me beyond his reach. As we wrestled like this, the other rafts tried to get closer so I could save myself by jumping onto one of them. I couldn't help him (I couldn't leave him like that), wouldn't be able to help him. Now he was all by himself. Absolutely alone. Jivan was the person I loved the most in life. I understood that better, and more than ever now, on this raft. And I couldn't even touch him. He no longer could be restrained; he was foaming at the mouth. We were approaching the most turbulent bend of the river. The raft would not hold us anymore, it rocked back and forth like a cradle. Jivan's rabid strength exhausted me. The grief I felt exhausted my strength and everything else in me. I wanted to push him back, to make him stop, to tire him out, or at least make him shrink back into his corner and stay there. But the raft was rocking faster than it had before, and wouldn't hold anything on it, like a foal newly saddled. With my last bit of strength, as I tried to push him back, get him away from me, he slid off, and I saw the waves catch him. For a time, he wrestled the waves but soon disappeared entirely . . . I grabbed one of the ropes the men threw at me and made it over to a raft.

For some time I refused to accept what the men had told me. I was paralyzed. I had lost a part of myself when Jivan was placed on that raft and sent downstream to overcome the river. One of the sheiks he had been taken to had ordered the cure. From then on, I couldn't truly live any of my emotions anymore. They have all lost their wholeness, their realness, their intensity.

"The water jinn didn't let us pass!" said the villagers. "No one's fault!" The rushes covered the flames in which I had burned the devil.

I gave my jereed pole to the river.

My prayer beads, my *poşi*s, my *agal*s.

What good is there in standing here and remembering all this? It turns out all of it was a dream, a nightmare, an illusion. At a distance, across the upper banks, is the bridge, now too real to allow any of this.

I walk there and, standing on the bridge, watch the river flow beneath me.

1983

The Serpent and the Deer

> You know that, in parks,
> The corners that call to you correspond
> To people's secret dark corners.
>
> —Edip Cansever, "Parks for the Hopeless"

In the corner of the park, they found his dead body.
    In the corner of his face, a faint smile.

Like a kite, still attached to his face.
    His face like a childhood, like the sky, like a kite. Like all this at once.
    It was as though he had rescued something out of the clutches of death, as though this secret happiness froze in the form of a smile and remained there in the silence of his face.
In the silence of the park   His face as silent as the park   Silence, like a park and like a face. Like an evocation.
Evocation. Evocation.   Evocation. Evocation.
Like solitude. Like all solitudes. Does this smile carry in it the peace that comes from going head-to-head with death?
Is it death   he's smiling at?
                    at what he lived out
                    at the living
at what he left behind too
                                        possibly
              at whomever he left behind?

Whatever the case, it's clear he'd been smiling at something. Is he wanting to say that he is not a defeated corpse?
    His face is not like that of a dead person; rather, it's like he's sleeping.
    As if something has resumed. As if embraced with death, each in the other's loving arms, in the corner of the park,
    in the corner of life.

The corner of the park: as much as the corner of life and death,
      The corner of being alive and being dead
      The other side of the park: life
      The other side of the fence
      The other side of all fences.

As if sleeping on the other side.

Torn right from the middle   The sky is bleeding . . .

a smile.   Like a bleeding kite in the sky . . .
Wedged among the tree branches   death caught, is it a kite gliding
a kite caught   in the sky?
        while rising?   in death's sky
        while falling?   is it the flight map of a kite gliding?

or is it while doing both?
if it is both: Showing up just as he was dying
the wounds he sustained   that image of a kite
how will we tell them apart   his entire childhood
the ones sustained while rising   called back to him
from the ones while falling   an entire childhood. Death
how will we tell them apart   an entire childhood
      Just as he was dying
      like a heavy downpour

all the images of his childhood   rained onto this park
      onto the corner of this park.
      With his childhood.
      He died. Evocations.

when he can tell nothing apart anymore Evocations.
when he can tell nothing apart anymore Evocations had ceased.
      as if he is sleeping there.

  The park, a city fairy tale.
  Little city forest.
  Solitary. Quiet. Dense. Hid/den.
  In the lonely corner of the park that looked out onto the back entrance, where the vegetation grows dense and turns dark, they found his dead body.

One could say he was a happy corpse.

At least that's the impression he left.

From the position of the body, how it'd been toppled over, how he'd slipped while holding onto something (while holding on to his face, his shoulders, his arms, his chest, his waist, his hips, his calves, his knees, slipping) one could tell he had struggled quite a bit, and he had not submitted to death easily.

Toppled over, lying on his side, as if he'd propped his head up on a rock and gone to sleep, at peace for having cut off all commerce with the world, with life. As if before dying he'd wrestled with death quite a bit, but while dying he'd dragged death off with him. As if embracing death, holding death in his arms while dying.

Never again would they separate.

The dead, found early in the morning.

He'd been a park regular. Living at night. Hiding in his forest. A deer. Running away.

The park, the forest, the hidden fairy tale of cities.

The forest of the cities' hidden fairy tales.

Where the prey hunted their hunters,

the hunters their prey.

A forest park of the hunted:

A hunt heaven.

He had been strangled.

Dark, livid bruises around his long swan neck, a serpent wound around his neck.

A black, pitch-black serpent, as black as its legend.

Who knows once upon when?

When the whole world was (still) a forest,

they were going to divide up the forest for sure, to each his own forest, each settled in a separate part of the forest. While each forest lived its own adventure, its own history, its own geography,

                              if the two met one day,

met one way or the other, then they would battle. The forest. And each other.

If each lived in his own forest

    lived with his own forest,

no trouble. But one day,

                any which day,

if a forest grew

                                    inside them
then the battle would begin
                                    inside this forest
                                        for this forest, too . . .

    The serpent spoke: solitude, secrecy, darkness is my place. I slither,
advance, coil into myself.
    Don't cross my path!
    This path is my being.
    I know: you are bigger than me, large, beautiful, magnificent.
    But I am stronger than you
        I, too, am stronger than you
        I can swallow you
        make you my prey.
    You'd disappear in your forest.
    You'd disappear with your forest.

The serpent spoke all this before meeting him, before knowing him.
    Without meeting, without knowing, he spoke.
    Fearfully, he spoke.
    He spoke, for fear of meeting him, of knowing him, of seeing him.
    He spoke, fearful of being afraid.
    These were things that threatened to undo the adversarial laws of the
forest. If they met, if they saw, if they knew each other, if they loved,
    strife would be threatened.
    This is why without ever meeting
                        ever knowing,
                        ever seeing,
                            he spoke.

Everyone's forest was enough to them
To everyone this forest was enough.
This forest was enough for everyone.
        While walking in the forest, don't let the trees of others' forests get
                        tangled in your trees
                        wound around your feet
Do not set foot in others' forests, those forests grow. Every track in the
forest is an evocation. It grows through fear. Forests grow through fear.
In all the fairy tales, children always get lost in the forest. Evocation.
Evocation is a thing that gets lost. It is what makes the forest a forest.
Evocations that call down from who knows which age are assigned

nebulous names. Dark, deep, complicating evocations, buried in forgetting. Evocations that resurrect those gripped in forgetting. Evocations that wind other forests around your feet. Evocations if you wander. Evocation of a footprint you left in another's forest. It grows on its own,

growing its own forest.

Do not wander off in the forest. Your forest.

But the deer did.

He'd go down to the water.

Gazelles go down to the water.

It was the gazelle season.

He was alone. Solitary. Solitude was akin to being hunted. Something unredeemable. Walking around, one day or another, he would enter another forest.

It was fate.

He turns and looks behind him.

At how, during the day, it looks like another country.

For those who didn't know its nights, the park was lovely, docile, soft, restful. Unassuming, calm, crisscrossed by paths wide or long, diagonal or perpendicular, narrow or broad trails intersecting one another. There were even sycamore trees. In every direction, the smell of linden. Built around some of the trees were wooden benches decorating the park. It's impossible to resist sprawling oneself under a tree or on a bench, giving in to the hypnotic invitation of the dense shadows, on autumn days that simply cannot shake off the summer heat. In daylight, everything is easy and reassuring. (A dangerous animal asleep.)

Built in one of the city's busiest sections, it even has a giant monument in front of it. In the back, the park enjoys, or so it seems, the official protection of various Institutions of the State like the Ministries, and everything else around appears to add to this air of safety, although when the night arrives, as the night arrives,

How the night changes everything.

People commend to the night all the secrets they are never able to tell anyone. Night, a sovereign power, rewrites everything anew and to its liking, in its own black ink.

Night draws people out into their own darkness.

Evocation.

Waiting at the taxi stop, he turns around and, for a moment, watches the park in daylight—in the truest sense of daylight. The serpent sleeps soundly, satisfied for having unburdened itself, released its venom, spewed its bile. At night, it will pull up its skin up over its body to return to the forest.

When the taxi arrives, he jumps in and rides away from there. For now. It's still daytime. Not the blood hour yet.

The animal inside everyone is asleep. Every day is a very long winter sleep. That wounded animal who sees at night, who sees with the night, who lives in the dark, is asleep now, nestled behind our daytime, our daily masks. It gathers itself. It gathers itself lying behind the mask.

The park stretches out like a docile cat by the feet of the city. It sleeps; in this daytime sleep, the park is lovely.

He knows this, too.

He will return. He knows that this park he walked through, in front of, alongside, while going or coming back from somewhere, this place he always passed, a tangent to the daily flow of life, becomes a forest at night knows very well the irresistible call of bloodlust.

His name was Ilhan.

Depicted on flags, banners, pennants, ancient tablets, leather engravings, miniatures, dragon-head door knockers, figurines, reliefs, the serpent entered people's history, became their history. Lived with their power, in their imagery.

Hid himself in them.

Hid his venom inside.

For itself.

He became the emblem of revenge, hatred, terror, of that boundless and inexplicable rage, and of the killer, the strangler, the piercer.

It is told and known that there are some easygoing kinds—indeed, that inside the baskets in the Far East, some even dance to a poor man's flute.

But in the history of human evocations, the serpent we know is the one from the mountains. He lives in his hideaway, alone.

If you don't cross paths, he does nothing,

and if you do . . .

One night, they crossed paths.

He suddenly saw him on a path—one of those wide or long, diagonal or perpendicular paths—in the park.

Coming from the darkness.

From the unknown.

A pair of green eyes, deep as emeralds, he thought. In the starless, silvery night, the partially lit park looked as dark as a trap. He was returning home from somewhere. For some time now he had been walking home by way of these paths that meandered and disappeared in the darkness of this long and narrow park . . .

He had come down from Meşrutiyet Avenue to the boulevard and, crossing the park, would be heading for Saraçoğlu. He was about to leave the park. On the perimeter. He could have taken one of the better-lit—therefore safer—main streets above the park. But, as of late, he had been choosing to walk through the park. Though, in his consciousness, this "choice" had not yet turned into an admission. A tiny thing stirring inside him—so very tiny that it could be covered up with the smallest possible excuse—was nudging at his heart. Like the things that, heeding a call, began to gently stir inside those baskets in the Far East, the tiny thing inside him, too, still stayed inside its basket, invisible. Its presence could be felt from time to time, though so faintly that it could be quickly forgotten. Everyone knew more or less what went on in that park. He had known it for a while, too. Yet, knowing it felt to him like a stain on his consciousness. He carried the guilt of knowing something that he should not have learned, he should not know. Why did he feel burdened for knowing so commonplace a fact? Why did knowing it make him so unhappy? Make him guilty in his own eyes? He was overlooking the actual source of his burden; what made him miserable wasn't what he knew but what it reminded him of. A buried memory. And perhaps he never understood this. Or by the time he understood, it was very late, for everything.

To keep living on guilty streets, one must develop immunity very early. Those who are out of step with their lives become early victims. When those people, fugitives in their own lives, come out on the guilty streets, looking to complete their selves, they will find their killers instead. Killers, living or dead.

There had to be a reason for the night people to sit alone smoking cigarettes for hours on the benches under the darkness of trees, or to walk up and down these paths that go along, across, or diagonally through the park. A reason for this silent film . . .

Everything was an action-packed, black-and-white silent film.

By day, safe, without danger, but by night, charged with the secrecy and danger of darkness. Demure trees that embody the quiet beauty of a landscape painting, at night their limbs multiply like an octopus. The snare that grips his heart in its claws every time he passes through will not release it until he leaves that park. And when it does—that is, when he crosses the boundary—an equally intense longing begins. He passes through that park to be released. Released? But from what? He doesn't know that either.

He was just about to leave the park. On the perimeter. About to release a breath trapped in his heart. He would hold his breath while walking through the park. He was underwater, holding his breath. Just as he was about to surface, a fish passed him by and then disappeared, diving into the dark, deep waters. As it passed, they came eye to eye. He forgot his breath. Pushing back the heavy blanket that had left him breathless, he moved his head back on the pillow, breathing in the cool air of their room, breathing in and out evenly again. That's the dream he had that night. The night they first met.

He thought about the aquarium air of the park. The fish suffocating.

The pair of green eyes, deep as emeralds, crossed his mind. On one of the last paths, near the perimeter.

Passing through the park as if testing the limits of his secret.

Maybe that's why passing through the park was, for him, one of the dangerous underwater games.

He must have thought, if secretly, about how the park had the power to reveal. If not, why would he recall all day, with a longing akin to home-sickness, this hellish oasis in the middle of the city?

He knew that, on his way home through the park, he would run into one of them, if not several. One of the heroes of that silent film. Par-ticularly if it was well into the night, at one of those hours when no one just happened to walk in the park for no reason, the possibility of such an encounter would increase significantly. True, among those he encountered, some were actually passing through, and others who pre-tended like they were, walking fast, paying no heed to others, to give the impression that they were trying to get somewhere, and these people could deceive him, adding to the muddled uncertainty. But besides those who created such puzzling situations, he could also run into people who walked not quickly but, on the contrary, ever so slowly, enjoying every step of the walk, eyeing the passersby with great interest, even looking intently into their eyes, and still unsatisfied, even turning around after a few steps and looking back at them. Or he could meet people who sat on dark benches, waiting for you to approach them, and, just when you were passing by, taking a deep drag on their cigarettes, signaling their presence, inviting you by showing you their face in the glow of their cigarette.

Passing through this park that he saw as a shortcut to his house became a nightly thrill for him after a while. When he realized that what sent inexplicable tremors and excitement into his heart already at dusk was the prospect of passing through the park at night, he began to experience feelings of disillusionment, anger, hurt, and spite directed at himself along with this fluttering ethereal happiness. His feelings divided into two enemy camps. This gray city he watched from the window of his depressing office became meaningful in his eyes, his drab life gained color, his humdrum days that resembled one another took on a new life thanks to this nightly thrill, bringing back an excitement, a joy of being alive he'd so long ago forgotten.

What sustained the greatest joy of being alive was a state of perpetual suicide; he would understand this much later, when he lost everything he'd been clinging to.

This guilty pleasure,
  this passion for danger,
  the accursed adventure of that path a few minutes long,
  started becoming something that threatened him and his life. He felt this with great pleasure and pain.

A guilty and dangerous pleasure,
  his walk back home, through the park at night. The darkness that descended early in winter kept him from dillydallying here and there, inventing little errands, little distractions while waiting for the night. As soon as he left work and checked a few shopwindows, he would dive into the park, which had already started coming alive, finding its groove with the descending darkness. In truth, the thick traffic of people scattering from work at those hours could lead to mistaken encounters, but the trial and error from day to day on the path decreased the ratio of error. By now, he'd acquired an intuition, an instinct, a certain feeling. He learned to distinguish those who were truly passing through from others who, for one reason or another unable to swallow their pride, pretended to pass through. Signs included the artificiality of their speed, the lack of confidence in their gait, their belabored frowns intended to appear disinterested, or the twinge of pain they experienced between eyeing you and not eyeing you. They tried hard to maintain, to rescue, the delicate balance between themselves and their pride by playing such childish games. They longed to experience large-scale excitements and adventures that they were unwilling to pay the price for and which they didn't have the heart for. And much later he would learn that those pretenders would then tramp around Kızılay's various streets before returning to the park to resume their game of pretense. Along with the fear of running into an acquaintance, they carried in them a more fundamental fear: of gaining in that park the confidence needed to live their own life. Of becoming a shameless regular of the park till the end of time.

Doesn't the magic spell of fear lie in frightening oneself?

The panic he felt on recognizing the reason behind the joy that visited his heart in the afternoons soon dissipated. He had built mighty castles to defend himself against himself. That's why he could withstand for so long. And this time, he was able to reassure himself with ready consolations. Perhaps all this was just a curiosity, a curiosity about an animal garden. The secret charm of encountering people one can only see there. A harmless thing, as long as one didn't go too far. Nor was there even an opportunity to go too far. He felt a terrible hatred and loathing. His mind resisted, couldn't imagine.

It was on one of those nights when his quick steps took him across the park that he came eye to eye with the pair of green eyes in that pitch-black darkness. They glowed like a giant pair of emeralds. He couldn't understand why his heart or his steps quickened. A young hotblood, dark as death, walked past him. Then turned and looked back. As he walked into the light, his eyes lost their glow and became muted. Maybe this was because his face and entire body came into view. He had come up to him as if swimming through the darkness; he was like a spell, like a mirage. As he came even closer, as his face and body came into view, this spell dissolved a little, as he became just another of life's details. Still, the young man had come from death's country and landed on the face of the earth. He trembled at the thought. He thought about death. He knew the ways of this place; he'd learned it by now: if he turned and looked back, he'd have encouraged him, signaled him to follow. That's why he didn't turn around. He recalled Lot's wife. He feared that if he turned around and looked, he would turn to stone and stay there forever. Even if he didn't admit this to himself, he didn't turn around and look because he was afraid. He was afraid of being afraid.

The doormat first caught his foot and then his eye. Every time he returned home, it caught his foot and brought him down to earth, shaking him out of his dreams. The mat meant home. It reminded him of the existence of home, of homes, of families. Of the reality of everyday life, the reality of the daytime . . . This mat that caught his foot was his common sense.

But the very moment he entered his house, he felt a great longing, a deep regret and emptiness. An emptiness he didn't know how to get rid of or cope with. He didn't know what he was longing for or what he regretted. As if he had jumped over something. As if his regret derived from a millennium of times past. So it seemed to him. His regret contained all continuums, all the emotional and mental continuums.

The next day, working in his office, every object or detail that glowed reminded him of that pair of eyes. It was the end of autumn. With the evenings arriving sooner, his excitable heart made him uneasy. He felt a sweet uneasiness. By now he'd become accustomed to his palpitations. Even without investigating its cause, he took care to live in peace with his heart. It was like a little toy; he didn't know how it worked and he didn't want the toy taken out of his hands. Either that night or the next, he didn't see that pair of jade-green eyes, nor did he ask himself whether he wished he saw them or not. And yet every night when entering his house, he felt that emptiness, that aching regret. Though after a while, he'd forget about it, go into the kitchen and attack dinner as if starved. Once at the dining table, following the traditional order of dishes from soup to dessert, he'd forget that glow entirely. He felt a certain satisfaction, the deceptive satisfaction of no longer seeing, of forgetting something he had experienced so intensely. A deceptive satisfaction that usually accompanied a feeling of escape.

Having buried his memory deep in his consciousness, returning home one evening from a get-together over drinks at a friend's house, he turned toward the park, seized again with the same palpitations. His steps were steady, slow, and confident, maybe because the park was silent and deserted. His steps carried him like an actor walking a theater stage after the audience had let out. He even found in himself the strength to look all around him. Suddenly, on the right side of the path, at the edge of one of the half-moon-shaped wooden benches, he saw nestled in the tar-black darkness of the night the same pair of green eyes. In the dark, his gaze flashed like lightning. Sitting alone there, he was smoking. Waiting. He could not stop the rumbling of his heart. Stunned by the bends. As if he'd been betrayed. Both the night and the park, silent and deserted, had played a trick on him. They had fooled him by hiding this pair of eyes for a long time.

"It's a cat's eye," he said.

"It signals danger. Like the phosphorescent, glow-in-the-dark signs on a cliff's edge. Like a cat's secret vengeance."

Behind him was a bushy tree crowded with limbs. Nestled nicely into that tree's dense shadow, he was staring at the grass, at him, at the path, with traitorous eyes. As for him, he was caught in the glare of the lights that illuminated the path. He felt insecure while the young man had found refuge in the darkness and

while he sat and waited with expectation, he walked slowly, gravely, under an avalanche of light that exposed all his secrets. He felt naked, entirely naked. As if his whole life had been laid bare. He walked slowly, gravely. He could no longer pretend to be merely walking through the park. He experienced conflicted but equally intense feelings, torn between walking up to him and running away and saving himself. Had he dived quickly into the park, maybe he could have kept walking. The rhythm would have saved him. Our entire life was at the mercy of a rhythm. No matter which rhythm. But now he was walking too slowly. He'd been caught. And he couldn't quicken his steps. He thought that speeding up would expose his fear and that would have hurt his manly pride. He was afraid to escape, afraid that his escape would be known. He was afraid.

He still escaped.

Ever since he'd been haunting this park, this was the first time he felt defeated.

When the world was one vast forest, how was it?
                                    how is it now?

It's hard to know. How much can prewritten history help us? How far back can material discoveries take us?

Is history as instructive as we assume it is?

But as the area of the world's forests kept shrinking, this "historic confrontation" only became likelier.

The forests were shrinking, at least in the sense of their area. The contiguities were being disrupted. Other things appeared in those gaps. Concrete Institutions. Geometric Order. Precise Calculations. Mathematical Data. Easy Classification Codes. Weights and Measures. Dictionaries. Materials. Statutes. A distribution that disperses the forests but doesn't dissolve the forest. The lake region of our expropriated lives. Dam Laws. Barriers and Ramparts. Beflagged Bastions. Housing and Mortgage. Canals and Undergrounds. Castles and Overgrounds. Rites and Migrations. Our union divided by Migration Routes. The forest, itself divided, still harbored those who carried with them the possibility of meeting face-to-face again someday. When cement was first poured, people dispersed across the places they traveled to; every footprint caused its forest to burgeon in another forest. Yet these can no longer be gathered back and reconstituted.

This must be how the first comparison of forests and trees emerged. The quandary about missing the forest for the trees or the trees for the forest,

That is, for seeing and being seen

or not seeing and not being seen,
the forest was the most suitable setting.
Revealing while hiding, hiding while revealing,
neither understood nor explained unless experienced,
it was the longest-held secret of the world's geography.
Because meeting face-to-face
was the first step in facing oneself. The encounter carried in it a grudge, a bottomless hatred, rage, violence that could turn it into a battle.

Bloodlust is perhaps a defense instinct left over from those times. Who/knows?

The park had by now become a symbol of a fundamental disquiet he felt. The park: the smallest unit of the diminishing forests in our day. Paths lined with trees. Games of miraculous encounters. The destiny you pass by. Manly games of forcing the boundaries of relational geography. The dark prelude to battle. In the astrology of these dark, tree-lined paths, in the gravitational force of a meteor falling before you, what kind of life awaits you . . . What kind of life? You cannot know.

That park by now,
seeing and being seen,
                                        the thing that made him so uneasy, he had been walking through it for so long. It was no longer about pushing himself. It was something else. Perhaps he wanted to prove a certain fearlessness. When pushing himself, his limits, he had seen how afraid he became. Now he wanted to overcome this fear. He tried to banish his doubts.

By pushing and pushing
he wanted to validate himself. He would rejoice if he saw that he was no longer afraid. He wanted this even if he had to forfeit all his joy.

If he could walk through the park, if he crossed it, he'd be exonerated, he thought. It would mean he was right. That he justified his values to himself.

But no one in this park (in this forest) is that strong.

He wasn't.

A moment after the stranger passed by him, he'd turned and looked behind him. He saw the fish gliding. It was swimming into the heart of the sea. For a moment he thought the fish would never return from there. Even a fish would have drowned in the water's depths. The park had a "No Parking" sign. He'd lost time. He was breathless; the fish had distracted him. He had almost drowned. He pushed the blanket off his body. He'd awoken. Reached the surface of the water.

The deer knew he was larger than the serpent. Maybe not stronger, but he was certainly bigger. The serpent was more daring, nimbler, and deadlier. In this battle
in a battle
the deer's death was something expected. It was something known.

That the deer also knew this seemed to have lifted a great weight off him. Hence his lightness, his bounce.

He left his death in the hands of others.

And perhaps this was a different manner of killing.

The very moment he sat down next to him, he already knew that his excuse the next day would be that he was drunk. The power of alcohol could explain many things, make them forgivable. Returning home after a night of drinking, he had decided—resolutely and deeply—that the time had come for him to meet someone, to talk with him. His decision meant that he had taken another step. Or that yet another of the defensive ramparts had fallen. In his eyes, his reasons were valid enough to justify his actions.

This reticence, this silence enchanted him completely. If he talked with one of them, one of his nightly excitations, he hoped it would subside, that he would
make it subside.
Talking with someone, talking with any one of them, would break the spell, he must have thought, render the experience perfectly ordinary, and he would have solved a mystery that needed solving.

If the spell is broken, maybe he would never again come to this park,
to this forest.
He'd have jumped through. Overcome an imminent danger. This would be a release, a liberation. Just as his marriage was approaching, he would have rid his life of a significant threat. This threat wasn't about becoming something. Anything. Nor was it about holding something or someone by its edges. It was a more fundamental thing that threatened his being more deeply. Something so delayed that it couldn't be resolved by simply choosing to be any which thing . . . something that had long besieged his entire body, captured his soul.

Talking, yes, merely talking would be enough. He would have experienced it, jumped through it. And to jump through, he had to step on someone's shoulders. This gave him a feeling like touching a leper. Talking would be a form of liberation for him. But how would he approach them, get close to them, without ridding himself of this infinite hatred he felt? He wanted to grab a sharp knife and butcher every one of them here. As if he would not know peace without scraping their kind from the face of the earth forever. The fundamental dependency he felt toward them exasperated him. He would not let them walk away scot-free. The one he chose to talk to was also important. He needed a person who would be helpful in getting him through this ordeal, though, doubtlessly, someone unaware that he was helping. But who, what kind of person did it have to be? He didn't know.

He searched his heart, he kept searching. He could find no feelings, none he could express. It was a confused jumble in there.

He resorted to drinking more than before. Sitting down on the bench, he knew that alcohol was what would lend him the courage, and tomorrow's excuse.

On their first meeting
the deer reminded the serpent of something the serpent didn't know.

Something unknown, or something that the serpent wouldn't want to know, or something that would otherwise remain unknown or unknowable.

You are powerful, you have the venom, and you are hungry.

you can swallow me if you want, the deer said.

But there's something you forget: I am larger than you, and after you swallow me, until you digest and dissolve my body, you will have to live for a time in my form, live like me. Then, later, I will certainly dissolve, dissolve in you. I will be mixed into your flesh, blood, and soul.

You won't be the same old serpent.

Killing me will make me live in you.

For no one ever forgets whom they've killed.

No one has been able to forget.

Was this the same bench?

He tried to recall this while the other was talking. Was it the same bench?

"So you're going to leave me. This time you're sure! But will you be able to forget? All the experiences, will you treat them like they never happened? Even if you marry, I don't think you will forget me so easily. No one can forget so easily a person whose life they've ruined. From the very start, there was something about this relationship that you couldn't bring yourself to accept. I was aware of it but thought it would pass. All of us have had periods we've gotten over in our lives. We've all known animosity, brief or extended. Inside us, in our forest within, our divided selves have at times battled each other.

"One has to leave this battle without dying.

"I know you think there is something about me that threatens you, threatens your being. You think I'm depleting you, killing you little by little. I know, loving is something that threatens a man. This is why you see yourself as my enemy.

"But we are the black people of the night.

"No other place but the forest accepts us. Without burning it down you'll never be able to get out of here. But no one will survive the conflagration. No one can. And this you need to know. At least after having dived into this forest once.

"So many times you've tried staying away. How many days does it last? How you come back every time with new sorrows and even bigger problems. Both of us know this and both of us pay the price.

"I know you're afraid. Trying to scrape away these fears, you end up tearing your soul to threads. Because they permeate your soul. Do I even know your real name? What are you? What do you do? What line of work? Where do you work? I haven't been in your room, I don't know your childhood, your relations, which foods you like, even what makes you laugh. But I love you. I love you as wide as this forest.

"I know it, I can sense it, this time you will stay away longer. Just to prove to me and to yourself that you can stay away, and stay away longer, and if necessary, leave me for good. Leaving is a very manly act, is it not? Three months, five months, hey, let's even say three years, five years, maybe ten years at the outside. And then what? One day you will return here. You will want to return to that forest homeland you carry inside you. Will I be here then? Will I be where you left me? Maybe you will call out to me: 'Ilhaaaan, where are you? Where are you in this forest?'

"I will not answer.

"I will not hear you.

"I will mix in with the tree, the soil, the water. Mixed in the city noise, in the night's lit-up streets. Other lives will have depleted me, I will be smothered in other sheets. My tongue will be parched from licking my own wounds, and even if I wanted to, I won't be able to answer you. We cannot hold our wounds up to the sun. We hide during the days. Take cover. But there is no sun at night. It falls only to us, to our depleted strength, to cope with our wounds.

"So, you say you're going to go. You say you're not going to come back. You say you're never going to come back. Fine, go then, leave, but if one day you come back—and you will come back—what a crying shame for me, what a sin.

"What a sin for both of us.

"I have no strength left, I won't endure another separation, the silently passing forest nights.

"You can neither leave nor stay; neither at night nor during the day will you be able to make a life for yourself. You can't find a place for yourself in the world. What's worse, you make me live your misery with you. What I overcame so long ago, the problems, the sorrows I met and left behind, you've made me relive them. I now must relive all of them once again on account of you. You again set me up with the hurdles I once jumped over. You tire me out, Nejdet. You tire me with things I've become tired of understanding.

"I would have liked to talk for many more hours. To talk with all the words. I would have liked to find deep, stunning, staggering sentences. To come up with metaphors that have the power to sum up everything. So I can explain to you in a flash everything I learned up till now. But it won't help, I know. Nothing, nothing will help, it seems. Love isn't enough for everything.

"Love isn't enough for anything."

And because the serpent didn't have any other way, didn't know any other way, he attacked the deer that came upon his path,
and swallowed it.

The serpent knew no other way of being. Had not learned. No one had taught the serpent.

The forest had no room for the two of them.

The battle lasted long. The forest shuddered.

The serpent shuddered.

The deer's eyes pierced the serpent first.

Then, the serpent's fangs.

The forest shuddered. Then the forests, then all the evocations shuddered.

The serpent, having swallowed the deer, was much heavier now. Tired. The forest was heavier. Now the serpent had to carry the deer's weight too. For a while, the serpent felt as if dying. In the quiet of that forest, where it had swallowed the deer, the serpent didn't move, he couldn't budge. He saw that he had taken on the shape of the deer. A serpent in the form of a deer. As if the deer's eyes glistened on the serpent's scales.

Digesting and dissolving, the serpent remained still until he could feel the deer mix with his flesh, his blood, his venom.

The deer lived within him like a vengeance.

He had said it right.

It had been told long ago.
He wasn't the old serpent anymore.

In the corner of the park, they found his dead body.
In the corner of his face, a faint smile.

January 1983

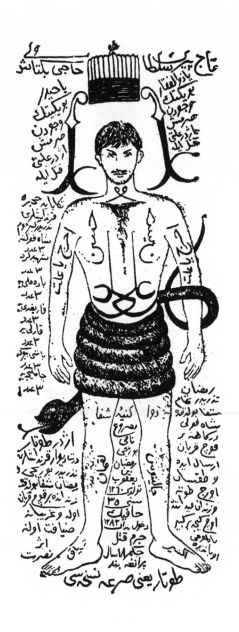